Sara settled back as the conversation went on around her. It was turning out to be a very good trip. And grudgingly, she admitted Jaime had a lot to do with it. Perhaps it was good, having an outsider with them. It would help though if she didn't look like a damn model. Maybe that was what was bothering her. She was attractive. In fact, she was one of the cutest women Sara had met in a long, long time. And she was a flirt. And Sara felt a tug of attraction for the other woman. She rolled her eyes. *God, did I just think that?* But yes, she couldn't deny it as she watched Jaime rise from the water and sit on a rock, laying out flat and letting the sun dry her. She very nearly groaned as her eyes landed on Jaime's breasts. She made herself move, dipping under the water again. She wasn't even sure she liked the woman. How could she possibly be attracted to her? She stood in the middle of the springs, her eyes again landing on the prone body of Jaime Hutchinson. How? Jesus, you'd have to be dead not to notice her. Well, dead or straight. And she was neither.

Visit

Bella Books

at

BellaBooks.com

or call our toll-free number

1-800-729-4992

the TARGET

gerri hill

Bella
BOOKS
2007

First Edition

Editor: Anna Chinappi
Cover designer: KIARO Creative Ltd.

ISBN-10: 1-59493-082-1
ISBN-13: 978-1-59493-082-9

About the Author

Gerri lives in East Texas, deep in the pines, with her partner, Diane. They share their log cabin and adjoining five acres with two labs, Max and Zach, and four cats. A huge vegetable garden that overflows in the summer is her pride and joy. Besides giving in to her overactive green thumb, Gerri loves to "hike the woods" with the dogs, a pair of binoculars (bird watching), and at least one camera! For more, visit Gerri's Web site at www.gerrihill.com.

CHAPTER ONE

Jaime Hutchinson stared at her captain, raising one eyebrow. Surely she misunderstood.

"Come again."

Captain Morris sighed. "I'm fairly certain you heard me."

"You want me to . . . to *babysit* some woman?"

"I did not say *babysit*. I said keep an eye on her. Big difference." He shoved a file across his desk and pointed. "Everything you need is there."

She flicked her glance at the file, then back to him. "She's the daughter of a senator and she's had a death threat. Doesn't this fall to the FBI?"

"They claim they don't have a female agent in the area who is an accomplished backpacker and certainly none that knows the backcountry as well as you do. It's as simple as that."

She narrowed her eyes. "Give me a break."

He shrugged. "They said it was important."

She stood quickly, pacing in front of his desk. "Look, Captain, I've got cases pending. I don't have time to goddamn babysit some senator's daughter, for Christ's sake!"

"Sit down, Hutchinson."

She pierced him with dark eyes. "I'm serious."

"So am I. Jesus, you'd think you'd love this assignment. You get to go out to the woods and you don't even have to take vacation time."

"That's not funny."

"Jaime, sit down. Please?" He took off his glasses and rubbed his eyes, wishing for once she'd just accept an assignment and be on her way. But no. Always had a thousand questions. If it wasn't for the fact that she was so damn likable, he'd have suspended her a hundred times by now. But the ever-present smile was absent. "Look, Senator Michaels has received threats against him and his family—Sara Michaels in particular—ever since he announced his run for the presidency. Special Agent Ramsey says Sara Michaels has refused protection, for whatever reason. She's a private citizen. They can't exactly force her into protective custody, now can they?" He pointed at the file. "From what I've gathered, she and her father are estranged. The FBI thinks it's just some bullshit political ploy—the threats. But of course, they have to check them out." He watched as she finally picked up the file. "Read the file. Then you're to meet with Ramsey in the morning. He'll go over the particulars. You might also want to do a little background on her. I don't think the file covers much."

"So basically, it's a nothing case that's going nowhere and they don't want to waste one of their agents in this babysitting gig?"

He nodded. "Afraid so. Like I said, think of it as a vacation."

Jaime reluctantly opened the file and found herself staring back at a beautiful blond woman whose bluish-green eyes reached out and captured her. She raised an eyebrow and lifted one corner of her mouth in a grin. Looking up, she met her captain's eyes and laughed.

"Yeah, thought you'd like that part."

"Well, gotta find your perks where you can." She got up to go but he called her back.

"Look, Jaime, one more thing. This assignment is undercover, okay? The Feds want it that way. It's just between you and me."

"Simon?"

"Not even Simon."

"How am I going to keep this from my partner?"

"Tell him you're going on vacation."

CHAPTER TWO

"Vacation?" Russ Simon rubbed his two-day stubble, then shook his head. "No, Jaime, you can't take vacation now. We've got three cases pending. You know that. The captain's never going to go for vacation."

"Sorry, man. An opportunity just came up. He's already approved it." She hated lying to Russ. They were damn near best friends. But she would obey her captain's orders. Especially since he appeared to be watching them right now.

He leaned forward. "Jaime? There's something you're not telling me. I can see it in your eyes. Hell, you never could lie worth a damn."

She gave him a forced smile. "Vacation." Then she glanced toward the captain's office. "I'll explain later," she whispered.

"I see." He, too, looked the captain's way. "So, when does this vacation start?"

"I'll know tomorrow."

He frowned. "You're not in any trouble, are you?"

"No. Not yet, anyway." She stood and grabbed her backpack, shoving a few personal items inside, then the file.

"What's that?"

"Nothing."

He nodded. "You're leaving already?"

"Yeah. I've got some things to take care of. I'll be in early, if you want to get in a workout."

"Sure. I'll blame you when Amanda wants to know why I'm leaving her bed early," he said as he leaned back in his chair.

"As if. I happen to know that Amanda is not a morning person and she'll most likely thank me, big guy, for saving her from your advances."

"Very funny, Hutchinson. She likes my advances."

"Yeah, yeah." She walked away, then tossed over her shoulder, "See you in the morning."

CHAPTER THREE

It was unusually warm for early September. And dry. Denver hadn't seen a rain shower in more days than she could remember. At least it would be cooler up in the mountains. And thankfully, the Collegiate Peaks area had rain recently. The burn ban was lifted above eight thousand feet. At least they could have a campfire at night. She didn't think these women could make the trip without one. Sara slowed her pace, waiting for the others to catch up with her. She had been pushing them harder the last week, trying to get them into good enough shape to handle their two-week trek on hiking trails. And she thought they'd be fine. All but Sandra. She would have to keep an eye on Sandra.

"It's hot, Sarge," Abby panted as she came alongside Sara on the jogging trail. "I haven't sweated this much since I went on a walking tour of Atlanta one July."

"Ms. Michaels? Maybe a break?"

Sara stopped and allowed everyone to catch their breath, hiding her smile at the use of the nickname they'd given her. Sandra was several yards behind them, still struggling to keep up.

"How you doing, Sandra?"

"I'm coming."

Sandra Kellum was the oldest of the group and the most out of shape. But in the ten weeks they'd been training, she'd made progress, shedding nearly twenty pounds. Unfortunately, she could stand to shed another thirty.

"You'll be fine, Sandra. We'll take it nice and slow on the trails."

"You keep saying that," she panted as she bent over at the waist.

"Don't worry, Sandra. We'll all help," Abby said.

Sara stared at the group of ten women, all of varying ages and backgrounds, all with anticipation on their faces. They wanted to change their lives. In the three years she'd been doing the program, she always felt a sense of accomplishment in the tenth week, knowing that the counseling sessions were over and their two-week sojourn into the mountains would mark a rebirth for them. But for some reason, this time, she felt uneasy. The group was not unlike the one before them and most likely no different than the next one would be. They all came because of the same circumstances. They were overweight or they were unhappy in their life, unhappy in their job, unhappy in their marriage. Most of them lacked self-esteem and confidence and nearly all of them simply wanted a new outlook. And in only ten weeks, they changed from timid, unhappy, overweight individuals to confident, independent women, ready to face the rest of their lives. But this time . . . this time something wasn't right.

She shook off the feeling, telling herself it was just the recent visit she'd had from the FBI. Well, she was used to threats. Mostly from her father but still, she was used to it. She would not be intimidated. She was accomplishing too much to stop now.

"Okay, ladies, one more mile and then we're done." Her announcement was followed by a chorus of groans and she headed down the trail in a fast jog, knowing they would follow.

CHAPTER FOUR

"The Feds requested you?"

"Will you keep it down?" Jaime hissed. She lowered the dumb-bells to the floor and walked over to the stationary bike.

"But that's good, right?"

"Russ, it's a chickenshit assignment that they didn't want themselves. Didn't have a female agent that backpacked? Give me a break. They're trained to do all kinds of shit."

"It might be true."

She gave him a wry glance then started peddling. She'd read the file last night. It was brief. Too brief. She'd read FBI files before and they were thorough and detailed, nothing like the crap in this file. And she didn't like it. It just didn't make any sense. A senator running for president gets death threats and the FBI requests a lowly Denver detective to guard the daughter? They obviously knew it was a dead end.

"Look, this is supposed to be some big secret, okay? I promised the captain I wouldn't say anything to you. As far as you know, I'm on vacation."

"No problem. I guess I'll have to handle the gang killing by myself," he said dramatically.

Jaime rolled her eyes.

"And the old woman who was mugged."

"Gonna miss me, huh?"

"I'll request Susie to work with me," he said with a grin.

"Sure you will. Amanda will have you sleeping on the sofa. Besides, I don't think you're really Susie's type."

"What do you mean by that?"

She grinned and peddled faster.

"No. She's not? Please God, say she's not."

"Sorry, big guy, she is."

"What is this world coming to? How the hell are we supposed to tell you apart if someone like *her* is gay? She's model material."

Jaime shrugged. "You're married, remember? It shouldn't matter to you."

"Great. Now you've just killed about five fantasies of mine." Then he grinned. "But you may have added a couple new ones."

One of the uniformed officers knocked on a locker not far from Jaime's. She pulled her T-shirt over her head then looked up.

"Hey, Sal. What's up?"

"Captain wants to see you."

Jaime checked her watch. "It's not even eight."

"He's got some suit in with him."

Jaime nodded. "Okay. Be right there." Apparently, the FBI was punctual.

After tossing her backpack on her desk and punching Russ playfully in the arm, she knocked on Captain Morris's door.

"Hutchinson, good. Come in."

Jaime nodded and took a seat next to an impeccably dressed man in his mid-forties, she guessed. With thinning hair and a slight film of perspiration on his brow, he didn't seem the least bit intimidating. Standard black suit, blue tie, shiny black shoes. She looked at her own jeans and boots, thankful she'd decided to add the lightweight blazer over her T-shirt. She looked somewhat more presentable that way. After all, it *was* the FBI.

"Special Agent Ramsey, this is Detective Hutchinson."

Their eyes met and Jaime childishly waited until he extended his hand before offering her own. His handshake was brief.

"Sorry about the short notice, Detective," he said. "Sometimes things move quickly."

"Sure." She held back the sarcastic comments that were threatening to spill out, instead crossing her arms and glaring at her captain.

"I trust you read the file?"

"I did. Although it was extremely brief. Not a lot there."

He patted another file in his lap. "This is a little more in-depth. Until we were certain you were on our team, we didn't want to divulge too much."

"I see."

"Sara Michaels is owner of The New You. She's sort of a self-help guru, if you will. You may have seen her on Oprah when she was pushing her book." At Jaime's blank stare, he continued. "She is Senator Michaels' only child. If we didn't feel these threats were legitimate, we wouldn't be so concerned with getting someone on the inside. As it is—"

"Wait. On the inside? What do you mean?"

"Her program caters to women only. Her clientele consists mostly of middle-aged women with . . . with issues," he said with a wave of his hand. "She does group sessions, not one-on-one. Ten weeks of counseling mingled with some sort of exercise program. That's followed with a two-week backpacking trip."

"Exercise?"

"The New You," he said sarcastically. "The book was a best seller, not to mention the video. But we're not really concerned with all that. However, two weeks in the mountains leaves her very vulnerable."

"And you want me to get into one of her classes?"

"That's not possible. She's in week ten already. They head out on Sunday for the two-week trip."

"Okay. So what? You want me to crash their backpacking trip?" She looked at Captain Morris with raised eyebrows. He simply shrugged.

"Detective, how you do it is up to you. Surely you can find a way. Your job is to protect her."

"Well, *surely* the FBI has powers beyond our comprehension here," she said, letting a little of the sarcasm get through. "*Surely*, you have a way to get me inside?"

"Unfortunately, no."

"I see. Because if you did, you'd have your own agent on this, right?"

"Captain Morris, you assured me that she would not be difficult," Special Agent Ramsey said with a pointed look at him.

"Difficult?" Jaime asked. "This is not being difficult. You want me to protect some woman who you can't get close to and you expect *me* to get close to her?"

"Detective, we have already approached her and she refused. I talked to her personally, in fact, and she was adamant that she was in no danger." He shrugged. "She's a private citizen. She and her father do not speak. The threats that have been received have not been made public. We intend to keep it that way. In fact, only a handful of people in the Senator's inner circle know. The Secret Service will protect the Senator when he's out on the campaign trail, of course. But the Senator expects protection for his daughter, so . . . you're it."

"Unbelievable," she murmured.

"My suggestion would be to intercept her somewhere on the trail. That seems to be the only way to stay close."

"Have you determined who has made the threats?" she asked.

"I'm sorry. I'm not at liberty to say."

Jaime stared at him, then flicked her gaze to Morris. "You're what? You're not at liberty to say? I'm just supposed to traipse into the mountains without a clue as to who might be trying to kill her?"

"We don't have a concrete suspect, no. Several groups, perhaps, but nothing that should concern you. Your job, Detective Hutchinson, is to simply watch her. And make sure she doesn't get killed, of course."

Jaime stood, leaning on the chair that she shoved close to Captain Morris's desk. "Well, this is just great, *Special* Agent Ramsey. You've been a wealth of information. I'm sure I won't have any problem keeping Sara Michaels safe from unknown assailants. In fact, it'll be just like a fucking vacation!"

"Detective, we don't expect miracles. We know you're not . . . FBI," he said, grinning.

Jaime clenched her fists and Captain Morris stood quickly, spreading his hands across his desk. "We're all on the same team here."

"Of course we are," Jaime murmured.

"Detective, in all likelihood, any assailants that may be targeting Ms. Michaels won't be able to accomplish anything while she's in the mountains. This is simply precautionary. Most likely, you'll make the trip without any problems."

Jaime stared at him. "You guys are unbelievable."

Ramsey lowered his eyes. "The best thing she's got going for her is that she rarely takes the same route twice. In fact, the planned route is kept a secret. As far as anyone knows, her destination is up in the air. Any professional hit man would be able to take her out while she's going about her daily activities, if that was his desire. I doubt seriously anyone would go to this much trouble to track her into the mountains."

"So, this is just precautionary?"

"Exactly."

Jaime walked to the door then stopped. "There's just one thing. If she winds up dead, I'm not like . . . going to get a demotion or anything, right?"

"Of course not, Hutchinson. You're on loan to the FBI. This case has no bearing on your record here."

"Well, thanks, Captain. That makes me feel so much better."

Ramsey exited the police station and flipped open his cell phone while jogging down the steps. At the bottom, he paused, waiting.

"She's a go."

"She bought it?"

"Yes, sir."

"Good, Ramsey. Good job. I'll notify him."

Ramsey nodded and closed his phone, slowing his pace to the black sedan parked along the street.

CHAPTER FIVE

"Sara?"

Sara looked up, smiling wearily at her secretary. "Yes?"

"It's almost six."

"Six? Then what are you still doing here?"

"I wanted to get all the notices out, reminding everyone that you'd be gone."

"Good. Now go home."

But instead, Tracy walked into the office, plopping down in the visitor's chair. "If I go home, there'll be no one here to remind *you* to go home and you'll end up staying until midnight."

Sara sighed. "There's just so much to do."

"And it'll be here when you get back. Just like always." Tracy stretched out her feet. "What's wrong? Is it the FBI thing?"

Sara put down her pen and ran both hands through her hair, finally resting her elbows on her desk and meeting her secretary's eyes.

"I . . . I don't know what's wrong. I feel restless." She waved her hand. "And the FBI thing, no. If my father has had a death threat, it doesn't involve me. We've not spoken in years."

"What about your mother?"

"I spoke with her a few weeks ago. I did try calling her yesterday but she's not returned my call."

"Well, you look really tired. More tired than I can remember."

"That goes without saying. I've been averaging about four hours a night of sleep for the last couple of weeks." Sara relaxed, pushing her chair back far enough to rest her feet on her desk. Her once pressed slacks were wrinkled and her feet were bare, having shed her shoes an hour earlier.

"Then this trip is coming at a good time, right?"

"I suppose."

"Are you worried about it? I know you said Sandra may have a hard time."

"I think she'll be okay. She's really excited about it. No, I'm not really worried. And if things go bad and she can't make it, we can always turn around and head back down. There are always options."

"Well then what's wrong?"

Sara smiled. Tracy had been with her since she'd opened her business and probably knew her better than anyone. And in the last year, Tracy had become one of her closest confidants.

"I'm just in a rut, I guess," Sara finally admitted with a heavy sigh. "I'm tired. I feel like I've lost my spark. I spend so much time here—"

"Ah. No personal life."

"No personal life, no nothing. I've put so much effort into this business, time just got away. I feel like I'm on a merry-go-round sometimes."

"Well, then maybe it's time you slowed down. I mean, you've got a two-year waiting list for your classes. You've hired three counselors to help. Book sales and videos are through the roof." Tracy grinned. "And you've been on Oprah, for God's sake!"

"That doesn't mean things are going to change. The women I get introduced to simply bore me to tears."

"Maybe you just need to stop allowing yourself to get set up with these women who everyone thinks would be perfect for you. I mean, just because your father is a senator, why do they always insist on setting you up with someone who has political aspirations?"

"Because they think we would have that in common."

"Well, you hate politics. If they don't realize that by now, then your friends don't know you very well." Tracy leaned forward. "I wish you could just meet someone that's more like you. You have so many outdoor interests. You jog, you work out. You love to hike. Why don't you ever date anyone like that?"

"Have you seen some of the women at the gym? They scare me. Besides, it's not like I have time. Maybe in a year or so." Sara swung her legs to the floor and shoved her chair closer to her desk, waving her hand dismissively. "This will pass, Tracy. It always does."

"Sure. It always does." Tracy stood. "How long are you planning on staying tonight?"

"I've got a few letters I need to write. I'll e-mail them to you. I'll also work up our itinerary and e-mail that to you as well."

"Okay. Leave anything else you need and I'll do it. I mean, I'll have two weeks." She walked around the desk. "Now, give me a hug."

Sara complied then went to work on the stack of papers that littered her desk. She really was tired, but there was little time to relax. She'd not yet packed and they were leaving for Buena Vista tomorrow.

CHAPTER SIX

"Senator Michaels? A moment of your time, please?"

Peter Michaels smiled one last time and waved to the crowd, then turned to a member of his entourage. "Who is he?"

"FBI."

He straightened his tie then offered his hand to the stranger. "What can I do for you?"

"I'm Special Agent Erickson, Senator. I'm involved with the task force that's looking into the threats, sir."

"I see. And what have you found out?"

"Unfortunately, not much. Your daughter has refused protection so that's made it a little difficult. We're going to, of course, try to persuade her. But I wanted to discuss your wife's planned fundraising dinner tomorrow night. It's at a public hotel. I'm wondering if perhaps we might change venues. Your home, for instance? It would be much easier to monitor the guests that way."

Senator Michaels gave his best political smile and shook his head. "Special Agent Erickson, I assure you, we won't be intimidated. My wife feels the same way. Do what you must, but we won't change our plans."

"Of course," he said politely. "Could we then at least have the list of guests? We'll need to do background checks."

"Certainly. Get with Daniel. He'll get you anything you need."

"Thank you, Senator."

Peter Michaels watched him walk away and motioned for his campaign manager.

"Arthur, call Mr. Dodds, please. I need to have a word with him."

CHAPTER SEVEN

Sara stood at the trailhead and surveyed her surroundings, deeply inhaling the sweet air of the mountains. She was thirty minutes early but that was okay. It would give her some alone time, time she doubted she would have for the next two weeks. They had all met for dinner last night at a small restaurant in Buena Vista and the women were very excited about their upcoming trip to the backcountry. Sara was excited too. It was her first trip to the Collegiate Peaks. From what she'd heard, the trails were moderate, except where they ventured up to capture the fourteeners—mountain peaks above fourteen thousand feet—trails that Sara would not venture with this group. They would climb up to Cottonwood Pass then hike south along the Collegiate Peaks toward Monarch Pass. They should have plenty of time to explore the old mining town of St. Elmo along the way and perhaps some hot springs, if they were lucky. It would be a good trip, one she'd been planning since last spring. She'd almost taken this route during the summer but had instead taken the Colorado Trail to the north, ending up in Rocky Mountain National Park and spending a week exploring there. It had been a pleasant trip, not strenuous at all and they had made it back to Denver without mishap.

It was an easy trip. Maybe she should have taken that trail again. No doubt Sandra could have managed the hike without problems. But this? Who knew? They could stick to moderate trails but then again, moderate was damn close to difficult. She shook her head. If they ended up going slower because of Sandra, so be it. But she would not push. And if it took them a few days longer, all the better. Who was she to complain about a few more days in the mountains?

That sense of unease returned and she tried to shake it off. She normally trusted her intuition but she couldn't simply call off this trip because something was nagging at her. Resting her backpack against a boulder, she walked off into the woods, listening to the birds that called. She glanced into the trees, trying to spot one of the mountain chickadees that were darting between the two pines. She shoved her hands in the pockets of her jeans and absently kicked at a rock with her boot, wondering at the apprehension she felt. Surely, once they were out on the trail, the peacefulness she normally felt would settle in. Surely. If not—

"It'll be a hell of a long trip," she murmured.

She was pulled from her thoughts by the sounds of vans approaching and she walked back to the trail, waiting. Soon, familiar voices filled the air and she smiled. They were so looking forward to this trip. Even Sandra. Ten long weeks. They had hashed over their lives until each of them knew the others' stories by heart. But they were done. Now, two weeks of solitude, away from family and friends, TV and radio. Two weeks to absorb nature at its best. And two weeks of *not* talking about their past lives. As she'd told them yesterday, they were done with it. It was in the past and it was time to embark on a new life. They would leave these mountains new women with new confidences, unafraid to face their futures. *The New You.*

"Ms. Michaels? Sara?"

"Over here," she called. She walked to her backpack and waited. Soon, all ten women appeared, each carrying nearly identical backpacks. The anticipation on their faces practically made her laugh. She wondered if any of them knew how much they'd changed in ten short weeks. Self-confidence showed on almost every face. The eagerness with which they approached the last two weeks of their group sessions was reward enough for Sara, but looking at them now, all standing tall and proud, ready to face the world—and this two-week trek up the mountain—made all those long nights and weeks worthwhile.

Abby was the first in line, as usual. A young mother, she had suffered constantly at the hands of her abusive husband, only escaping when he had finally put both her and her two-year-old in the hospital. She had been beaten but her spirit did not break. Next to her stood Lou Ann, an attractive grad student in her thirties who had been on the verge of alcoholism when she'd joined the program. Then Megan and Ashley, the youngest two of the group, both slightly overweight and lonely—they'd blossomed the most. Their energy inspired most of the others during the hardest sessions. Behind them stood the others, all looking at Sara with expectant faces. The biggest smile came from Sandra, standing at her usual spot at the back of the line.

"What are we waiting for, Sarge?" Sandra asked. "Daylight's wasting. Let's start this trek you've been talking about."

Sara laughed. "You're right. Okay, everyone filled up water bottles, yes?"

"Yes," they answered.

"And we've got meals to last a month?"

"Yes."

"Nobody forgot a sleeping bag?"

"No."

"Okay then. I checked with the weather service this morning. You'll be happy to know that there is no chance of an early season snowstorm, so we won't have that to worry about."

"Then let's hit the trail!"

Sara laughed, her earlier unease fading at the exuberance of the ten women around her. She grabbed her backpack and slipped it over her shoulders, starting out on the trail at an even pace, listening to the chatter behind her with a satisfied smile. This moment made all the hard work worthwhile. They'd cried more times than she could count but over the last few weeks the tears had turned to smiles. They all knew the significance of this trip. It was a new beginning for each of them. And hopefully, they would each emerge back into the world as more confident women, not focusing on the past, but looking forward to the future.

CHAPTER EIGHT

Jaime tightened the straps on her backpack then checked the trail map one more time. She'd been to the Collegiate Peaks before, many times in fact, but had never been on this trail. She'd always started near Cottonwood Pass, not the trails near Buena Vista. But hell, none of that would matter if Michaels had decided on a different route at the last minute.

"No. She wouldn't do that."

Not planning a trip for ten women, you don't change plans at the last minute. And Andy at the downtown sporting goods store, not far from Sara Michaels's office, had talked nonstop about how he caters to The New You clinic. In fact, he's been supplying new backpacks to them since the beginning. And yeah, Sara Michaels may have mentioned the Collegiate Peaks a time or two in the last week. That and she'd purchased a new topo map for the area. Yes, good old Andy could put two and two together. He'd even suggested which trail they might start out on. But Jaime had done her own research for that. The New You clinic had rented two vans with drivers. Destination, Buena Vista.

Jaime shook her head. The more she thought about it, the more convinced she was that no one in his right mind would hike into the backcountry to assassinate the daughter of a senator. Especially if they couldn't be assured of which trail to take. And of course there would be ten potential witnesses. As Special Agent Ramsey had said, it'd be much simpler to just whack her as she left her office one day.

"Then what the hell am I doing here?" she murmured. Then she smiled. "Oh yeah. Vacation."

She shoved the trail map into her back pocket and walked down the hill to wait. If her guess was right, they'd be upon her within the hour. Then, it was just a matter of her joining their group. At the stream, she took off her backpack and leaned against a rock. It was warm and she shed the flannel shirt she'd worn over her T-shirt that morning. Folding it neatly, she tucked it into her pack then took off one boot. A sprained ankle was as good an excuse as any. She pulled out an Ace bandage and wrapped it around her ankle and waited.

And waited. And waited. Jesus, how long could it take them? She frowned. What if her guess was wrong? What if they hadn't taken this trail at all?

She picked up a rock and tossed it into the stream, wondering how long she should wait for them. It was quiet and peaceful. Normally, she would relish this time. Usually twice each summer she escaped for an extended trip, saving her vacation time during the year to allow at least a weeklong trip each time. She normally went alone, only occasionally joining others. But she always enjoyed her solitary trips the most. And truthfully, she'd never been out two weeks straight. She'd done a ten-day hike once between Aspen and Crested Butte and had thoroughly enjoyed the time alone but had welcomed the company when she'd reached the old mining town of Crested Butte. She'd spent two whole days in the bar, she recalled, with a redhead named Gretta.

Finally, nearly an hour and a half later, she heard voices. Female voices. She shifted her position, sticking out her supposedly injured leg and waited. She felt like an idiot and she very nearly started laughing. Why would she assume Michaels would stop for her and even then, ask her to join their group? She couldn't very well tag along uninvited.

Could she?

Sara saw the woman sitting by the rock and slowed her steps. Of course, it was not uncommon to come upon other hikers but still, she was wary.

"She looks like she's hurt," Abby said.

"Uh-huh," Sara murmured.

"Can we rest?" Sandra called from the back.

Sara smiled. They'd only been on the trail a little more than an hour and most of that had been level, only rising slightly in the last fifteen minutes.

The woman raised her hand in greeting and Sara did the same, stopping a few feet away.

"Are you okay?"

"Oh, just twisted my ankle a bit. Nothing too serious."

Sara took off her pack and the others did the same. She squatted down beside the woman.

"I can take a look if you want."

"Thanks but I've wrapped it. It should be okay."

Sara surveyed the woman, noting worn jeans and scuffed hiking boots. Her light brown hair was cut short and brushed away from her face, a face that was marred only by a smattering of freckles on each cheek. Sara glanced at the woman's pack, noticing that it had seen a trip or two and she relaxed. This woman obviously meant them no harm. She offered her hand.

"I'm Sara." Her hand was captured in a warm grip and she squeezed back.

"Jaime. Nice to meet you."

The woman's eyes were dark but friendly. "Where you headed?"

Jaime smiled. It was just too easy. "Taking the trail along the Collegiate Peaks. Just starting out, actually." She raised her foot. "This might set me back a day or so."

"We're heading the same way," Abby said. She knelt down beside Sara. "Are you alone?"

"Yeah. I enjoy the solitude. Gives you time to think."

"I can't imagine coming out here all alone."

"Well, you get used to it."

"I was going to say you could join us," Abby said, motioning with her arm to the others. "But this isn't exactly being alone."

Sara stood quickly. "I doubt she'd want to tag along with us, Abby."

Jaime looked up and smiled. "Well, I might not mind the company for a day or so," she said. "If you guys don't."

"What's one more?" Abby asked.

Sara cleared her throat. "Actually, I don't want to be rude . . . well, I will be rude. You can't join us."

Jaime raised her eyebrows. "Oh?"

"We're . . . a group. It's kind of a . . . a therapy hike."

"Therapy hike?" Jaime grinned. "I see. All women. You're either doing a male-bashing session or you're all lesbians. Which is it?"

"Excuse me?"

"I'll fit into either, I assure you."

Abby and Lou Ann laughed. "Come on, Sarge, she's injured. We can't leave her here alone."

She turned and looked at the expectant faces around her. She'd been taking these trips three times a year for the last three years and never once had they happened upon a stranded hiker. Was it just a coincidence or was her earlier uneasiness getting the best of her? The woman looked harmless enough. She was obviously a seasoned backpacker judging by her worn pack and hiking boots. And no doubt, once her twisted ankle improved, she would be leaving the group. She shrugged. What could it hurt for a day or so?

"Okay. You can tag along with us for the day."

Jaime smiled. "I appreciate it. I hope I don't slow you down."

"No, no. You can hang back here with me," Sandra offered.

Abby reached down to shake her hand. "I'm Abby." She turned to the woman beside her. "This is Lou Ann. I won't bother you with everyone's name, you'll never remember them. But that's Sandra at the back. She'll talk your ear off."

"Great," Jaime said with a smile. She turned and met the blue-green eyes of Sara Michaels. Suspicious blue-green eyes, she noted. Well, that's good. At least she wasn't so trusting as to allow just anyone to get close. Jaime assumed she'd have her work cut out for her as Michaels took off down the trail, leaving the women to follow. She quickly put her boot back on and laced it, looking up as a plump older woman with god-awful bleached hair stared back at her. Then the woman offered her hand and she allowed herself to be pulled to her feet.

"What's your name?"

"Jaime."

"Well, nice to meet you, Jaime. You just limp all you need to and I'll stick right beside you. They won't leave me behind."

"Thanks." Jaime took a step, reminding herself to go slow. "It actually feels better already."

"Can't be too careful. I had a broken foot once. Had it run over by a motorcycle, cast up to here," she pointed to her knee. "Was on crutches for five weeks. My arms were so sore . . ."

Jaime rolled her eyes as she let Sandra's monologue drift away. Up ahead, the others walked, most in single file, with Sara Michaels leading the way. She was certainly different than Jaime imagined. The woman in the picture had been in a business suit, not faded jeans and a denim shirt. And the blond hair had been styled, not the short, windblown look she sported today. She was sexy as hell. Jaime grinned. Yes, you have to get your perks wherever you could.

Jaime nodded at the appropriate times during Sandra's nonstop talking, trying to listen to conversations up ahead. The others, mostly in groups of two or three, talked quietly among themselves. Except for Sara Michaels. She walked alone, a few feet ahead of the others.

Sara kept an even pace, ignoring the desire to go faster to test their tagalong hiker. She glanced back occasionally, seeing the woman nodding at something Sandra was telling her. She only hoped Sandra wasn't revealing who they were or why they were up here. The last thing they needed was some outsider asking a hundred questions. Everything they'd learned in the last ten weeks should be embedded by now. There was no need to talk about it. Once the last session ended, that was it. Even among themselves, these last two weeks hiking was to be among friends. They weren't to discuss the sessions.

But now, they had an outsider. And it would be too easy to undo all the weeks of hard work they'd been through, with just a few innocent questions. No, she couldn't allow it. Tonight, she would speak to this Jaime person. She would tell her about their group and ask her to use discretion when talking to the others. If not, she would just refuse to allow her to join them.

"Right," she whispered. *And how do you propose to do that?* She grinned. Tie her to a tree?

"Sarge?"

Sara turned.

"Sandra and Jaime are lagging behind," Abby said.

"Of course they are," Sara murmured. She stopped, allowing the others to catch up. Sandra and a slightly limping Jaime brought up the rear. "How are we doing back there?"

"Just . . . peachy," Jaime said, forcing a smile to her face. Sandra had not stopped talking the entire time.

"Oh, this isn't hard at all, Ms. Michaels. Just trying to keep a slow pace for Jaime," Sandra said as she labored to catch her breath.

"How about we stop for a little lunch?"

"Now that's a good idea," Sandra said, shrugging off her pack.

They all crowded under the shade of a ponderosa pine and rummaged into their packs, pulling out apples and cheese. All but Sandra. She pulled out a slightly smashed sandwich.

"How many of those you got in there?" Jaime asked.

"A couple. Ms. Michaels said to pack light. This tuna sandwich weighs less than an apple."

Jaime laughed. "And tastes better too."

"What you got in there?"

"Bananas and apples."

"Rabbit food. I swear, I'm going to lose twenty pounds on this trip," Sandra said, then patted her ample stomach. "Not that I couldn't stand to do that, mind you. But I figured, at least the first day, I could eat something other than fruit."

"Yeah. By the end of the trip, you're going to hate freeze-dried meals."

"Sandra, what the hell are you eating?" Abby demanded.

Sandra looked up sheepishly as she chewed. "Tuna sandwich," she said around a mouthful.

"Tuna?" Abby waved her apple. "Tuna? Did you pack a steak for dinner too?"

"I would have, if I didn't think I'd have to share it ten ways."

Sara shook her head. If anyone bucked the fruit and cheese rule, it would be Sandra. She watched as Jaime peeled a banana and took a bite, then looked away as brown eyes tried to capture her own. She bit into her apple, instead looking up the trail. It would be their first real climb. Soon, they would leave the scrub oaks and pines behind and climb higher into the mountains, spruce and fir trees replacing the ponderosas that dominated the lower elevations. And they would pass through stands of aspens, the colors just now changing to the golden hues that made them famous. She hoped the women would enjoy the colors of the mountains as much as she did. Autumn was her favorite time of year. The days still warm enough to enjoy and the nights had a crisp, invigorating feel. And, if the trail maps didn't lie, they would pass hot springs along the way. She'd instructed them all to bring swimsuits so they might enjoy a soak. She preferred to soak in the nude but she thought in a group such as this, they might all feel more comfortable in suits.

Then she looked at the stranger. The woman was sitting cross-legged next to Sandra, quietly eating her banana. Wonder what she brought to soak in? Sara let her eyes travel over the woman, the T-shirt tight against her skin, sleeves rolled up to reveal well-muscled arms. She was tan and looked fit. No doubt, the woman would feel quite at home walking completely nude into one of the springs.

"Whatever," she murmured. There was just something about the woman that bothered her.

"What?" Abby asked.

Sara frowned. "Nothing. Sorry." She stirred. "Everyone about ready? We've got a pretty good climb coming up."

"When do we stop for the night?"

Sara laughed. "In about four hours."

Jaime looked at the women around her, thinking there was no way they'd make it another four hours. But they all stood up, eagerly putting on their packs, even Sandra. Well, it was the first day. She couldn't imagine this group being this eager for two weeks straight. Of course, once they were out there, it wasn't like they could call a bus to come pick them up.

She stood, too, easily slipping on her pack and joining Sandra on the trail. The older woman, for once, seemed to be at a loss for words as the trail headed straight uphill. Jaime slowed her pace, not wanting to get too far ahead of Sandra but they were lagging behind the others. Sandra labored for breath and several times Jaime took her hand as the older woman slipped on a rock.

"They tell me the view will be worth it," Sandra gasped.

Jaime smiled. "It'll be out of this world. Up on top, you can almost see forever."

"You been up here before?"

"Yeah. A few times."

"I hope I live to see it," she gasped, finally stopping and bending over at the waist. "You're not limping any more."

"It's still a little sore."

"Uh-huh. Not hanging back here just to make sure I'm okay?"

Jaime grinned. "If I said my ankle was okay, your boss up there might kick me out of the group."

Sandra laughed. "That she might. Don't take it personally.

We've been through a lot with her. This trip is sort of a . . . a celebration. She's afraid you might set us back."

"Yeah? Well, whatever you've got going on here, I don't want to get in the way."

"No, you won't. We've all got our own demons we're trying to shed. Maybe it's good you're here. You can keep Ms. Michaels occupied so she won't be so worried about all of us."

"What's she worried about?"

"Ladies? You okay?" Sara yelled.

"Yeah. Coming," Jaime called. She nudged Sandra. "Ready?"

"Yeah. Let's go." Sandra fell into step beside Jaime. "She's worried we're going to revert back to our old selves," she finally said. "But not me. Not any of them, I think. And I don't know why she's worried. I mean, she gets paid whether this works for us or not."

"If what works?"

"I'm really not supposed to talk about it." Sandra glanced quickly up ahead. "Secret group therapy," she said with a grin.

"Okay. I understand."

They climbed on, still several feet below the ridge that the others had already disappeared below. Jaime grabbed Sandra's hand and pulled her up, resting at the top for a moment.

"Look."

Sandra lifted her head, her eyes opening wide.

"Good heavens."

"Yes. Beautiful, isn't it?"

Beyond the ridge rose the Collegiate Peaks mountain range, stretching for miles and miles in every direction.

"We're going up there?"

"Yep. Well, not to the top, no. The trail travels along the sides of the mountains and if I remember, to the backside of Mount Princeton."

"Wow. It's . . . breathtaking."

"That it is. Makes you feel good to be alive, doesn't it?"

"Yeah. Yeah, it does. No wonder she wanted us to come out here."

"What do you mean?"

"A lot of us weren't really living, you know."

Jaime frowned. "I don't understand."

"We've all got our own issues to overcome. Like I said, I'm not supposed to talk about it. Especially with an outsider." She paused. "But me, I lived my whole life with parents who abused me." She shrugged. "I didn't know any better. So when I got married and my husband turned out to be an asshole, I thought it was just more of the same."

Jaime nodded. "I'm sorry."

"Oh, I got away from him. Divorce is a lovely word," Sandra said with a laugh. "But I was down in the dumps. I was on my third different antidepressant drug when I saw Sara Michaels on Oprah one day. She was just so positive and full of energy. I learned a lot from her book but I wanted to experience the real thing, you know. I was on a waiting list for over a year."

"Wow."

"Yeah. And it cost a tiny fortune but I feel better about myself now than I have in my whole life. She's so wonderful."

Jaime nudged Sandra as Sara Michaels was making her way toward them. "Better look alive. Sarge is coming."

Sandra laughed.

"You two okay?"

"Great, Ms. Michaels. Isn't this view something?" Sandra asked.

"Yes, it is. Do you need to rest for a bit, Sandra?"

"No, no. I'm okay. Jaime, with her hurt ankle and all, is kinda slowing the pace."

Sara met the amused eyes of the stranger and let a small smile touch her face.

"I see. Well, we've got another couple of hours to go. Do you think Jaime can make it?"

"I'm sure she can manage," Sandra said. "Can't you?"

"I'll try my best."

CHAPTER NINE

Jaime shed her pack along with the others, leaning it against a tree as she rubbed her shoulders. She was winded after the climb, no doubt they all were. Sandra had said very little in the last hour, but she was a trouper and had only requested to rest a few times. Jaime had stayed with her. For some reason, she liked the woman. Perhaps it was because of the courage she saw Sandra muster up each time they crested a ridge only to have another in front of them.

"Okay, ladies. Let's call it a day, shall we?"

"Shall we?" Abby mimicked. "Gee, let's hike for another couple of hours, Sarge."

"You're all doing great. Getting into the mountains is the hardest part. Now that we're here, the trail will be more level," she promised.

"You said that two hours ago."

"Can we have a campfire?" Lou Ann asked.

"Sure can. The fire ban has been lifted up here." Sara unhooked her tent from her pack and found a level spot a few yards away from the group. "I'd suggest setting up your tents first. Once we eat, most of you will want to crawl into bed and sleep."

"Why bother with eating," Abby murmured. "I could fall into bed right now."

Jaime surveyed the area, wondering how they were going to fit eleven, no twelve tents there under the trees. She nudged Sandra. "Where's your tent?"

"Oh, I'm sharing with Celia. Two to a tent."

Jaime nodded. Made sense. Less weight, too. Soon, six tents—blues, greens and one bright yellow—dotted the trees. She took her own a little ways from the group, thinking she'd give them some privacy. Maybe Sara Michaels had some sort of session planned for later. Although judging by their conditions, most would be asleep as soon as the meal was done, campfire or not. She pulled over a flat rock and brought out her tiny propane burner. She soon had water heating and sorted through her freeze-dried meals, trying to find one that seemed appetizing. Spaghetti? Why had she bought spaghetti? She hated freeze-dried spaghetti.

Leaning back, she took a long drink of water and watched the others. The dark-haired Abby was hanging on Sara Michaels' every word as she showed them how to light their stoves. Buddy system again. She counted only five stoves.

"Need some help?" Jaime finally called as only one stove was burning.

"No. They need to learn," Sara said, turning her back to Jaime and watching the women.

"I see." She shrugged. Apparently Michaels was still not too thrilled by her presence here. Well, she wasn't exactly having the time of her life either. If she was alone, she would still be hiking. There was at least another hour of daylight. Then she'd set up camp, eat and maybe read a little. Camping was the only occasion that she took time out to read. Her busy days left little time for such pleasures.

Conversation was sparse as everyone settled down to eat and Jaime kept her distance, allowing them their time. Even Sandra seemed completely exhausted as she quietly ate, sitting by herself on a downed tree, a little ways from the small campfire. She'll never make two weeks, Jaime guessed. What in the hell was Sara Michaels thinking?

"I know what you're thinking," Sara told the group. "You'll never make it two weeks."

Jaime looked up. Could the damn woman read her mind?

"But you will. The first day is always the hardest. Tomorrow will be a short day. We'll camp by some hot springs. You can soak for hours, if you like. We're going to take it nice and slow. I know the hike up today was hard. I only saw Abby pull out her camera, although I know you all brought one. But trust me, in the days to come, you'll want to stop and take pictures and just enjoy the scenery. And before you know it, we'll be walking up Monarch Pass and you'll wonder where the time went."

Jaime wondered if this was a pep talk she had to relay to each new group when they started out. But, she'd been doing it for three years. Apparently, she knew what she was doing.

"How high up are we?" Celia asked. "It's already starting to get cool."

"Eighty-five hundred, maybe nine thousand feet."

Jaime fingered her watch, then pushed one of the side buttons, reading the digital altimeter. 8,794. She shrugged. The Sarge was pretty good.

"Well, ah . . . anyone need a pee break?" Lou Ann asked. "I'm going."

Jaime smiled as four women got up. Just like at a bar, there was safety in numbers. Well, she'd take her own break in private, thank you very much.

She was just wiping clean her dinner pot when Sara Michaels walked over. Jaime met her eyes for a moment then went back to her cleaning.

"May I . . . may I have a word with you?" Sara asked.

"Sure. It's your party."

Sara nodded. She sat down cross-legged opposite Jaime and waited until the woman looked up again.

"I need to apologize. About earlier. And also, I wanted to thank you."

"Thank me?"

"For being such a good sport about Sandra," Sara said quietly.

"Ah, hell. I like the woman. She's got spunk."

Sara nodded. "Yes, she does." Sara hesitated, wondering how to approach this woman. She took a deep breath. "Look, I wanted to tell you a little about our group. Let you know why we're up here."

"Well, you've got quite an assortment, that's for sure."

"I'm their counselor. Sort of a therapist."

Jaime grinned. "I know what the word means."

"We have a clinic in Denver. The New You," she said. "You may have heard of it."

"No."

Sara shrugged. "Well, we're not really mainstream. For most, they can only afford the book and video. But at the clinic, we offer hands-on counseling and group sessions, for ten weeks."

"The New You? What is it? Fat farm?"

Sara bristled. "Not a fat farm. What gave you that idea?"

Jaime shrugged. "Some in your group aren't your typical back-packers."

"A lot of people with weight issues do come to us. But most of the weight problems are simply symptoms of deeper issues. Self-esteem issues, no self-confidence, difficulty relating to others, any number of things."

"I see."

"We go through ten weeks, kind of a crash course. They all live at the clinic and we provide nutritional meals. There is, of course, counseling and lessons. And I incorporate workouts in our sessions, from light weights to walking to eventually jogging. It gives them a sense of purpose, a goal. They all know that at the end of our ten weeks, we take a two-week trip, away from society, away from our discussions."

"Two weeks is a long time, especially for women not accustomed to it," Jaime said.

"Yes, it is. But we go as slow as we need to. Our sessions are over with. There's to be no talk about it up here. I imagine most of them privately reflect on their past but after a few days on the trails, they forget. It's hard to keep that pain with you up here, where you're away from it, away from reminders. You find that you can do things you never thought you could. And when they get back home, they'll have the confidence to go on with their lives."

Jaime nodded. "You must be good."

"I'm only telling you this so that you won't ask questions of them. Especially Sandra. She's probably the most vulnerable of the group, also the oldest. She will find it the hardest to get on with her life. But her self-confidence has grown each week. I just don't want you to say something or ask something that will set her back."

"So I shouldn't tell you that Sandra's already told me some of this?"

Sara's eyes widened. "What did you say to her?" she demanded.

"Whoa, Sarge. I didn't say anything. I just asked—"

"You asked? You asked what?" Sara's eyes flashed and she leaned forward, pointing her finger at Jaime. "This is exactly why I didn't want you to join us. Especially the first few days. They're still . . . *raw*."

"Give me a break. You underestimate her. She's very strong-willed. Hell, I thought she was going to pass out on that climb but she kept going. And you know why? Because it was expected of her. She didn't want to let you down. So lighten up."

Sara stood quickly to her feet. "Do not presume you know *anything* about this. We've worked too hard for you to . . . to disrupt this."

"Disrupt?"

"Yes, disrupt. And I think perhaps in the morning, you should just be on your way."

Jaime watched the angry woman walk away. Hell, she should be the one upset. She'd gotten jumped on for absolutely no reason.

"Way to go, Jaime. Got kicked out of camp on the first day," she murmured. But damn, Sara Michaels was some kind of cute when she got angry. There was not a hint of blue in the green eyes that flashed at her. Jaime shrugged. Well, the Sarge was just going to have to get over it. She wasn't going anywhere.

CHAPTER TEN

Sara stretched inside her sleeping bag, finally opening her eyes. It was still dark. And quiet. Her favorite time of the morning, that hour or so before daybreak. Leaning up on her elbows, she listened. Something had woken her. Then she heard it. Rustling on the rocks. She cocked her head. Perhaps someone needed an early morning bathroom break. But no, it wasn't footsteps.

"Shit." She sat up and tossed the sleeping bag off. Probably a bear. Had she told everyone to wash up after dinner? Did they leave food out? In the darkness, she found the small flashlight in a side pocket of her pack and quickly unzipped her tent, flashing her light in the direction of the noise.

She caught her breath when yellow eyes glowed in the beam of the light. Then she smiled and lowered the flashlight. Only a fox. It scampered off up the hill and she relaxed, making a mental note to remind everyone about leaving food out. A fox was no problem but it wouldn't do to have a bear come visit.

She looked at her watch, the illuminating hands reading only four thirty. Crawling back inside her sleeping bag to chase off the cold, she closed her eyes, hoping to grab another hour of sleep, but she was wide awake. She hardly felt rested. Last night, she'd lain awake for hours it seemed, going over her conversation with Jaime. She knew she'd probably gone overboard with the woman. Sandra seemed to have taken a liking to her and vice versa. She doubted the woman would say or do anything to upset Sandra. Not intentionally at least. But sometimes, the most innocent of statements could be taken the wrong way.

Well, it didn't matter. She'd asked the woman to leave. And if she had any trail etiquette whatsoever, she'd be gone before everyone was up and about.

Sara sighed and rolled over. There was just something about the woman that she couldn't put her finger on. She seemed nice enough, Sara supposed. Not that she'd bothered to have a normal conversation with her, but still, she seemed friendly. She doubted there were very many strangers who would willingly hang back with Sandra as she labored up the trail. And Sara hadn't missed the few times that Jaime had offered her hand to Sandra when she'd slipped.

"Hell, you're an ass," she whispered to herself out loud. The woman had done nothing wrong and all Sara had done was yell at her and demand she leave. Okay, so if she was still around at daybreak, Sara would apologize again and ask her to stay. If she wanted to, that is. Then Sara shook her head. Why would she stay? She'd come backpacking alone, she liked the solitude, she said. Why in the world would she want to hook up with a group of eleven women?

Sara sat up again. What if she had something to do with the threats? What if the FBI was right? What if she was a target and this woman was . . . what? The assassin?

"That's just crazy," she murmured. But she rolled over and faced the zippered door, eyes wide open.

❧

Jaime unzipped her tent and stretched her arms over her head, listening with satisfaction as her back popped. It was barely light enough for her to see the other tents and she assumed no one else was awake. Slipping a sweatshirt on over her T-shirt, she fired up her stove and put water on to boil before taking a discreet trip behind the trees. Hopefully, she could have a cup of coffee in solitude before the others were up and about. And maybe it would give her some time to think of what she was going to say to Sara Michaels. Hell, she could always just tell her the truth.

"Bet that would go over well," she murmured to herself.

While her water heated, she brushed her teeth and ran wet hands through her hair. It was cold but not nearly as cold as it would be if they intended on camping above ten thousand feet. She squatted down beside her small stove, warming her hands over the boiling water. Normally, she hated instant coffee but up here coffee was coffee and she couldn't start her day without it. She filled her cup to the brim with hot water, then walked up the hill and found a rock to sit on to watch the sun creep over the ridge. She'd seen a lot of sunrises over the years and more often than not, she'd seen them alone. But now, right at this moment as the pink rays reflected off of the distant peaks, the tall spruce in front of her silhouetted against them, she wished someone was there to share it with her. Someone to admire the grandeur of it, the simplicity of it.

Sara leaned against the tree, looking past Jaime to the sunrise as the mountains reflected the colors, then casually moved her eyes back to the woman. She looked so peaceful, sitting cross-legged on the rock, staring intently to the mountains. Sara couldn't help but smile. Apparently Jaime was a kindred spirit. Watching the sunrise had become a ritual for Sara on these camping trips and she never had to worry about company before. This morning was no different. Her group of ten was still sound asleep. This stranger, however, had beaten her to it.

Sara was about to turn and go back when Jaime spoke to her. The woman hadn't turned around and Sara was surprised that Jaime even knew she was there.

"You could have shared my rock, Ms. Michaels. I wouldn't have minded."

"Sunrises are . . . private. I wasn't sure you'd want company."

Jaime turned and tossed out the rest of her coffee. She flashed Sara a smile. "Well, it might be the only chance we get, seeing as how you're kicking me out of camp and all."

Sara finally walked closer, allowing a smile to touch her face. "Yeah, about that." She shrugged. "Seems all I do is apologize to you. But I am sorry for jumping on you like I did."

"I understand."

"Do you?"

"Are we about to get into another argument?"

Sara stared at her. "Why are you here?"

"Pardon me?"

"You obviously came up here to go hiking alone, for whatever reason. Why would you want to tag along with the eleven of us?"

"I always like meeting new people. Don't you?"

Sara sighed. "What's your name?"

Jaime frowned. "Er, it's Jaime. Don't you remember?"

"Are you intentionally trying to piss me off? You have a last name, don't you?"

"Oh, I see. In case you want to look me up after we leave here? Tell you what, Sarge, I'll even write down my address and phone number. Hell, I'll throw in my e-mail address too."

"Look, is it too much to ask to know a little something about you? I mean, for all I know, you could be a . . . a serial killer or something. I just think if you're going to travel with us, it wouldn't hurt to share a little about your life. And why the hell are you smiling?" Sara demanded.

"A *serial* killer?"

"You know what I mean."

"Okay, so if I tell you something about me, how do you know

I'm not just making it up to pacify you? Then tonight, perhaps, I'll sneak into your tent when you're asleep and—"

"Are you enjoying yourself?"

"Oh, very much. Don't you want to know what I plan to do when I'm inside your tent?" Jaime asked quietly.

Their eyes met and even though Sara could see the amusement in Jaime's, she still had a nearly uncontrollable desire to knock the smirk off her face. "I teach a self-defense class. Don't try it."

"A woman after my own heart."

"Don't flatter yourself. You're not my type," Sara said as she turned and walked quickly away.

"Oh yeah? So who's your type?" Jaime called.

Sara couldn't resist. She turned and stopped. "At this moment? *Anyone* but you."

She walked back to the tents with Jaime's laughter following after her.

"I may very well push her over the next cliff we come to," she muttered to herself.

"Who are you talking to?"

Sara gasped and jumped back as Abby materialized from behind a tree, discreetly holding toilet paper in one hand.

"Don't litter," Sara said as she zipped up her tent. She wanted to throw something. Actually, she wanted to scream. She didn't know why but the damn woman got on her nerves. And it made no sense. They'd hardly spoken. It was just that whenever they did the woman drove her nuts.

Sara was still perturbed an hour later when they finally broke camp and headed out. The ladies were chatterboxes this morning and more of them than not were hanging back, listening to a story Jaime was telling them about a previous camping trip. Their laughter rang out on more than one occasion and Sara resisted the urge to double-time it down the trail, knowing that would at least shut them up.

But she was being childish. Geez, was she ever being childish. She was a professional, for God's sake. These were her people. And apparently they'd all taken a liking to this Jaime what's-her-name. Sara should be thankful. And in all honesty, having another person on the trip who was an accomplished backpacker gave her some sense of relief. Should something happen, should something go wrong, at least Sara wouldn't be forced to face it alone. She rolled her eyes. Who was she kidding? She knew absolutely nothing about this woman other than she was an attractive, apparently like-able woman that the others had flocked to.

Attractive? No. She was nothing but a flirt. As if Sara would be interested in looking her up after this was over with. *Please.*

While they walked, Jaime pulled out a small notepad from a side pocket on her pack and began writing, nodding occasionally at what Sandra was saying. She nearly started laughing as she finished the note. She didn't know why but she got extreme pleasure out of teasing Sara Michaels. She suspected the woman was much more at home here on the trails than back in the city, yet she hadn't seemed to relax a bit. For her group's sake, Jaime assumed she was trying to hold on to her I'm-the-counselor-I'm-in-charge attitude. And that was just it. These were not her friends with whom she was enjoying a relaxing hike. These were paying clients. She was responsible for them. And she was trying to lump Jaime in with them.

Well, that won't work. She folded the note in half and reached out and poked Celia.

"Pass this up to the Sarge, would you?"

Jaime grinned as she watched the note being handed from one woman to the next, finally reaching Abby's hands who hurried to catch up with Sara. She tapped her on the shoulder then silently handed her the note.

What the hell? Sara kept walking, unfolding the note slowly, wondering what idiot . . .

Jaime Hutchinson. Age 34.

Oh. That idiot. Sara's eyes narrowed at the information that followed, including Jaime's address, home phone number, work number, cell number and e-mail address. Slashed below that: *Call me sometime, we'll get together! I guarantee a good time!*

Sara wadded the note into a ball and tossed it on the trail.

"Hey, don't litter," Abby reminded her. She picked up the crumpled piece of paper and handed it back to Sara. "Dispose of your trash properly."

Sara squeezed the paper in her fist, trying to ignore the rather loud chuckle coming from the back of the group.

"What was that?" Celia whispered. "I've never seen her face get that red before."

Jaime grinned. "I asked her out."

"Oh my."

"Does Ms. Michaels . . . well, does she do that sort of thing?" Sandra asked.

"Date?"

"Well, date women?"

Jaime shrugged. "I'm hoping. That's why I asked."

"Well, judging by her reaction, I'd say no."

Jaime only smiled, keeping her eyes fixed on the back of Sara Michaels. Well, it'd be a damn shame. Then she mentally shook herself. She was supposed to be *protecting* her, not playing with her. Jesus, have some decorum, she told herself. She should at least pretend to be working. With that, she glanced over her shoulder to make sure no one was following them. Nope. They were alone.

So she fell back into step beside Sandra, her eyes scanning the horizon, not looking for would-be assassins but instead enjoying the splendor of the fall colors of the Collegiate Peaks mountain range. She nudged Sandra with her elbow.

"Take a look at that," she said, pointing to their left. "The mountainside looks like it was dipped in gold."

"Yes. Aspens, right?"

"Yep."

"Where are you from, Jaime? You've never said."

"Denver. You?"

"Originally from Michigan—Grand Rapids. But after my divorce, I moved to Chicago."

Jaime nodded but didn't ask anything else. She didn't want to totally piss off Sara Michaels by asking questions. And really, she didn't understand all this need for secrecy.

A short time later they came to a stream and Jaime saw the tell-tale sign of hot springs as steam rose out of the cold water not thirty yards upstream from where they stood.

She watched as Sara turned and faced the group.

"Everyone had enough for the day?"

"Already? We're stopping?"

"Well, I thought you might like to spend the afternoon soaking in the hot springs."

"Oh, God. We're here?" Abby dumped her pack where she stood. "Thank you. I could easily spend the next four hours perched in the water."

"Thought you would." Sara took off her own pack. "The rest of the afternoon is yours, ladies. Soak, take a nap, explore around a bit. Whatever you like. We'll camp here."

"Now this is my kind of camping trip," Jaime said. She walked underneath a large spruce and tossed down her pack. They'd only been on the trail three hours and had not yet stopped for lunch. As she expected, Sandra pulled out another smashed sandwich. She turned up her nose. "Please say that's not tuna."

"Ham and cheese."

Jaime sat down and pulled out an apple, pausing to shine it on her shirt before taking a bite. She watched as most of the others unfolded and pitched their tents. All but Abby. She was fishing inside her pack, finally pulling out a swimsuit and waving it over her head. Suits? They were going to soak in suits? What was the fun in that?

Sara sat inside her tent, holding the rather conservative one-piece swimsuit she'd packed. For some reason, she was hesitant to change, even when she heard the excited laughter of the others as they prepared for their first soak in a natural hot spring.

And it wasn't as if she was ashamed of her body. The hours and hours she spent at the gym and on the jogging trails made sure of that. But still.

Oh, hell. She was being silly. Just because Jaime Hutchinson was here, there was no need to alter her plans. She'd been looking forward to the hot springs as much as anyone. With that, she pulled off her boots and socks and stripped the T-shirt over her head, then lay back to slide her jeans off. She heard the first splash and squeal of laughter and smiled. Yes, this was good for them. She put thoughts of Jaime Hutchinson from her mind and slipped on the suit.

Once outside her tent, she walked purposefully to the springs, where all the others, minus Jaime, were already gathered. Even Sandra stood, completely unself-conscious in her swimsuit, anxiously watching the water.

"What do you think?" Sara asked Abby who was splashing about.

"This is glorious, Sarge. What the hell are you all waiting for? Hop in."

That was all it took as nine other women climbed over the rocks and submerged under the warm water.

"Oh my. I could sleep in here," Sandra said as she settled on a rock, the water rising up to her neck.

"What causes hot springs, Ms. Michaels?" Celia asked.

Sara smiled. "Sorry. Geology was not my strong suit. Maybe we should ask one of these two college students."

"Are you kidding? I was an English major," Megan said.

"Music," Ashley added. "What about you, Lou Ann?"

"Sorry. Business major."

"I bet Jaime knows," Sandra stated.

Of course she would, Sara thought sarcastically.

Jaime watched from a distance, her eyes glued to the buff body of Sara Michaels as she stepped over the rocks and into the water. Wow. She had runner's legs, long and muscular. She shook her head. It just wasn't fair, covering that magnificent body with a swimsuit. Then she grinned.

"Oh, hell. Might as well shake things up a bit."

With that, she pulled off her boots and walked barefoot to the springs, still clad in her jeans and shirt.

"Well, you look like you're having fun."

"We are," Celia said. "Aren't you going to join us?"

Jaime flashed a grin. "Of course I am."

She unbuttoned her jeans and let them slip down her legs, stepping out of them in one motion, then pulled her T-shirt over her head and tossed it on the ground. "Move over, Sandra honey, I'm coming in."

The older woman laughed as the very naked Jaime splashed down around her.

"Jesus Christ," Sara murmured, but her eyes refused to obey her command to turn away. She stared as Jaime dropped her jeans then nearly gasped as she tore her T-shirt off, revealing a tanned torso and two unbelievably perfect breasts unencumbered by a bra. Surely to God she's not going to . . . *strip.* But she did, purple panties joined the pile of clothes and a completely naked Jaime Hutchinson splashed into the hot springs full of straight women.

"Holy shit, but she's got some body," Lou Ann whispered.

Sara only nodded, still unable to take her eyes away from the lithe body that had disappeared under the water.

"Why are you all wearing suits?" Jaime asked as she emerged from the water, slicking her short hair back. "That's not allowed in hot springs. We're out here in *nature*," she said. "This is God's gift, intended to be enjoyed in the most natural way possible." She raised her arms up and grinned. "In the buff."

"I haven't been skinny dipping in thirty years," Sandra said.

"I've *never* been," Celia added.

Sara looked up to the sky. Surely they weren't buying this garbage? But, oh yes, they were. Before long, ten fairly conservative, heterosexual women were shedding their swimsuits and tossing them on the rocks, frolicking naked in the water like children, all at the beckoning of this . . . this *stranger*.

"Oh my God! This is fabulous," Judith shrieked.

Sara shook her head. Judith, always the quietest of the group, rose out of the water bare-chested and did a belly flop into the springs, splashing everyone around her. Sara stared. She never would have believed this. They were . . . free, exuberant, happy. Laughter rang out as they all splashed and played. Even Sandra, not one bit shy, stood out of the water and raised her arms overhead, her ample breasts swaying, then crashed down into the water, splashing the others.

Sara finally laughed. She could do nothing else as these grown women were reduced to ten-year-olds. She looked across the water, meeting the laughing eyes of Jaime Hutchinson. She nodded and smiled, sending a silent thank you to her.

"Sarge? What are you doing? Come join us," Abby insisted, grabbing Sara's hand and leading her deeper into the pool.

"No, no. I'm doing just fine," she said.

"Come on, take it off. It's so wonderful like this," Lou Ann said as she playfully splashed Sara.

"I can see that. But, actually, I'm pretty shy," she lied. She moved to another rock, sinking to her chest. Finally, she ducked under the water, wetting her hair. When she opened her eyes, dark brown ones were staring back at her. She pulled her eyes away, laughing as Sandra did another belly flop into the water.

For the next hour, they splashed about, enjoying the sunshine and the warm water, content to laugh and play as they'd not done in years. She listened as Jaime explained how the springs were formed—most likely some made-up nonsense about thermal water being forced to the surface through cracks in the earth—and then had them engrossed in a story, telling about another trip she'd taken to these mountains and how she'd been chased from the springs, stark naked, by a bear.

"Climbed the first tree I came to, scared to death," she said. "I thought the bear wanted me for dinner and all he wanted was a drink."

"They don't really attack, do they?" Celia asked.

"Black bears? Not as a rule, no. But if you have food in the tent with you, I'm sure they might want to come in and check it out. You need to remember to put up all the food."

Sara nodded. "We actually had a fox in camp with us last night."

"A fox? Really?"

"Yeah. He woke me up about four thirty. I was afraid it was a bear."

"Is that something we should worry about?" Beth asked.

"No. I'm sure eleven snoring women would scare him off," Jaime teased.

"I do not snore," Abby said. Then she turned to Lou Ann. "Do I?"

Lou Ann laughed. "How would I know? I passed out as soon as my head hit the ground."

Sara settled back as the conversation went on around her. It was turning out to be a very good trip. And grudgingly, she admitted Jaime had a lot to do with it. Perhaps it was good, having an outsider with them. It would help though if she didn't look like a damn model. Maybe that was what was bothering her. She was attractive. In fact, she was one of the cutest women Sara had met in a long, long time. And she was a flirt. And Sara felt a tug of attraction for the other woman. She rolled her eyes. *God, did I just think that?* But yes, she couldn't deny it as she watched Jaime rise from the water and sit on a rock, laying out flat and letting the sun dry her. She very nearly groaned as her eyes landed on Jaime's breasts.

She made herself move, dipping under the water again. She wasn't even sure she liked the woman. How could she possibly be attracted to her? She stood in the middle of the springs, her eyes again landing on the prone body of Jaime Hutchinson. How? Jesus, you'd have to be dead not to notice her. Well, dead or straight. And she was neither.

CHAPTER ELEVEN

The sun had just sunk below the western mountains but dinner had already been eaten and they were all sitting on the ground, enjoying the coolness of the approaching evening.

"This was one of the best days I can ever remember," Ashley said.

"Me too," Judith agreed. "It was fun."

"Well, we should be able to do it again. The Collegiate Peaks are famous for their hot springs," Sara told them.

"Where are those springs you were telling us about, Jaime? The one where the bear chased you," Sandra asked.

"Actually, we'll come across it," Jaime said. "It's on the eastern side of Mt. Yale, before we get to Cottonwood Pass."

"Is that why it's called the Collegiate Peaks? You mentioned Mt. Princeton earlier. Now Mt. Yale."

"Yeah. There's Mt. Oxford and Mt. Columbia too. All four-teeners," she said. "And of course, Mt. Harvard. Actually, the

Collegiate Peaks wilderness has the most concentration of four-teeners in the Rockies."

"Fourteeners?" Abby asked.

"Mountain peaks over fourteen thousand feet tall," Sara supplied.

"Can we hike them?"

Sara and Jaime both laughed.

"Not this group, no."

"If you want to hike up a fourteener, Pikes Peak has a trail that starts in Manitou Springs, about seven thousand feet and climbs right up to the top."

"Or you could always just drive the road to the top."

"But people do it, right?"

"Oh sure," Jaime said. "Colorado has fifty-six peaks over fourteen thousand feet. I've bagged a few myself. Some are relatively easy, with established trails going right to the top, like Pikes Peak. Others, well, once you get above tree line, you rely on your compass and luck." She looked at Sara. "What about you?"

"I've bagged a couple. Longs Peak was my first."

"Yeah, Longs Peak is popular. My favorite trip was up the Maroon Bells, though. Barely over fourteen thousand but still, the prettiest views I've ever seen. It's almost spiritual up there," Jaime said quietly.

Sara nodded, watching the others as they all watched Jaime. She had a presence about her, Sara realized. Tall, attractive, confident. And friendly. The others just seemed to be drawn to her. Like herself.

"Can we drink the water here?" Abby asked out of the blue. She was looking at Jaime and Sara bristled just a little. She'd already told them they had to purify it first.

Jaime grinned. "Oh, it's the best tasting water you're ever going to put in your mouth. But I wouldn't," she added. "It looks crystal clear but there's this little nasty organism that lives up here. If you get it and you're up here without a bathroom, trust me, you're going to want someone to shoot you."

"Have you had it?"

"No. But a lady friend who was hiking with me got it."

"Gross."

"That it was. Let's just say when we got back down the mountain, we didn't see each other again." She looked across at Sara and winked. "So the lesson is, drop the little iodine tablets in your water just to be safe."

"What do you do back in the real world, Jaime?" Abby said. "You're from Denver, right?"

Jaime smiled and looked across at Sara. "Actually, I'm a cop," she said.

"No kidding? A cop?"

"Well," Jaime met Sara's eyes. "A detective, really."

Sara shook her head. A cop? A detective? Next thing you know, she'll tell them she's the chief of police. Geez, couldn't she have made up something a little less far-fetched?

"That must be exciting," Lou Ann said.

Jaime shrugged. "Sometimes. But it's nothing like TV, trust me."

"But still, I bet it's dangerous," Sandra said.

"It can be, yes. But hey, we're up here now. None of that really matters, right?"

"Right you are." Abby stood up. "In fact, because none of that matters and because there is no TV to watch, I'm going to hit the hay. I'm sure the Sarge has a busy day planned for us tomorrow."

"Yeah. We'll have a pretty good hike tomorrow. We'll go above ten thousand feet," Sara said.

Everyone dispersed, leaving Sara and Jaime sitting alone in the darkness, their campfire nearly out. Jaime thought she should be polite and retreat to her own tent but why start now? So instead, she stretched her legs out and leaned back against the rock, watching as Sara Michaels did the same.

"I can't believe you got them to strip," Sara finally said.

"Well, all but one," Jaime teased.

Sara smiled. "I'm not that easy." She cleared her throat. "A cop? Couldn't make up something a little less threatening?"

"Threatening? Well, should I have told them I'm just a boring old CPA? Not much fun in that."

"I see. No, we wouldn't want them to think you're boring. Although I don't see how that would be possible, considering the entertainment you provided today."

"What about you, Ms. Michaels?"

Sara frowned. "What about me? And please call me Sara. I don't know why some of them continue to call me Ms. Michaels."

Jaime nodded. "Are you having any fun out here or are you technically working?"

"Technically? Yes, working. I'm supervisor, tour guide, chaperone, whatever you want to call it."

"So you have to continue being a counselor out here. I guess it's not like you're just out hiking with a group of friends."

"Exactly. They've become friends with each other, of course. Good friends, in fact. Abby and Lou Ann are nearly inseparable and that's something that they'll carry with them long after I'm forgotten. But up here, this is just the culmination of our sessions. I'm still the Sarge, as they call me."

"It must be exhausting . . . and very lonely."

Sara stared. She couldn't believe that this stranger had hit on the truth so quickly. She took a deep breath then let it out slowly. "It's been," she smiled. "Yeah, lonely. I spend twelve weeks total with these women, meeting every day, some days two or three hours at a time in sessions. And then there's the physical activity we do. A spare hour here or there is spent planning the next day's session." She leaned forward, holding her hands out to the fire. "Sometimes I feel nearly overwhelmed by it all. So, this two-week trip is my down time, I suppose. It gives me a chance to get away too."

"Surely, you're not the only one running your clinic."

"No. We have nutritionists on staff, trainers. We have a trained psychologist who meets with the women once a week."

"I thought you did the counseling."

"I do. I don't have a Ph.D. but I have extensive training. But having Dr. McNally on staff is a bonus. And I've recently hired three more counselors to take on sessions."

"So, you don't really have a private life?" Jaime guessed.

"No, not really. But for other reasons than I just don't have the time." Sara pulled her knees up and leaned on them. "Have you heard of Senator Michaels?"

Jaime shrugged. "I've heard the name, of course. I'm sorry, but I'm not really into politics. You're related?" Jaime was thankful it was too dark to see. She never could lie worth a damn.

"He's my father and please don't apologize. I absolutely abhor the profession. And I've had more people than I can count pretend to take an interest in me personally just because he is my father."

"Using you for what?"

"You would be surprised how many political groupies are out there and what they hope to gain by getting in good with a senator's daughter. The fact that I have a thriving business doesn't seem to hurt." Sara peered into the darkness trying to see Jaime's face. "For as long as I can remember, my father's been in politics. I grew up in Colorado Springs. He was on the city council. Then mayor. Then elected to the state legislature. And he's been a two-term senator." She let out a heavy breath. "Now, he's decided to run for president."

"Wow," Jaime murmured.

"I hated being a senator's daughter. I can't imagine being the *president's* daughter."

"Well, what are his chances of being elected?"

"Realistically, I'd like to say none. He's extremely conservative and has the backing of most of the major religious groups. But he's so far to the right, I can't imagine him being elected. On the other hand, he's never lost before."

"So I take it you don't work the campaign trail," Jaime said.

Sara laughed. "When Mayor Michaels became State Representative Michaels, I was camping out on Barr Trail on my way to the top of Pikes Peak. He sent one of his aides up to get me. We were going to go as a family to Denver. He found me in a tent with another girl." Sara laughed again. "We weren't sleeping."

Jaime laughed too. "Shook his conservative image?"

"Had it gotten out, sure. I mean, you've heard of the Family

Values Association? They practically paid for every one of his campaigns. They're also, still to this day, the most outspoken opponent of gay rights. They would have hung him out to dry."

"So you're . . . in the closet?"

"Oh, God no. I would never allow my father to do that to me. I owe him nothing. I put myself through college." She smiled affectionately. "Well, with help from my grandmother and my mother. He refused. He wanted me to go to a religious university. He still insisted I was pretending to be gay to get back at him for some reason and if I went to a *school of God*, I'd come to my senses." She shook her head. "No. My father and I don't speak. We don't really have a relationship at all anymore. Most people probably don't even know that he has a daughter, which is fine with me. I like my privacy and I like my separation from him. But I don't know how he intends to pull this off. When you're a presidential candidate, everything about your life is scrutinized and everything is open for public debate. I doubt that he can hide the fact that he's got a gay daughter."

"You said you're not close to your father. What about your mother?"

"Oh, I love her to death. We have lunch whenever she's in Denver and when she's in Washington we talk several times a month."

"And how does she feel about you?"

Sara smiled. "You mean my being gay? My mother's been nothing but supportive. She loves me, regardless of how my father feels. And her political views don't necessarily mirror his. She's actually terrified he's going to get elected."

"Terrified? She doesn't want to be first lady?"

"She thinks he'd be an awful president. I have to agree."

"But if he did get elected, wouldn't you be required to participate?"

"Participate in what?"

"Hell, I don't know. Like I said, I'm not really into politics. It just always seems the daughters get air time."

"What I'd be required to participate in would be a Secret

Service escort. Can you imagine having someone around every single hour of the day?"

"What about your clinic? Your sessions?"

"Yes. We'd have an agent here with us right now."

"Well, maybe you'll get lucky and they'll assign a female agent," Jaime teased.

CHAPTER TWELVE

It was a cloudy, cold morning and Sara looked up, wondering if the forecast of no snow was wrong. Everyone had donned sweat-shirts and some had even slipped on gloves. But within an hour, the skies began clearing and the sun warmed them. At the first stop, Sara pulled off her sweatshirt and shoved it into her pack. Most of the others did the same. She noticed that Jaime replaced her sweatshirt with a flannel shirt that she left open over her T-shirt. Their eyes met and Sara smiled slightly before looking away.

She hadn't intended to reveal quite so much to the other woman last night but it had felt good to just talk with someone. She spent most of her time listening to others talk and she rarely took the time for casual dinners with friends where she could share some of her thoughts and feelings. There just wasn't enough time. In truth, there really weren't that many friends. And that was her fault. She had a hard time trusting people. She'd been burned too many times when she'd found they were more interested in her father's name than in her.

Maybe that's why she was starting to take a liking to Jaime. Jaime didn't care who her father was.

"Wow. Look at that," Sandra said, pointing overhead. "What is it?"

They all looked up, watching the large bird as it circled over them.

"It's a golden eagle," Jaime said. "Isn't he beautiful?"

"He's *huge*."

"I guess so. Six-foot wing span."

Sandra stared at her. "You know a lot, don't you?"

"What do you mean?"

"Out here. You know what the trees are, what the mountains are, the birds. Like that little bird we saw this morning, the one with the black cap. What was it again?"

"Mountain chickadee," Jaime supplied. "And I don't know all that much. You just learn as you go. Next time you're out here, you'll know a bird and impress someone, huh?"

Sandra laughed. "It's beautiful out here but I can't imagine doing another hike like this one."

"Why not?" Jaime asked as they fell into step again.

"Oh, you look right at home out here. So does Sara. But I'm an old city girl. Never been camping a day in my life."

"So this is a crash course, huh?"

"But I'm having fun. Yesterday in the hot springs was wonderful. I hope we can do that again."

"I'm sure we can." She pulled out the trail map that was folded in her back pocket. "Look here," she pointed. "I'd guess we're about right here," she said, moving her finger across the map. "See all these blue dots? They're springs. See where the trail goes? Once we cross over the Mt. Harvard trail, we'll be crossing all sorts of streams and most of them have hot springs."

"Where did you camp before?" Celia asked as she looked at the map.

Jaime unfolded the map one more time. "Over here. We've probably got about two more days hiking before we get there. But it's beautiful. The springs are about as big as a swimming pool. It would be a great area to spend two nights."

Sandra poked her elbow against Jaime's ribs. "Why don't you mention that to the Sarge?"

"Well, she's probably got an agenda. Might not be enough time to stop for two days."

"Yeah, but ask anyway, would you?"

Jaime nodded. "Sure. I'll give it a try."

"By the way," Celia said quietly. "I heard you two up talking last night."

"Yeah, we visited a bit."

"Making any progress?"

"With what?"

Celia smiled. "You know. With your date?"

Jaime burst out laughing, causing the others to stop and turn.

"What's going on back there?" Abby demanded. "If you're going to do jokes, you have to share with everyone."

Sara turned around too, her eyes finding Jaime's at the back of the line. She raised her eyebrows, waiting.

"Nothing," Jaime murmured. "It's private," she added.

"Uh-huh." Sara noticed the amusement on both Sandra's and Celia's faces and wondered what they were up to. "How about a break?"

"Don't have to ask me twice," Abby said, already tossing her pack on the ground.

"Sorry about that, honey," Celia whispered as both she and Sandra leaned against the same tree as Jaime.

"No problem."

"You know, I don't recall Sara ever mentioning a special some-one," Celia said. She nudged Jaime with her shoulder. "You might have a chance."

"Well, you'll certainly be the first to know." Jaime slid her eyes to where Sara was sitting, alone. The mountain breeze was blow-ing the blond hair onto her face and she watched as slim fingers reached out to try and tame it. Jaime stared, wondering when the last time was she'd found someone this attractive. Actually, she realized it had been months since she'd even gone out on a date and that was someone her friend Carol had set her up with. It had turned out to be a nice dinner but there wasn't even a tiny spark between them and she had never called the woman again.

But Sara? Well, she would have given just about anything to have had Sara strip off her swimsuit yesterday. She closed her eyes and smiled. Of course, then she'd probably have just made a fool out of herself.

They hiked until nearly four o'clock, through stands of golden aspens and along ridges dotted with spruce trees. The views were incredible and most of the women pulled out small digital cameras to capture the scenes. Once, Sandra handed her camera to Celia and wrapped her arm around Jaime's shoulder, smiling big as Celia snapped their picture.

There would be no hot springs this evening as they weren't even near a stream but they would at least have a campfire. And they would need it. As soon as the sun dipped below the mountains, the cold returned. Jaime traded her flannel shirt for the sweatshirt again, then helped to gather downed wood for their fire. Sara made a fire ring out of rocks and piled pine needles and cones inside before adding smaller twigs. She handed Abby a book of matches.

"Want to do the honors?"

"Absolutely."

All the women watched as Abby knelt down and struck the match, cupping it to keep it from blowing out. Soon, the flame licked at the pine needles and they had their first big campfire going. Cheers and claps resounded and Jaime looked up, right into the smiling eyes of Sara Michaels.

After they ate their dinners and cleaned up the pots, all twelve of them crowded around the fire, trying to keep warm. But one by one, the cold chased them off and the women retreated into the tents and sleeping bags, until only Sara and Jaime remained.

"It's barely eight," Jaime said from across the fire.

"They're not used to this much activity. But I thought having a fire might keep them up longer."

Jaime nodded although she hadn't missed the wink Celia had given her when she'd left them alone. The older woman was apparently playing matchmaker.

"You seem to be in pretty good shape for a CPA," Sara said.

Jaime laughed. "I hate that stereotype. I'm a gym rat, actually."

They were both quiet, staring into the fire. Then Sara leaned forward, watching Jaime.

"Can I ask you something?"

"Of course."

"What are you doing here?"

Smiling, Jaime raised her eyebrows. "Are we back to that again? Still think I'm a serial killer?"

"I haven't made up my mind. But surely, this can't be your idea of a quiet backpacking trip. Why are you still traveling with us?"

Jaime stirred the fire, watching embers dance as they rose from the flames. "You want me to make up something witty or just tell you the truth?"

"I'm a big advocate of the truth."

"Okay." Jaime leaned forward too. She met the blue-green eyes across from her and held them captive. "The truth is, I think you're cute as hell and I find myself extremely attracted to you."

Sara's breath caught. "Excuse me?"

"Besides, I have a great view from the back of the line. I think you have a very sexy walk."

"*Excuse* me?"

"You said you wanted the truth."

Sara was at a loss for words. Jaime Hutchinson had to be the most conceited, arrogant . . . *flirt* she had ever met. All she could do was stare at her.

"No comment?" Jaime finally asked. "You're not going to tell me the feeling is mutual?"

Sara smiled and shook her head. "I'm not sure I even like you."

"You've got to give it time. I'm sure I'll grow on you."

"I don't think we have that much time." Sara stood and brushed off her jeans. "Make sure the fire is out."

Jaime nodded and watched as Sara retreated into her tent. "Damn, but she's cute. Sexy and cute," she murmured as she stirred the fire again.

CHAPTER THIRTEEN

Three days later, they were crossing the Mt. Harvard trail at ten thousand feet. They had explored a large rock formation for nearly an hour and everyone sat on the edge of the cliff, feet dangling over the side as they enjoyed the views. Everyone except Sara, who insisted they were entirely too close to the edge.

"Well, while you're standing back there, Sarge, why don't you take our picture?" Jaime suggested.

"You're insane."

"It's not that bad, Sara," Abby said. "It's a gradual drop-off."

"This would make a great picture," Sandra said, turning around to hand Sara her camera. "Make sure you get all of us."

Sara took a step closer to grab the camera, too embarrassed to tell them that she had a slight fear of heights. She walked backward, trying to fit them all into the frame. They turned their heads and leaned into each other, the same smiles on all their faces, Jaime included.

"One, two . . . three," she called, snapping the picture. She lowered the camera. "Happy now? Will you please come away from the edge?"

"I think she's worried about you," Celia teased quietly.

"I think she's worried about a lawsuit," Jaime said which caused Sandra to burst out laughing.

Sara scowled at them. Jaime was a troublemaker, she decided.

But Sara was as excited as the rest of them. They were within an hour of the springs Jaime had been telling them about. Springs as large as a swimming pool, she promised. Hopefully, they wouldn't have to share it with bears.

"And you know, Sara, if we stayed for two days, we could do laundry," Jaime suggested, remembering Celia's request for an extended visit.

"Laundry? God yes," Abby said. "I'm afraid if I take these jeans off one more time, they're going to walk away on their own."

They all laughed and Sara looked down at her own dirty jeans. She'd instructed them all not to bring more than three changes of clothes. Yes, probably a laundry day in the springs would be a good idea. That and a bath.

"Okay. I suppose we can stay two nights there," she agreed. Her announcement was met with cheers.

"I like her more and more every day," Jaime said. Sandra was a few steps behind her and she turned to wait for her when something caught her eye. A reflection, perhaps, high up on the ridge behind them. As she watched, it disappeared. "You going to make another hour, Sandra?" Jaime asked, her eyes still scanning the mountainside behind them.

"No problem. Not when I know we'll have two days to play."

Jaime nodded. What could have caused the reflection? Glass? Metal? Could be anything. She turned to walk on but she had a nagging feeling that it wasn't just anything. She stopped and scratched her head, then turned back again, seeing nothing out of the ordinary, just the scattered spruce and fir trees that had found footholds in the rocks. She had convinced herself that these threats against Sara Michaels were bogus. Hell, even the FBI suggested they were. But what if they weren't? What if someone had been following them the whole time? Watching them? And all the while, she'd been more concerned with having a good time and teasing Sara, not protecting her.

"Goddamn," she murmured.

"You coming?"

Jaime looked back at Sandra and shook her head. "You know what? You go on ahead. I'll catch up. I know the way. I want to do a little exploring around here, maybe chase up a bird or two."

"A bird?"

Jaime grinned. "Yeah. It'll be quieter without all you guys running your mouths."

Sandra waved. "Okay. Go on. But I'll expect you in the hot springs later."

"It's a date."

Jaime's smile faded as soon as Sandra walked away and she turned back toward the trail, wondering where to start. Up this high, the vegetation was thin. She decided to go down between the two ridges, trying to conceal herself as much as possible behind the boulders that dotted the area. She slipped once on a rock and landed on her ass, stopping her downward slide by grabbing a tree.

"Nice and quiet, Jaime. You're doing great," she murmured sarcastically, getting to her feet again. She circled around, constantly watching the mountainside for movement. Then there it was, the reflection again. She whipped out her binoculars, scanning the trees and rocks, seeing nothing.

"Shit."

She studied the area, wondering what it could be. She looked up. The sun was at her back, shining directly on the mountain, no doubt reflecting off of . . . something. Then she looked at her binoculars. Could be reflecting off of the glass of a binocular lens or spotting scope. Her eyes widened. Or off of the scope on a rifle. She shook her head. She was letting her imagination get the best of her. If they'd been followed for the past six days by someone with a rifle, surely they could have taken a shot by now.

"I hate this job."

She waited another half-hour but saw neither movement nor the reflection again. Well, regardless, it was time she let Sara Michaels in on it. It was only fair. After all, she was the target of this supposed threat.

As Sara walked, she noticed something was missing. The constant chatter at the back of the line. She stopped and turned around, looking for the laughing brown eyes that were normally there waiting for her. She found none.

"Where's Jaime?" she asked. Everyone turned around and looked at Sandra.

"She went off by herself," Sandra said as she tried to catch her breath.

"Off where?" Sara demanded.

Sandra shrugged. "Just off. She was looking for some bird or something."

"A bird?"

"That's what she said."

"Is she coming back?"

"Yeah. She said she knew the way, Ms. Michaels. I think maybe she just wanted a little alone time."

"Uh-huh." But Sara shrugged. She shouldn't really care. It wasn't like she invited her on this trip to begin with. She started walking again. According to the map and Jaime's directions, they should be at the river any minute.

And fifteen minutes later, they heard water cascading over rocks. At the water crossing, Sara turned upstream as Jaime had told her, easily finding the well-worn trail between the trees. Apparently, these hot springs were popular. A short while later, she saw the steam rising.

"Oh my God," Abby said. "It's beautiful."

Yes, it was. Practically an oasis stuck high up in the Rocky Mountains. The river dropped some twenty feet onto boulders that were strewn about then flowed into a pool that was nearly bubbling as hot thermal water escaped the cracks underground and formed the springs. It was as Jaime had said, the size of a swimming pool.

"I vote we stay three days," Sandra said.

Sara smiled and dropped her pack, her eyes still glued to the water. It was absolutely beautiful. One of the prettiest sights she had ever seen. Again she turned, looking around for Jaime. Damn the woman. She'd only been with them six days. How could she possibly have gotten used to her being around in that short of time?

After the tents were set up, everyone changed and hurried into the hot springs. Sara noticed that not one woman discarded her swimsuit this time. She, too, changed into her one-piece suit and joined them. They were all enjoying the water, but not like they had the last time. Conversations were quiet and she realized that in only a few short days, Jaime's presence, or lack thereof, was a major influence on the group. Again, she looked down the trail, hoping to catch sight of her.

Submerging into the warm water, she let out a satisfied moan as her body was enveloped. She, too, missed the chatter of the other woman—and the unlimited stories she seemed to have at her disposal. Jaime was able to reach them on a different level, Sara realized. Instead of telling them not to leave food out, she told them of a time a bear had come looking for food. Instead of simply telling them not to drink the water, she told them of a time when someone had taken a drink. Sara knew with this group, and with all the others, she had missed connecting with them on that level. She was their counselor, teacher . . . but never friend. And she, like the others, missed Jaime's presence now.

Finally, after nearly thirty minutes of quiet talk, she spotted the familiar figure walking up the trail. A relieved smiled touched her face before she could stop it.

"It's Jaime," Celia said and pointed.

"About time," Sandra yelled.

Jaime waved and tossed her pack on the ground, then bent to

untie her boots. Sara knew that she was about to be confronted with another display of nakedness. So did the others. Jaime walked slowly toward them, hands on her hips.

"What have I told you about the rules, ladies? Clothing is *not* allowed in hot springs. Jesus, what am I going to do with you?"

Sara stared as jeans were dropped and T-shirt was flung. Then, almost in slow motion, black panties this time were shed and a completely naked Jaime Hutchinson stood on a rock and executed a perfect shallow dive into the hot springs. She rose out of the water like a goddess, her eyes finding Sara's immediately.

"I thought you were in charge," Jaime teased. "Why do they all have clothes on?"

"Not for long," Abby said loudly as she dipped below the water and came up flinging her swimsuit upon the rocks. Soon, nine others followed and the pool was reduced to a playground for eleven naked women.

Sara laughed at their exuberant play, especially Sandra, who was floating on her back in the middle of the pool, not at all self-conscious as she splashed water on Jaime only to have the other woman dunk her under. Sandra came up spitting and laughing.

"God, I love this." She splashed down again. "I feel almost thin in this water."

"Sandra, honey, you look great just the way you are," Jaime insisted.

Sandra beamed a smile at her. "Now why can't I find a man just like you?"

Jaime's eyes widened in mock disbelief. "A *man*? You're comparing me to a man? I'm very offended."

"If I was into women, I'd already have you wrapped up, young lady," Sandra teased the other woman.

Everyone laughed, including Sara. It was only then that Sara realized they all must know Jaime is gay. And even then, here they were, all stripped naked without a concern in the world. She never would have thought it possible. Not with this group.

"Sarge? Why don't you join us?" Celia asked.

Jaime walked closer, eyebrows rising mischievously. "Yes, Sara? Why don't you?" Jaime playfully captured her hand and tried to pull her deeper into the water.

"Behave or I'll be forced to hurt you," Sara said.

Jaime laughed but did not release her hold. "What if I promise I won't look?"

Celia laughed and clapped her hands. "Don't believe her!"

"Hey, whose side are you on?" Jaime asked.

"Yours, of course."

"I see. Ganging up on me, huh?" Sara tried to pull her hand away.

"Yes, we are." Jaime smiled, refusing to let her go.

Jaime stood up, the water reaching only to her waist. Sara's breath caught at the sight standing before her. Droplets of water clung to her breasts and Sara stared as one slowly traveled down Jaime's breast to her nipple. The hand that was still holding hers tightened and she brought her eyes up, colliding with Jaime's. The brown eyes darkened and she felt her heart quicken its pace.

"Take it off," Jaime whispered.

Sara shook her head.

"Please?"

Sara was aware of how quiet it was, aware that the others were watching them with anticipation. She knew it was pure insanity but she wanted to be a part of their group. So, she took one hand and slowly slipped her straps off her shoulders. She saw Jaime's breath catch and she smiled.

"Turn around," she instructed quietly.

"What would be the fun in that?"

But Jaime released the hand she had been holding and obediently turned around, pausing to wink at Celia. The other woman smiled broadly at her. Jaime finally heard a splash and quickly turned, just in time to see a nicely rounded backside dip under the water. Sara resurfaced in the middle of the pool, water up to her shoulders.

"See? Isn't that better?"

"Much." Sara slicked her hair back and let out a contented sigh. Yes, it was glorious. But as Jaime came closer, Sara laughed and splashed water in her face. "Behave."

The other women laughed and Jaime splashed back at Sara then moved a safe distance away.

"Ms. Michaels? Are you dating anyone?" Celia innocently asked.

Jaime hid her smile as Sara stared at Celia.

"Actually, no. I'm not." Sara cleared her throat. "Why do you ask?"

"Oh, just . . . curious."

"Uh-huh," Sara murmured. She slid her eyes to Jaime, raising an eyebrow. Jaime only shrugged and dipped below the water again.

They stayed in the pool for another hour, then one by one they started getting out, most to grab dirty clothes to rinse out in the springs. It was only then that Sara realized her position. Her swimsuit was flung on a faraway rock. And Jaime was still in the water, a satisfied grin on her face.

"Now what are you going to do?" Jaime asked with a laugh. "Can't stay in here all night."

"Yes, you're right. I can't, can I?" So, she gave Jaime a dose of her own medicine. She stood and walked slowly to the edge of the pool, the water dripping off her naked body. She had the pleasure of seeing Jaime slip on a rock as she stared. Serves her right, she thought.

"Oh my God," Jaime whispered. She looked around for Celia. "Did you see that?"

"Sure did."

"She's beautiful."

"Nice body."

"Nice? That's not nice. That's . . . magnificent."

Celia moved closer to her. "I think she likes you."

"Oh yeah?"

"Yeah. She kept looking for you when you were gone. And she

must have asked Sandra a hundred times if you were coming back."

"She did?" Then Jaime playfully nudged Celia. "Thanks, even though this conversation is fast approaching the high school level."

Jaime watched as Sara disappeared into her tent and her smile faded. She would have to tell her tonight. Tell her that she was only here because she was a cop and she was supposed to be watching her. And then, no doubt, all the fun would be gone. Sara would be furious.

Sara changed into her one pair of sweatpants, then took her dirty jeans and underclothes back to the springs to wash them. She smiled, thinking they looked very much like pioneer women on wash day. All but Jaime. She was nowhere to be found. Sara dipped her jeans into the warm water, trying to scrub the dirt off as best she could. Before long, tree limbs and shrubs held their wet clothing as it blew in the breeze. She helped the others gather wood for the fire they'd have later, all the while looking around for Jaime. Finally, she could stand it no longer.

"Celia? Have you seen Jaime?"

"She changed and walked back down the trail again. She didn't say where she was going."

Sara nodded, wondering at Jaime's odd behavior today. Oh, well. The woman had a right to her privacy. It would just be courteous to let someone know where she was going.

In fact, it was nearly dark before Jaime joined them again. Everyone had already eaten and were gathered around the fire, relaxing. Sara watched as Jaime quickly assembled her tent, then moved closer to the fire with her small stove.

"Where were you?" Sandra asked.

"Just exploring." She grinned. "Miss me?"

"Well, it's just kinda quiet when you're not around."

"Oh yeah? Thanks. I think," she added. "Actually, you know, I'm crashing your party so I thought I should give you guys some alone time. Sara might have had something planned that I shouldn't be a part of."

"We don't need any alone time," Abby said. "And you're not crashing our party. We invited you."

"Well, thanks." Jaime sat next to Lou Ann on a log they had moved up. "This reminds me of a trip I took when I was a kid. My older brother organized this backpacking trip with a bunch of his friends but I wasn't invited. In fact, I was instructed they didn't want me within ten miles of them." She bent down to add her freeze-dried meal to the boiling water. "So, I snuck out of the house and followed them for two days before showing myself. I knew he couldn't send me home alone but he was mad as hell, let me tell you."

"How old were you?"

Jaime grinned. "Eight."

Sara rolled her eyes. "And your parents didn't miss you?"

Jaime laughed. "Hell, yeah. They had the police and helicopters out looking for me. It was all over the news. Volunteers had already organized to search the woods."

Sara laughed with the others. "How old was your brother?"

"Seventeen. We came walking home five days later—tired, dirty and hungry. We should have known something was up by all the cars parked along the street."

"Please tell me you were grounded."

"Me? No, but my brother got his car taken away from him."

"Your brother? But you were the one who snuck off," Abby said.

"I was *eight*. You can't be punished when you're eight."

"And your return made the news?"

Jaime grinned. "My mother made me put on a dress for the event."

Sara watched the women as they hung on Jaime's every word. She was enjoying the story too. God, how boring would this trip have been if Jaime hadn't tagged along? Then she frowned. Were all of her trips boring?

Jaime stirred the pot one more time before pulling it into her lap. "Has everyone already eaten or are you planning on sharing mine?"

"We've eaten," Lou Ann said. "Tell us another story."

"Another story? If I bore you with more than one story a night, I'll run out before too long." She looked at Sara. "Are you planning on taking us to St. Elmo?"

"I was, yes."

"What's St. Elmo?" Abby asked.

"It's a ghost town. It's in really great shape. Even some of the wooden sidewalks are preserved. Went there once. Hiked up alone. Saw the ghost town, all right. But saw a ghost too."

"No way."

"Yep. Sure did." Jaime stood with her empty pot and walked toward the springs to clean it. "Remind me to tell you sometime," she tossed over her shoulder.

"Why not now?"

"Oh, no. None of you would get any sleep if I told you a ghost story before bedtime."

Sara smiled at the other woman. Yes, she was certainly full of stories. Sara wondered how many of them were true and how many were made up on the spot. It didn't matter. They were at least entertaining.

Before too long, as the fire was burning down, the women started getting ready for bed. But Sara wasn't tired. She added another small log to the fire and moved closer, holding her hands out to warm them. Actually, she hoped Jaime might stay up with her awhile. The previous evening, Jaime had joined the others at bedtime, leaving Sara alone. In fact, they hadn't spoken a whole lot since the night Jaime had confessed she was attracted to her. And Sara had run. But Sara found she was interested and she hadn't been flirted with this shamelessly since college. It felt good. It didn't hurt that the woman doing the flirting was attractive and fun to be around. Then she frowned. Hadn't she called her arrogant and conceited just a few days ago? Arrogant, yes, as she stripped naked in front of everyone, knowing full well the affect she was having on Sara. And then the nerve to insist that Sara strip as well. Yes, shameless. But it was all in good fun. It wasn't like Sara was going to fall for it.

"Hey."

Sara looked up. She had been staring into the fire and hadn't noticed Jaime approach. "Going to tell me about the ghost now?"

Jaime shifted nervously then glanced at the tents. They were within hearing distance, should anyone care to listen. And she knew full well that Celia and Sandra were probably sitting at their tent door this very moment.

"Actually, I need to talk to you," Jaime said quietly. "Can we maybe take a walk?"

"A walk?"

"Just over to the springs," Jaime suggested. "I'd like some privacy."

Had she not been so serious, Sara would have teased her about her lame attempt to get her alone. So she nodded.

They walked along the footpath to the edge of the springs. The continuous flow of the river as it crashed across the rocks and boulders gave Jaime just the sound barrier that she needed.

Jaime turned and faced her, the moonlight strong enough for her to see Sara's face. "Listen, first of all, you've got to promise me you won't get mad."

Sara crossed her arms across her chest and raised her eyebrows. "That depends."

"No, no. It can't depend," Jaime said. "I need to tell you something."

"Okay. Fine. Tell me."

Jaime took a breath then reached in her back pocket and pulled out her detective's shield. She squeezed it tight, then handed it to Sara.

"What's this?"

"What does it look like?"

Sara held it away from her into the moonlight. "Is it real?"

"Of course it's real," Jaime said as she snapped on a small flashlight and shone it on the badge.

"You said you were a CPA," Sara reminded her.

Jaime shifted. "Not exactly. If you recall, you asked why I hadn't made up something a little less threatening, I believe you said. So I insinuated that I might be a CPA. Big difference. Because in reality, I did say I was a cop."

"You said you were a CPA. You lied."

"No, I didn't lie. I told the truth. I'm a cop. You just didn't believe me."

Sara handed the badge back. "Fine. So you lied and you are a cop. The two are not supposed to mix. Cops are not supposed to lie."

Jaime raised her hands up. "Look, it doesn't matter, okay? That's not what I needed to talk to you about."

"It's not? Okay. Then what is it?"

"Remember, you promised you wouldn't get mad."

"I don't recall making that promise, but . . . what . . . *is* . . . it?" Sara asked loudly.

Jaime hesitated. Sara was going to kill her. In fact, she wouldn't be surprised if the woman never spoke to her again.

"You asked me once why I was here." Jaime took another deep breath. "Well, I'm working for the FBI." At Sara's widening eyes, she hurried on. "You know, the death threats."

Sara stared, her eyes finally narrowing. "How dare you? How dare you come here, befriend us, *lie* to us?" Sara pointed her finger at Jaime. "Do you have any idea how much those women look up to you? And it's all been a fucking game?" she yelled.

"Will you be quiet?" Jaime hissed, glancing toward the tents. "They don't need to know."

"They most certainly *do* need to know," Sara continued to yell. "I cannot believe you!"

Jaime stepped forward, moving behind Sara and clamping her hand over her mouth to keep her quiet. It seemed like a good idea at the time. But that was before an elbow to her midsection took the breath from her and a closed fist connected with her face. The next thing she knew, she was being tossed over Sara's shoulder like a rag doll and landing with a thud on the ground.

She ran her tongue over her lips, tasting blood. "Damn," she murmured. "Forgot about that self-defense class."

Sara stood back, her eyes wide. She couldn't believe she'd just done that but it was an automatic reaction. One minute they're . . . they're talking, well, she was yelling and the next, Jaime was . . . was manhandling her. Instincts just took over. She finally knelt down, touching Jaime's shoulder.

"I am so sorry. I never meant to do that, but you grabbed me and—"

"Yeah, yeah, yeah. It's okay. Really, it is. But you're under arrest for assaulting a police officer." Jaime wiped at the blood on her lip. "And as soon as I can stand up, I'm going to handcuff you."

Sara stood. "You're going to *what?*"

Jaime finally got to her feet. "I'm bleeding. I can't believe you did that."

Sara picked up the flashlight that had fallen and flashed the beam on Jaime's face. She touched her lips with a soft finger, finally finding the cut.

"You are such a baby." Sara let her hands fall away. "It's a tiny cut."

"Uh-huh. Don't think that'll get you off the hook."

"What hook? I'm the one who should be pissed off here. You lied to me."

Jaime snatched the flashlight from Sara's hands. "Fine. Be pissed off. It doesn't change anything. The only reason I'm telling you this is because we're being followed."

"What do you mean?"

"Well, they're behind us, following us. They're traveling on a higher trail or not on a trail at all. The map doesn't show anything but that doesn't mean there's not a trail up there. And it could be perfectly innocent. They might be hikers for all I know." Jaime turned the flashlight off. "But we can't take a chance. I've got to check it out. So, tomorrow, you stay here with the group, keep them occupied. I'm going to go out and see if I can find them. If it's just a couple of hikers, then it's no problem and we can be on our way."

Sara met her eyes in the moonlight. "And if it's not?"

"I don't know yet." Jaime rubbed again at her lower lip, shaking her head. A cop, for God's sake, and she gets tossed to the ground by a . . . a woman! Jesus. "Listen, what do you know about these threats? The FBI was strangely vague about them."

"Vague? That's an understatement. They showed up at my office one day, saying my father had received letters threatening my life. That's it. When I asked questions, they simply said they couldn't say more."

"Special Agent Ramsey said he practically begged you to accept protection."

"Who?"

"Ramsey. He said he spoke with you."

"No. I don't recall a Ramsey. There were just two. A man and a woman. The man was tall, black, with a shaved head. His name was Erickson. I remember because my secretary's last name is Erickson."

"Erickson? I spoke with Ramsey. Squirrelly white dude. He said he was heading the investigation. He said he talked with you and you refused protection. That's why I'm here. Your father insisted someone look after you."

"Oh, please. My death would be the best thing for my father's campaign. I can't believe he even notified the FBI. My father doesn't like me, Jaime. He never has. Even as a kid, it was like he was always angry at me for some reason."

Jaime walked away, pacing. "Why would Ramsey lie to me?"

Sara leaned her head back and looked at the sky. Why couldn't anything ever be simple?

"Look, let's start at the beginning, okay?" She sat on a rock and waited for Jaime to turn around. "Tell me what they said."

"My captain called me into his office last Thursday. He said the

FBI needed a female detective who backpacked to keep an eye on a senator's daughter who had received a death threat. The next day, Ramsey came in and basically said they thought it was a bogus threat but they had to check it out. That's when he told me he'd spoken with you and you refused protection. I asked him if they had any idea who had made the threats and he said he couldn't tell me." Jaime shrugged. "That's about it. Here I am."

"Well, you know more than I do. They showed up . . . not last week but the Friday before. Out of the blue, no call, nothing. They said my father had received several letters in the past month indicating that my life was in danger. They asked if I'd received any letters or phone calls. They suggested protection. And yes, I refused. I'm not involved in politics, I don't want to be involved. I'm not even involved in my father's life. I haven't been for years. Like I said earlier, we don't have a relationship."

"Did you tell anyone about the FBI's visit? Your mother?"

Sara shook her head. "No, I tried calling her but she wasn't available."

"And if she hasn't said anything to you, maybe she doesn't know about it."

"That could be. My father doesn't share things like that with her. She's window dressing, that's it."

"What do you mean?"

"My mother is a very attractive woman. The cameras love her. The press loves her."

"And she looks great on your father's arm?" Jaime guessed.

"Yes."

Jaime rubbed the back of her neck with her hand, trying to eliminate the stress that had settled there. It made no sense. First of all, why had Ramsey lied to her? Just to get her to accept this gig? Hell, it wasn't like she had a choice.

"Do you think it was a bogus threat?" Sara asked.

"I don't know. Hell, I don't know anything," Jaime admitted. "But today, while we were hiking, I noticed a reflection on the mountain behind us. Then it was gone. But I saw it again, that's why I left. I climbed up the hill and waited and then I saw it. But when I looked with my binoculars, it was gone."

"It could have been anything."

"Yes. But we can't take a chance."

"Look, I'm not going to alter my plans for this. We had planned on staying here another day anyway. If you want to go out searching, then fine. But tomorrow, we go on as usual. I can't have these women scared, Jaime. It'll undo everything I've accomplished in the last ten weeks."

"I agree. That's why I wanted to talk to you alone. But if I find anything, you've got to trust me. What I say goes."

Their eyes met and Sara finally nodded. "Okay."

"Who knows about your route? I understand there's some secrecy to it."

Sara nodded. "There are multiple reasons for keeping it a secret, especially from the group. They—"

"Wait. You mean none of these women knew their destination?"

"No. We've found if they know ahead of time, they dwell on it. Some worry if they can make it. Some contact friends, family, and let them know. On our first trip, we had four husbands show up wanting to go with us. And recently we've had more media attention. You'd be surprised at how many requests we get to have a film crew follow us around." Sara shrugged. "So, no. I plan the entire trip, right down to purchasing new packs for each member. We provide everything they need, but each woman packs her own gear, including meals. That's the responsibility they each take."

"So right now, who knows where you are?"

"I leave an itinerary with my secretary with exact details. Most everyone on my staff knew of the general location. They knew we were hiking the Collegiate Peaks."

"So did Andy at the sporting goods store. That's how I found you," Jaime said.

Sara smiled. "Andy and I have become friendly. I probably divulge stuff without even knowing it."

Jaime nodded, then kicked at a rock. "Listen, I'm really sorry I had to lie to you. I didn't know of another way to get close."

"Sprained ankle? You're a very good actor, I'll give you that."

"Actor? I've not been acting. Hell, I'm enjoying myself. I've had to remind myself why I'm here."

"So, the story about when you were eight? It was true?"

Jaime grinned. "Yeah. My mother hasn't forgiven me yet."

"I really hope this turns out to be nothing. You've been very good for them. I'm glad that you've joined us."

"Why, Ms. Michaels, I never thought I'd hear you say that."

"I'm still pissed off that you lied."

"Yeah? Well, don't forget you assaulted me. I'll hold that over your head."

Sara laughed. "I don't doubt it."

"Maybe we should share a tent from now on. I'll be able to keep an eye on you better that way."

Sara shoved off the rock and walked to Jaime, patting her face lightly. "Trust me. We will *not* share a tent."

CHAPTER FOURTEEN

Jaime left before dawn, moving quietly over the rocks, finding her way by the moon that had not yet slipped below the mountains to the west. It was cold, probably in the mid-thirties, and she slipped on gloves. In one hand she held her binoculars, in the other her small flashlight. She found the trail and walked back the way they'd come. She wanted to get to the base of the mountain before daybreak, then sit and watch for movement. If someone were following them, they would have no idea that they were camping for another day. They would move, thinking they had to keep up the pace. And Jaime would be waiting.

Thirty minutes later, dawn was breaking and she squatted behind a tree, leaning on a rock. She scanned the mountain, barely able to make out shapes in the waning darkness. It occurred to her then the possibility that whoever was following them had moved during the night and camped closer to her group. If that were the case, Jaime would be of no help. They would be vulnerable and

Sara would be on her own. It would be easy. She very nearly convinced herself that she should just head back and stay with Sara. But then she saw it. Smoke.

She squinted her eyes, trying to see through the shadows. But finally she saw the flicker of flame. A small campfire, about halfway up the mountainside. She felt her pulse rate increase and she reminded herself that it could be anything. Just hikers, for all she knew. Still, she moved her hands behind her and under her sweatshirt, touching her gun, making sure it was secure. From now on, she'd hike with it on instead of keeping it hidden in her backpack. She then pulled out her small cell phone and flipped it open. Battery was getting low. But that wasn't the real problem. She closed it again. The cell phone wasn't going to do them a whole lot of good without a signal. She let out a deep breath, then leaned against a tree and waited.

When the sun rose over the mountain, she moved back behind the tree, her binoculars trained on the campfire. Then she saw him. He stood and stretched. She couldn't make out his features and as quickly as she'd seen him, he was gone. Then the smoke from the campfire disappeared and she waited. But she saw nothing. No movement.

She waited nearly an hour then made her way higher, careful not to kick any rocks. She moved quietly, only a few feet at a time, using the trees for cover. Never once did she see movement or hear anything. It was like he just disappeared.

She was within thirty yards of where she thought the campfire had been. Instead of moving forward, she hiked higher, circling around. From above, she saw it, the circle of rocks. He had kicked dirt on top of the ashes. She waited again, then finally moved, reaching behind her back to grab her gun. She saw the impression under the trees where his tent had stood. Then she moved to the campfire, studying the footprints. There appeared to be only one person. Squatting down beside the fire, she picked up a cigarette butt and turned it over in her hand.

Not your average backpacker. Very few backcountry hikers

smoked. And those who did respected the mountains enough not to leave cigarette butts behind. But here, she counted ten, at least. She tossed it down with the others and stood up, looking down the mountain. He'd had a perfect view of the trail. She raised her binoculars to her eyes, pleased that she wasn't able to see as far as the river.

But he was on the move and she was not. She secured her gun in its holster under her shirt and hurried back down the mountain.

Sara leaned against the tree, watching the others as they frolicked in the springs. Most had slept late, knowing they would not be traveling today. But Sara had crawled out of her tent at daybreak, starting the fire and then going to Jaime's tent, finding it empty. She tried not to be concerned. All night long, she reminded herself that Jaime had lied to her, had lied to them all. More than once, she'd come to the conclusion that she didn't care what happened one way or the other. She didn't really believe that someone was following them, that someone would try to kill her. It was too farfetched. That only happened in the movies. She led a relatively simple life. And just because her father was running for president was no reason to kill her, for God's sake.

But as much as she tried to rationalize the situation, she was a little concerned. First the FBI and now Jaime—she'd have to be crazy to just dismiss the threat, which is what she wanted to do. She glanced once again toward the trail, wondering where Jaime was, wondering if she was okay. She picked up a small rock and tossed it.

I don't really even like the woman.

But that wasn't true. Despite the fact that she had forced herself on their group and the fact that she had lied about it didn't change anything. Jaime was still Jaime. And, well, Sara was still attracted to her. Her personality was addictive. She was fun. Jaime had been able to befriend Sandra within minutes. She'd turned Celia into matchmaker in a matter of days. And she'd turned the normally caustic Abby into a mild-mannered, playful woman. And all because she was a likable person with a somewhat warped sense of humor.

Okay, so maybe I do like her, Sara thought to herself. She leaned her head back against the tree, wishing she'd met Jaime under more normal circumstances. Perhaps then they could have gotten to know one another in an ordinary way instead of through lies and deception.

Her eyes widened. Jaime had lied about why she was here. It stood to reason, then, that she'd lied about everything, including her alleged attraction to Sara. She had said those things just to get close to her. Sara picked up another rock and threw it a little more forcefully than the last. It figures. No matter how or where she met women, there was always a hidden agenda for them, mostly involving her father. You'd think that just once she could meet someone who liked her for herself without there being underlying circumstances. But no. And that was why, at age thirty-two, she was still single and unattached.

"Hey."

Sara gasped and whipped around at the sound of that whispered word. She found herself face to face with Jaime, who was squatting down next to the tree.

"You scared me to death."

"Sorry. I thought you heard me walk up."

"No, I was . . . I was thinking, I guess." Sara relaxed again. "Did you see anyone?"

"Yes." Jaime folded her legs and sat down next to Sara. "There was only one guy camping. He was up on the ridge about halfway up the mountain."

"Do you think it's a problem?"

Their eyes met. "I think, maybe, yeah. He had his fire out before it was barely dawn and packed up and moved on. I couldn't follow his tracks in the rocks but he definitely went down the mountain."

"And you think he's close by?"

Jaime motioned with her head. "I think he's up there."

Sara followed her eyes, looking at the tree-covered hill about a hundred yards away. "Okay. So now what?"

Jaime sighed. *Yeah, Jaime, now what?* She didn't have a clue. Pack everyone up and head out? He would simply follow them, stopping when they did, biding his time until he could take his shot. No. As far as he knew, they were still oblivious to his presence.

"I think tonight, as soon as it's dark enough, we pack everyone up and move. Quietly."

"Tonight? And hike? Don't you think they're going to want to know why?"

"You want to tell them the truth? That there might be an assassin following us?"

"No, of course not. This is supposed to be a relaxing trip for them, not hell week."

"Look, I'm really sorry about all this. I really am."

"Did you ever think that you should have just told me the truth at the beginning? Then we could have stopped and gone back down and not have put them in danger."

"You're not serious? You didn't believe the FBI when they told you. Do you really think you would have heeded my warning?"

"Would it have hurt to try?"

"I'm sorry, *Ms.* Michaels, but I was following orders. And since we're trying to place blame here, how about you? The FBI warned you but you took these women up here anyway."

"How dare you? Do you think I would intentionally put them in danger?"

"No, I don't think you would intentionally do that but then I don't really know you, do I?"

Sara stood up quickly. "And I don't really know you, do I?"

She walked away quickly and Jaime scrambled after her. "Sara, wait."

"Go to hell."

"Oh great. We're going to have a fight *now*?" Jaime grabbed her arm and pulled her to a stop. "You can't go running off like that. Jesus! Stay behind the trees, for God's sake."

Sara's green eyes flashed at her but Jaime refused to release her arm.

"Let go of me," Sara said slowly.

"If you don't start listening to me, I swear to God, I'll handcuff you," Jaime threatened.

"And I'd like to see you try."

Neither noticed Abby as she walked over, not until she stood next to them, hands on her hips.

"Hey guys? Everything okay?"

Sara stared at Jaime another few seconds then forced what she hoped was a smile onto her face.

"Of course, Abby."

"Well, Sandra is threatening to strip without you." She looked at Jaime. "We thought you might want to come join us."

"Yeah? Need me to keep her in line, do you?"

Abby shrugged. "It's just more fun if you're around."

"Well, let's go then."

"Sara?"

"No, Abby, I think I'll—"

"She'll come too," Jaime interrupted and again wrapped her fingers around Sara's slim wrist. "Won't you?"

"Don't think I won't hold you under the water and drown you if I get the chance," Sara said under her breath as they followed Abby to the springs.

Jaime laughed but didn't release her hold. Oh yes, this was going to be a barrel of fun. She'd been teasing earlier about the handcuffs but she very well might need to use them. For a woman whose life was threatened, Sara could be so damn stubborn.

The only consolation was that the springs were hidden by the tall spruce trees. She looked around, knowing that he wouldn't be able to see them from the mountainside where she guessed he was hiding. Not here, anyway. Their tents, however, were well within view.

"Where have you been, Jaime? You've been gone for hours," Sandra complained.

"Just hiking."

"You haven't gotten enough walking in yet?" Lou Ann asked.

Jaime glanced quickly at Sara, looking for a little help.

"She didn't want you guys to know, but she's a closeted bird-watcher," Sara supplied with a smile. "Give her ten more years and she'll be wearing those funny little hats."

"*Very* funny, Ms. Michaels. Very, very funny," Jaime whispered. She stood back and motioned to the water. "You go first."

"Afraid I'll drown you, huh?"

"Trust me, Sara, if you jumped on my back completely naked, you wouldn't have to drown me. I'd pass out."

"And what would be the fun in that?"

"Fun? Want me to show you?"

"Stay away from me. Or have you forgotten your little backflip last night?"

Jaime grinned. "Well, I like my women a little rough."

Sara was about to shoot back a reply when she realized every eye and ear of the group was trained on them. Instead, she flashed Jaime a grin. "Rough? I can beat the shit out of you."

Jaime stared as Sara stripped where she stood, tossing her sweatshirt on top of her jeans and walking calmly into the springs.

"Hey. Close your mouth," Celia whispered, just loud enough for everyone to hear. Quiet laughter erupted.

"Thanks a lot," Jaime whispered back, stripping down and piling her clothes next to Sara's on the ground. She stood on the rocks, stark naked, and grinned. "Move over, Sandra honey, here I come!" She did a belly flop into the springs, splashing everyone within five feet of her, Sara included. She resurfaced next to Sara who was still wiping the water from her face. Without thinking, Jaime scooped up a handful and tossed it at her. Sara returned the favor and a water fight ensued. They both ended up laughing so hard that Jaime had to walk away, coughing up the water she had swallowed.

"You're vicious," Jaime said as she slicked the hair back from her face.

"Oh? So you thought I was teasing about drowning you?"

"Well, yes, actually. I see I need to keep my eye on you."

"As if you're not," Sandra said, causing howls of laughter among the others.

Jaime showed mock surprise and shot a handful of water Sandra's direction. They finally settled down and Jaime relaxed on a rock, stretching her arms out at her sides and closing her eyes. The professional side of her knew they shouldn't be out here playing. It was just courting danger. But she couldn't think of how to explain to everyone what was going on without causing panic. Tomorrow, though, they would need to be careful. If they were a smaller group, she would consider bushwhacking it across the mountain and forgoing the trails. But not with this group of twelve. They would never make it. No, tomorrow, she would most likely tell them all about the possible danger. They could decide then what to do. Unfortunately, they were a seven-day hike from where they started. Their best bet was the Cottonwood Pass Highway, although this time of year, traffic would be sparse. But surely, they could catch a ride down the mountain, if need be. The other alternative was the St. Elmo ghost town. There was a general store that operated during the summer months. Perhaps someone might still be about this early in September. And if they climbed higher, she might get service on her cell. That is, if the battery was still charged. Of course, if she wasn't just a lowly detective, if she was a *real* FBI agent, they'd have supplied her with a satellite phone or something. But no, just bogus threats, just a vacation.

Right.

"You're frowning," Sara said.

Jaime opened her eyes, finding Sara close by. "Was I?" Jaime looked away. "Just thinking."

"You're worried, aren't you?"

"You should be too."

"This is what? Day seven? Surely there's been ample opportunity," she said quietly.

"Maybe." Jaime turned back, meeting the blue-green eyes that were nothing but confident. "But we can't take a chance."

"I don't want to tell them."

"I think we have to."

"What good will it do?"

"Maybe nothing. But they have a right to know."

Sara flicked her eyes over the women, then back to Jaime. "It'll just scare them."

Jaime looked over at the women, seeing the contented smile on Celia's face, the relaxed look that Sandra sported. Yes, it would scare them. It would ruin the trip, that's for sure. But still, if someone ended up shooting at them . . .

"Let's just play it by ear, okay?" Sara suggested.

Jaime shrugged. No, she didn't want to play it by ear. They needed a plan. They just couldn't be sitting ducks. But now was not the time to discuss it.

"We'll talk about it tonight."

CHAPTER FIFTEEN

The small fire glowed hotly and he hovered close by, trying to warm himself. They were all doing the same, he was sure. All the little women ignorant to his presence. It'll be like ducks on a pond. He tossed his cigarette down into the fire, watching as the flames swallowed it.

Tomorrow. Dodds said to do it tomorrow. Good thing. Because he was tired of the mountains . . . and the cold. And it would be at least seven days before anyone missed them.

CHAPTER SIXTEEN

Jaime was nervous and she couldn't seem to shake it. She kept looking over her shoulder, wondering if he was watching them. It would be so easy. He could simply walk down the mountain and they wouldn't hear a thing. She looked at Sara who was sitting on a rock near the fire, hands outstretched to warm them. She didn't appear the least bit anxious and Jaime wondered if Sara even believed she was in danger.

"Are we going to make that ghost town?" Abby asked. "You never did tell us the story."

Jaime smiled. "Well, now that you mention it, Sara and I were talking about that just today." She glanced quickly at Sara, then back at Abby. "St. Elmo is about three and a half days from here. I was thinking, if we left early in the morning, like at daybreak, we could make Cottonwood Pass day after tomorrow."

"Daybreak?"

"Yeah. That would mean getting up before dawn and packing. What do you say?"

"What's at Cottonwood Pass?"

Jaime tossed a small pinecone into the fire, watching the embers dance before it was consumed by the hot flames. "Well, there's an overlook at the top. But I'm sure you'd be much more interested in the toilets."

"Real bathrooms?" Lou Ann asked.

"Well, not flush toilets, but you'd at least be able to sit down."

They laughed, then Celia poked her with a stick. "Tell us about the ghost."

"Ah, the ghost," Jaime said quietly. She looked around the fire at eleven faces staring at her. She smiled. "It scared the shit out of me, that's for sure."

"Tell us."

"Well, if you can't sleep tonight, don't say I didn't warn you."

"I don't believe in ghosts," Abby said.

Jaime picked up a rock and tossed it between her hands. "I didn't either. But I saw one." She leaned forward. "I was alone. I wanted to make St. Elmo by nightfall and I should have stopped earlier. But, as the sun was setting, I thought I was only fifteen, twenty minutes away so I pushed on. But full dark caught me and I still hadn't reached the old town." She bent down and picked up her water bottle, taking a sip. "All of a sudden, clouds moved in and covered the moon, the wind started blowing and I couldn't see a thing."

"How long ago was this?" Celia asked quietly.

"Three years." Jaime looked across the fire at Sara who met her eyes for a moment before looking away. "Anyway, I pulled out a little flashlight like this," she said, showing them the one she kept in her back pocket. "But still, I could only see a few feet in front of me. I turned around in circles, trying to find the trail but it was like it had just disappeared. I was standing among spruce trees on a bed of needles, no sign of a trail." She shrugged. "I thought, hell, might as well just pitch a tent right here. So I did. And I brought out my little stove and heated water and I sat there in the dark, listening to the wind," she said quietly.

"What happened?" Judith finally asked.

"I heard . . . I heard this banging, like a pickax on rock. Over and over." She looked up. "Do you know what a pickax is?"

"Miners used to use them," Sandra said.

"Yeah. Gold miners. So, I hear this noise and I think that surely there are other hikers close by—doing God knows what. I couldn't figure out why someone would be pounding at the rocks after dark. But then it stopped. And the wind stopped too. Just like someone had flipped a switch. But still, I didn't think anything about it really. I sat in front of my tent in the dark and ate my dinner. Then, through the trees, I saw this light glowing. And it was moving. At first, I thought someone was walking with a flashlight, but it had an orangey glow to it. It was a lantern. And it was coming closer," she nearly whispered.

"What did you do?" someone asked quietly.

"I thought it was a hiker, nothing more. I waited, thinking maybe he'd seen me earlier and was coming to visit or maybe he was in trouble. So, I just sat and waited. Then it stopped. It was like someone set the lantern on the ground. The wind started blowing again and all of a sudden . . . the pickax again. Over and over, pounding on the rocks. I couldn't stand it anymore. I got my little flashlight and walked toward the light." She paused, watching their faces. "He materialized right before my eyes. A miner. Ghostly white," she whispered. "And he saw me. The pickax was held over his head in mid-swing and he looked at me."

"Oh my God."

"I was shaking so badly, I dropped my flashlight. I just stared."

"What happened?"

"It's my gold," she whispered. "That's what he said. *It's my gold.* Then he swung the pickax down again and again."

"What did you do?" Celia asked.

"I ran. Back to my tent, nearly diving inside, as if that little tent could save me," she said with a laugh. "I didn't sleep a wink. All night long, the pickax worked the rocks and I could see the light moving outside my tent. Finally, thankfully . . . dawn. I went outside the tent and there, beside my little stove, was my flashlight."

"But you dropped it," Abby reminded her.

"Yeah, I did. And I ran without picking it up."

"You mean—?"

"Someone or some*thing* brought my flashlight back to me."

"Oh my God," Celia murmured.

Jaime smiled. "My one and only ghost and he turned out to be a nice guy."

Sara, like all the others, had hung on every word. Again, she wondered if the story was true or if Jaime just made it up on the spot. For some reason, as she watched Jaime's face, she thought it was true. And she, like all the others, moved just a little bit closer to the fire.

"Were you scared?" Judith asked quietly.

Jaime laughed. "I'm surprised I didn't pass out. Yes, I was scared."

Abby leaned forward. "And you're convinced it was a ghost?"

Jaime nodded. "I know it was. I wasn't hallucinating."

"I remember a story about Cripple Creek," Sara said. "You know, when they turned the old mining town into casinos, they just remodeled the original buildings. They have several accounts of security cameras capturing apparitions at the slot machines after closing."

"I'd heard that," Celia said. "I thought it was just a hoax."

"No, it's true," Jaime said. "I know someone who worked there once. They would shut the casinos down at two in the morning and open again at eight. But the security cameras ran all night. She said once, when they were watching the tapes, the slot machines started working, as if someone was feeding them coins. And one time, there was this vision of a lady, walking down the stairs and going to play at one of the machines."

"That's creepy."

"Yeah, it is," Jaime said. "But, it makes you think."

"Well, yeah, it makes you think," Abby said. "And how the hell are we supposed to sleep tonight?"

Jaime laughed. "I tried to warn you. Ghost stories around a campfire in the middle of nowhere are usually not a good idea."

"Now she tells us," Sandra said.

"Oh, you'll all sleep like babies," Jaime said. "At least you have a partner to sleep with. Sara and I are all alone."

Celia grinned. "Well, maybe you two should partner up then."

Jaime nodded. "I like the way you think. That's a great idea."

Sara shook her head. "I'll yell if I need you."

Across the fire, their eyes held. "And what if I need you?"

Sara grinned. "Yell. I'm sure one of these women will come to your rescue."

But later, as she lay wide awake in her sleeping bag, Sara wasn't sure if it was the ghost story that kept her awake or Jaime's insistence that someone was following them. And she knew she would feel much safer if Jaime was indeed in the tent with her.

"Ridiculous," she whispered and she purposefully rolled over, punching the tiny pillow that she carried in her backpack.

Jaime lay still, listening. Not for the sound of a pickax, but for the sound of footsteps. And she wouldn't get a moment's sleep knowing that Sara's tent was the farthest one away from hers. He could come during the night, no one would hear. And in the morning, they would find her.

"Oh, shit," she whispered. She finally tossed open her sleeping bag and sat up. "She'll kill me."

But it didn't matter. She couldn't take a chance. With her sleeping bag in one hand and her gun in the other, she walked silently among the tents, pausing outside Sara's zippered door.

Sara sat up at the sound of footsteps. Could be anyone. Maybe someone had to pee. But they stopped right outside her tent. Her heart pounded and she very nearly yelled out for Jaime.

"Sara? It's me."

Sara let out a relieved sigh, moving to unzip the door. "What?"

"I'm bunking with you tonight," Jaime said.

"The hell you are," Sara whispered as loud as she dared.

Jaime ignored her and shoved into the small tent, bumping Sara with her sleeping bag as she stepped over her.

"Have you lost your mind?"

"Perhaps. Move over. I'll take the door."

"You cannot sleep in here," Sara insisted.

"Why not? You're wide awake because you're afraid, and I'm wide awake because I'm way the hell back there and I'm worried about what might happen to you," Jaime reasoned.

"I am not afraid."

"Then why are you still awake?"

Sara moved her sleeping bag to give Jaime room. "Maybe your damn ghost story is running through my mind."

Jaime grinned. "I made that story up, so try again," Jaime said as she spread out her sleeping bag next to Sara's. She settled down, tucking her gun under her side.

"You have a gun?"

"Of course I have a gun."

"I don't feel comfortable sleeping with a gun."

"You're not sleeping with a gun. I am."

Sara lay down and jerked the sleeping bag over her. Obnoxious woman. God, she was actually sharing her tent with her. She shifted, moving as far away as possible.

"I don't bite," Jaime whispered. "Get some sleep. We need to head out early."

Sara took a deep breath. "Are you planning on telling them?"

"I don't know. Like you said, let's play it by ear."

Sara closed her eyes, hating the fact that she felt comforted by Jaime's presence. But she did. She had no doubt that if the other woman was not there, she would get precious little sleep. She also hated the fact that she was cold. She turned her head, noting the few feet that separated them. Jaime appeared to already be asleep and Sara chanced inching closer.

"Cold?" Jaime murmured.

"A little." *Damn!*

Jaime rolled over and unzipped her bag then tried to do the same to Sara's.

"What the hell do you think you're doing?"

"You're cold. I'm cold," Jaime said as she lay back down, now so close they were touching. "Roll over."

"What?"

Jaime sighed. "Just roll over. *Geez.*"

Sara did, facing away from Jaime. Then she jerked as she felt Jaime move behind her, pressing her warm body to her own. One arm snaked around her and pulled her close and she trembled. She could feel Jaime's breasts against her back and she closed her eyes. She should protest, she knew she should. Sleeping this way was far too intimate but she didn't have the willpower to pull out of the embrace. It felt too good. Sara sighed, relaxing as she felt Jaime's warm breath on her neck. She felt safe.

By dawn, they were completely entangled and she was horrified to find that she'd brought Jaime's hand to her breast. Her own hand still covered Jaime's. *Oh my God. Are you insane?*

A new warmth settled over her as she frantically thought of ways to remove the offending hand without waking Jaime. She would die of embarrassment if Jaime woke up. And no doubt the other woman would try to turn it into something it wasn't. For her part, it was a totally innocent gesture made without conscious thought while she slept. Suddenly the warm hand covering her breast squeezed and she stifled a moan as she felt her heart jump in her chest, but Jaime's even breathing told Sara that she was still fast asleep.

Finally, she took a deep breath, intending to just roll over and pretend nothing was wrong when she felt Jaime stir. The hand tightened once again then stilled. She could hear Jaime's sharp intake of breath and she was certain that Jaime could feel the pounding of her heart against her hand. She jerked her hand away and Jaime sat up.

"I'm *so* sorry. Really I am. I . . . I had no . . . no idea," she stammered.

Sara rolled over, her eyes meeting Jaime's in the dim light of the tent. In that split second, Sara made a choice. She could pretend outrage and bar Jaime from her tent for the duration or she could accept responsibility because she knew by the way she'd been gripping Jaime's hand that she'd pulled it to her. Or . . .

"What the hell are you talking about?" she murmured.

Jaime blinked several times then swallowed nervously. "I . . . well . . . I think I may have . . ."

"Are you always this incoherent in the morning?"

Jaime rubbed her face with both hands, shaking her head. "No. Not normally." She stared at Sara, looking for some sign of anger but saw none. Apparently, she'd pulled her hand away before Sara woke. She could only imagine the scene had she been caught. *Jesus! What were you thinking?*

"What time is it, anyway?"

Jaime looked at her watch. "Five thirty. I wanted to be on the trail before daylight but I don't guess we're going to make it." She cleared her throat. "How did you sleep?"

"Good. Warm." Sara felt herself blushing. "I guess I should thank you."

"Yeah, you should. Beats freezing to death." Jaime grabbed the edge of Sara's sleeping bag and pulled it off her. "Rise and shine."

She escaped out the tent before Sara could throw a boot at her. Her smile faded as she stared toward the mountain. As darkness still hovered over the canyon, she could make out a campfire through the trees. She stuck her head back inside. "Get dressed. Hurry. He's already up."

"What?"

"I can see a fire. Hurry. I'll get the others up."

CHAPTER SEVENTEEN

He sat close to the fire, warming his hands. Yes, he'd had enough of the cold. They weren't paying him enough for this shit. He would do it today. If he couldn't get a clean shot at Michaels, he'd pick them off one by one if necessary. And he'd start with the old cow that normally lagged behind.

He laughed quietly. Yeah. He could do them one by one. That'd be fun.

CHAPTER EIGHTEEN

The sun was breaking over the mountain when they climbed the next ridge. Sara intended to keep on but Jaime stopped.

"Hey, how about a rest?"

"Man, she's like a drill instructor today," Celia said. "You know, I haven't even peed yet."

"And I haven't had breakfast," Sandra complained. She punched Jaime on the arm. "You scared the shit out of me when you woke us up."

"Sorry."

"I thought we had a bear in camp or something."

Jaime smiled then looked over at Sara. Their eyes met and for the first time, she saw fear in Sara's. Pulling out her binoculars, she waved at them. "You go on ahead," she said. "I'm going to see if I can find . . . some birds." She looked at Sara, who nodded.

"Come on, ladies. Let's give our birdwatcher a little privacy."

"Are we going to have breakfast?" Sandra asked.

"No. But we'll stop early for lunch. Promise." Sara looked back once, silently telling Jaime to be careful.

Jaime nodded and as soon as the group moved away, she left the trail and moved behind boulders, trying to find a secluded spot. Her only consolation was that they had started out nearly two hours earlier than normal. She hoped the man following them assumed they would stick to their routine. With any luck, he would still be on the other mountain, waiting.

She stayed nearly thirty minutes, scanning the entire mountainside for movement and saw none. No reflections, no sound. Nothing. It was simply a gorgeous morning with autumn crispness still in the air. It was a beautiful time to be in the mountains, the colors just exploding around her. A perfect time if you liked solitude. Very few backpackers chanced the mountains this late in the year. She sighed. And that was why they were sitting ducks. They'd been on the trail nine days now and had yet to see another person other than their stalker.

After another hour, Sara finally stopped. She didn't want to get too far ahead of Jaime. She let her backpack fall to the ground and rubbed her shoulders while she looked down the trail. It was so beautiful out here—she had a hard time accepting that someone might be following them. But after this morning, she trusted Jaime. The constant teasing and flirting did nothing to change that. Jaime was a cop and if she said they were in danger, Sara would believe her. She shook her head. Still, it made no sense. She was estranged from her father. Her death would mean nothing to him. Her mother, yes. But him? He would probably thank the killer. One less lesbian daughter to account for during the debates.

"Ms. Michaels? Sara? Are you okay?" Abby asked.

Sara jerked her head, just now noticing the other woman. "I'm fine, Abby. And please, no more Ms. Michaels. Just Sara."

"Okay. But you've been acting strange this morning. So has Jaime, for that matter," she said, then lowered her voice. "Did she . . . did she make a pass at you last night or something?"

Sara smiled then laughed. "No, Abby. I can handle myself."

"Well, she's made it no secret, you know, that she likes you."

"Likes me?"

"You know what I mean."

"Jaime just likes to flirt. She means no harm."

"Okay, then." Abby shrugged. "I like her. I mean, if I were gay, God, she'd turn me to jelly."

Sara smiled. Abby, like all the others, had already been reduced to putty by Jaime's charm, gay or not. She slid her eyes back down the trail, looking for the familiar sight of the other woman. The trail was empty. She took a deep breath.

"Everyone ready?"

"Shouldn't we wait for Jaime?" Sandra asked.

"Let's go a little farther, then we'll stop for lunch. Jaime will catch up with us."

Amid groans, they all picked up their backpacks again and headed out, single file. The trail was going down the mountain and Sara felt no need to hurry. Until Jaime caught up with them, there was nothing she could do but go forward. Hopefully, they'd left early enough to lose their uninvited guest. But since they were simply following the trail, it wouldn't be hard for him to track them. She wondered if Jaime thought they could outrun him.

Jaime paused at the top of a ridge, turning to scan the area behind her. She'd still seen no sign of anyone. She looked at her watch. It had been an hour and a half since she'd left the group and she was beginning to worry. If he wasn't behind them, surely to God he hadn't made his way across the mountain to intercept them. No. Impossible. She'd seen his campfire.

And she knew they couldn't go on much longer like this. She would catch up with them, make sure they were okay then take off on her own. She had to confront this guy and find out what he wanted. And if he was the killer, she'd . . . what? Arrest him?

"Sure, Jaime, read him his rights," she murmured. *Shit.* A dead-end assignment that was supposed to be a vacation. A hoax. She couldn't wait to get her hands on Special Agent Ramsey.

After looking behind her one last time, she hurried down the trail, almost running. She didn't pause to notice the colors of the aspens or the chipmunks she roused. She kept her eyes on the trail except for an occasional glance behind her.

She was completely out of breath when she saw them, some fifty yards or more ahead of her. They were stopped, sitting down and she assumed they'd talked Sara into lunch. She stopped, resting on a rock as she caught her breath. Loosening the straps on her pack, she stretched her shoulders, thinking a soak in the hot springs would be just the ticket. Unfortunately, until they stopped this guy, they couldn't afford the luxury.

Finally, when her breathing was back to normal, she tightened her straps and shoved off the rock, walking nonchalantly toward the group. Sandra saw her first and waved.

"I was starting to worry," the older woman called.

"Oh? Was the Sarge double-timing it, trying to lose me?" Jaime found Sara's eyes, noting the relief she saw there.

"She was doing something. I was practically running to keep up."

Jaime grinned. "Trying to get rid of me, huh?"

"Obviously, we weren't quick enough," Sara said and returned her smile.

Jaime let her pack slide off her shoulders as she made her way over to her. She sat down in front of Sara and pointed to her shoulders. "Could use a little shoulder rub there."

"In your dreams," Sara murmured.

"Yes, you've definitely been there," Jaime teased. She rolled her shoulders several times, trying to loosen them up. Jogging with a full pack was not much fun. She felt like she'd hiked a full day already. She nearly jumped when warm hands touched her shoulders and began to squeeze.

"Not one word or I'll stop," Sara whispered.

Jaime nodded, squeezing her eyes shut. It was heavenly and the first moan escaped before she could stop it. "Sorry."

"Uh-huh." But Sara kept up her ministrations, squeezing the strong shoulders under her hands. She looked up once and saw the satisfied smile that Celia sported and she very nearly stopped. But it was another groan from Jaime stilled her hands. "That's enough. You'll get spoiled."

"Wow. You sure know how to use your hands. Are you that good at everything?"

"Can you behave for one second?" Sara asked quietly. "Did you see anything?"

Jaime shook her head. "Nothing."

"Then maybe we lost him?"

Jaime turned around. "How? We're still on the trail. All he has to do is follow it."

"Then what do you want to do?"

"We need to get off the trail, Sara. But I don't think this group can handle it."

"If there's no alternative then they have to handle it."

"Well, I've been thinking about something," Jaime said. She turned around and faced Sara, putting her back to the others. "We can't just keep running from him. I need to find him. I need to . . . disable him."

"*What?* Are you crazy?"

"No, I'm not crazy. Crazy would be to keep going like we've been. Eventually, something's got to give. We can't just sit around and wait for it to happen."

"You cannot go out there alone. It's too dangerous," Sara insisted.

Jaime grinned. "You're worried about me." She reached out and tugged playfully on Sara's jeans. "Thanks. I didn't think you cared."

"Of course I care. Who's going to keep me warm if something happens to you?"

"Ah. So we're talking body heat here. Well, I'm glad I'm good for something."

"Seriously, I don't think you should go out alone. Safety in numbers, right?"

"Sometimes. But not this time. I know this area. I can find him. You just stay on the trail until dark. I'll catch up with you eventually."

"I don't like it. What if something happens to you?"

"Well, you'll know soon enough, I suppose."

Sara shook her head and whispered. "If he is a trained killer, you won't stand a chance."

"Sweetheart," Jaime grinned. "I've got some skills of my own. I'm not just a pretty face."

"Can't you be serious for once?"

"Okay. Serious. I'm a detective. I've been on the force since I was twenty-one. I spent two years with the SWAT team. And when I say I know this area, I've been out here at least once every summer since I can remember. I doubt our guy has set foot out here before. I can find him." She tugged again on Sara's jeans. "Besides, we don't know for sure he's a bad guy, right? But we need to find out. The main problem is he's probably got a rifle with a scope. He won't have to get close. But I will."

Sara stared at her, noting the determination in her eyes. Very well. She wouldn't argue with her. "What do I tell the others?"

"How about the truth? I've seen someone following us and I've gone to check it out. They don't need to know anything about . . . about you or your father."

"Maybe we should just tell them."

"Let's see what I find out. There's no need to get everyone upset if it turns out to be nothing."

Sara nodded. "Okay. You're probably right. But I still don't like it. Like you said, he's most likely got a rifle."

"I'll be fine." Jaime got to her feet. "I'll walk with you guys a little ways, then split. How's that?"

Sara grabbed her arm as Jaime was leaving, pulling her back around. "How long will you be gone?"

"I'm not sure."

"After dark?"

"Yeah. Most likely, I won't see you until tomorrow."

Their eyes met for a second and Sara forced a smile onto her face. "Be careful, please. I've kinda gotten used to you being around."

Jaime laughed. "Better watch it, Sara, or I'll think you're flirting with me."

"As if." But Sara watched her walk away, back to where Celia and Sandra were sitting. The two older women laughed at something Jaime said, then Sandra handed Celia her camera. Sara grinned as Sandra wrapped an arm around Jaime while Celia took their picture. Sara wished she could be as free with her emotions as they were. But she'd grown used to being cautious over the years and it was a hard habit to break. She let her eyes travel over the lean figure of Jaime Hutchinson, remembering exactly what she looked like without clothes. If she were honest with herself, she'd admit that she hadn't been physically attracted to another woman in years. Not really. Mostly she went out with women who she thought she *should* like because of common friends or common interests. But there was never a physical spark. Most of the women she'd dated were now the best of friends because that's all they ever were destined to be. Just friends.

But Jaime—yes, there was definitely a spark. Just being near the woman made her heart beat a little faster. And whether or not Jaime really found her attractive or was just putting on a show, it hardly mattered to Sara anymore. She was insanely attracted to the woman, killer on their trail or not.

"Why are you leaving again?" Sandra asked.

Jaime kept up her even pace beside Sandra, knowing she should leave if she wanted to catch their guy before nightfall. "Would you believe me if I said I was looking for the three-toed woodpecker?"

"What?"

"Very rare bird. Found around here, I'm told."

"I see. Sounds exciting," Sandra murmured.

Jaime laughed and shoved playfully at Sandra. "Honey, someday I'll have you walking the parks with a pair of binoculars around your neck. You just wait."

Sandra stopped and stared.

Jaime did the same. "What?"

"Someday? Does that mean, you know, that we might keep in touch after this trip?"

"Well yeah, if you want. I mean, you know, we're buddies, right?"

Sandra grinned. "Buddies. Yeah, I like that." She walked on. "I think Celia and I will keep in touch but I don't know about the others. They're all younger and, well, they're different from us."

"I think it's great what you're doing up here. We've been on the trail nine days now and I've not once heard any complaints."

"It's all different up here. Sara was right, you know. You change up here. I'm not sure we really believed her. But this was just part of what we paid for. To tell you the truth, I've completely forgotten about my former life. We're hiking and playing in the springs and sitting around the campfire at night. It feels so great out here. By the time I crawl into the sleeping bag, I'm out like a light. It's wonderful. I mean, I feel so good about myself."

"I think that's the idea," Jaime whispered.

"Well, she's doing a good job, I'll say that. I'd recommend her to anyone."

"Yeah? And would you recommend this trip too?"

"Oh, yeah. I mean, it's work, sure. But I've never seen anything this beautiful before."

Jaime nodded. "You got that right. Take a deep breath, Sandra honey," she said, doing exactly that. She breathed out slowly. "They should bottle that smell. It's fresh, it's clean . . . hell, it's life." She looked at Sandra and smiled as the older woman breathed with her eyes closed. "Makes me want to break out into a John Denver song," Jaime said then proceeded to sing a verse. "That's how I feel about the mountains. Pity the poor soul who's never been up here before."

Sandra grinned. "I never thought about it like that before. But yeah, I do feel all the richer for having seen all this. It's something I'll always remember, that's for sure."

Jaime was about to reply when the rifle shot sounded. Instinct took both her and Sandra to the ground.

Sara whipped around, eyes wide. "Jaime! Sandra!"

"Get down! Get *down*," Jaime yelled. Leaning on her elbows, she looked back over her shoulder, seeing the reflection of glass on the mountainside. "Jesus Christ! Come on, Sandra. *Move!*" But she didn't. It was only then that Jaime saw the blood running down Sandra's face and her lifeless eyes staring back at her. Her heart stopped and she made herself roll over, diving behind a boulder just as the second rifle shot sounded, causing dirt to fly up where Jaime had just been laying. Oh dear God. *Not Sandra.* She closed her eyes for a second, fists clenched. *Goddamn . . .*

"Everyone, get the *fuck* down!" she yelled as heads poked up from behind rocks. She moved on her belly, sliding down the hill to where Sara and the others were hiding.

"Where's Sandra?" Sara demanded.

"She was hit."

"What?" Sara sat up. "No, *no*," she screamed.

Jaime pulled her back down, squeezing tight on her arms. "Listen to me," Jaime yelled. "We've got to move. Down the mountain, into the ravine."

"What the hell's going on?" Abby said, nearly hysterical. "Who is shooting at us?"

"Where is Sandra?" Celia asked frantically. "Where is she?"

Jaime moved closer, squeezing her hand. "She was shot, Celia. I'm sorry."

"Shot? What do you mean? Not Sandra."

Tears welled up and Jaime squeezed harder. "I'm sorry. We've got to go. Everyone, listen to me. Get down the mountain as fast as you can. Stay low to the ground. He'll be coming."

"Who? He who?"

"There's no time for that now! Move!" Jaime yelled, practically pushing Celia down the hill.

"We are . . . not leaving . . . Sandra," Sara insisted. She was shaking so badly she could hardly form sentences. "We're going to . . . to take her with us. We are *not* leaving her."

Jaime gripped her shoulders and shook her. "How the hell are we going to do that? She's *gone.* Now we've got to *move!*"

"We can't leave her!" Sara screamed.

"She's dead, goddamn it. There's nothing we can do for her." Jaime turned and pulled Sara after her, sliding down on the rocks and nearly losing her balance. The others were ahead of them, moving fast. Celia fell once to her knees and Jaime was right behind her, picking her up and urging her on. She looked back over her shoulder several times, thinking she would find him at the top of the trail, rifle trained on them. But there was no one. He had to have been at least two hundred yards away when he took the shot. It would take him a little while to get down the mountain and onto the trail.

"There's water," Abby gasped, pointing. She was bent over at the waist as they all were, trying to catch their breath.

Jaime pulled the trail map from her back pocket, trying to find out where they were. She turned a circle, then looked up, searching for the sun which was hidden by the mountain. "Goddamn it." She tossed her pack off and rummaged in a pocket, finding her compass. "Come on, come on," she murmured, looking at it and the map. "Okay. Yes, there's a stream up ahead but we're going to cross over it. Down in the ravine there should be a small river. That's what we want." She folded the map and looked at them, all standing around her with a look of shock on their faces, especially Sara. "Let's go. He'll be right behind us."

They moved on, over and around boulders and holding onto tree limbs as the mountain dropped dramatically into the ravine. The small stream was only four feet wide and using rocks for steps, they easily crossed to the other side.

"Stop," Jaime said when they'd all made it across the stream. She looked again at the map, studying the slopes. She wanted him to think they were going right down the mountain. "This way. We go straight down until we hit the river." As Sara passed her, Jaime grabbed her arm and spun her around. "How are you holding up?" she asked quietly.

"I'm afraid I'm not." Tears immediately formed. "It's my fault, Jaime. My fault."

"Stop it. It's not your fault. If anything, it's goddamn my fault.

Now come on." Jaime pulled her along, trying not to think about the woman they'd left up on the trail.

Only ten minutes later, they heard the water as it crashed down the mountain. For one moment, Jaime panicked. What if it was too big, too fierce? How were they going to manage the water? She hurried ahead of the others, shoving them out of the way, scanning the banks of the river and hoping her plan would work.

"Now what?"

Jaime turned and faced them. "Listen to me. We're out of sight, so he's going to be tracking us. But he can't track us in the water."

"You want us to walk down the mountain in the water?"

"No. Upstream."

"Upstream?" All heads turned and looked at the water that flowed and crashed along the boulders that littered the river.

"He'll assume we went down. So we go up."

Sara stepped forward, her eyes still on the water. "Jaime, I don't know . . ."

"It's the only way. Trust me."

"I want to know what the hell is going on," Abby demanded. "Someone shot at us! Sandra . . . Sandra is up there," she pointed. "What the hell is going on?"

Jaime grabbed her shoulders and squeezed. "We don't have time for this now, Abby. Someone's after us and we've got to move. Do you understand?"

Abby nodded. "Okay. Okay. Let's go."

"Good. Now, take your time, make sure of your footing. We only have to make it to the top of the ridge up there. We'll be out of sight that way."

"And what if he comes upstream instead of going down?" Lou Ann asked.

Jaime looked at Sara. "Then I'll kill him." She walked into the water and grimaced. It was like ice. "Come on. I know it's cold."

"Jesus Christ," Abby hissed when the cold water soaked her jeans.

Jaime ignored them, moving downstream several feet to where a tree grew close to the water. She grabbed a low limb, twisting the end until it broke, leaving it hanging. Hopefully, it would be enough to convince him they'd gone downstream. She looked at all the terrified faces watching her and raised her eyebrows. "Ready?" At their nods, she walked against the current, knees bent, concentrating on each step. The water was strong flowing down the mountain but at least the river wasn't deep. Like most high mountain streams, so many boulders littered the river that is was only a few feet deep in places. If you avoided the deeper pools, you could walk across most streams. She bent over once as she lost her footing and she looked behind her. The others were all using their hands to guide them. But they were going slow. Too slow. Looking at her watch, she wondered how much time had passed since they'd left the trail. Since they'd left Sandra.

"There's a deep pool right there," she pointed. "Stay to the left. Just follow me."

Sara found herself in the middle of the group, between Megan and Ashley. She was soaked nearly to the waist, as were the others. It felt like they were crawling at a snail's pace and she found herself looking over her shoulder constantly, wondering when the next shot would ring out. She followed the others around the pool, feeling the water swirling against her legs, pulling her downward. Her feet were so cold, she could hardly feel them but she pushed on, stepping on the rock that Megan had just vacated.

"Just a little farther," Jaime called. She noticed that Celia was lagging behind and shook her head. "Celia, come on, pick it up."

"I'm trying."

Jaime stood where she was, holding onto the branch of a spruce tree that was hanging over the river. The water was splashing over her thighs and she realized how cold she was, how cold they all must be. "Abby? Can you make it on your own?" Jaime pointed. "Get out right behind the two boulders there. Get low on the ground. I'm going to help Celia."

"Got it, Chief."

Jaime managed a smile at Abby as she left her, pausing to help Lou Ann before moving downstream.

"Where are you going?" Sara asked loudly to be heard over the rushing water.

"To help Celia. We've got to hurry. I feel like we've been out here for hours," Jaime said.

"I know. I keep expecting—"

"No." Jaime gripped Sara's arm and squeezed. "I'm not going to let anything happen to you. Now go."

Jaime passed the others, offering encouragement, urging them to hurry. Celia was several yards back, struggling over the rocks. She was drenched and Jaime knew she must be freezing. She reached out and grabbed Celia under her elbow.

"Let me help," she yelled.

"Not going to make it, can't," Celia gasped.

"The hell you're not!" Jaime pulled her forward. "I'm not letting you go."

"I can't feel my feet."

"That makes two of us. Just a little farther."

Celia slipped and Jaime pulled her up, holding her close. Celia looked into her eyes, her face frantic.

"I'm scared, Jaime."

Jaime leaned close to her ear. "Don't you be scared. He took Sandra. He's not taking anybody else."

"Promise?"

"I promise. Now come on. We don't have much time."

With Jaime pulling Celia, they finally made it to the boulders. The others were all on the ground, as she'd instructed. Sara got up and helped Celia out of the river, pulling her down beside her.

Once out of the water, the cold penetrated. They were completely shaded by the mountain and Jaime guessed the temperature was barely fifty up here. They would be chancing hypothermia if they didn't get out of the wet clothes soon. She knelt down close to Sara, touching her face, her cheeks.

"What is it?" Sara whispered.

"You're cold."

"No shit."

Jaime flashed a smile, then squirmed out of her pack. "Lay back down. Everyone. I'm going into the forest. I've got to find a spot where I can watch him. You've got to stay out of sight. No matter what."

"Out of sight. Yeah," Abby said. "I'm fucking cold. I don't think I could stand up if you begged."

"Good. I'll be back as soon as it's safe." She unzipped the side pocket on her pack and pulled out her binoculars. "Don't move," she said again.

CHAPTER NINETEEN

"Goddamn, goddamn, goddamn," he muttered as he hurried down the mountain. His rifle was slung over his shoulder but his pack . . . his goddamn backpack was still up on the trail, laying next to the old woman he'd popped.

He paused to catch his breath, studying the ground, seeing overturned rocks and dislodged dirt. He had their trail but they were ahead of him, running. His eyes narrowed. Oh, he had no doubt he'd catch them eventually. He just never thought they'd run like this, down the mountain. He assumed they'd stick to the trail, running for their lives like scared rabbits. Didn't matter. If he couldn't track a bunch of women, he was in the wrong line of work. And that, he was not. He'd catch up with them tonight as they huddled around their campfire, scared out of their wits.

He looked back, judging how far the trail was. His coat was with his backpack. He'd have to go back for it.

He studied the ground, seeing that they'd run straight down

the mountain. Nowhere to go but down. Yeah. But he was thorough. No sense taking chances.

He pulled out the small, electronic transponder and adjusted the frequency. Staring, he frowned, then lifted his eyes upstream from where the signal was transmitting.

"What the hell?"

CHAPTER TWENTY

Jaime moved silently through the forest, hiding behind trees and rocks, trying to find a hidden spot where she could observe the river down below. He should have been there by now. Surely, it wouldn't have taken him that long to get down the mountain to the trail. The trail had been relatively level, he could have jogged it in no time.

"He smokes," she whispered. So, he's not in the best of shape and the altitude is probably not helping. Well, that was one thing in their favor. Another thing in their favor was he had no idea one of them was a cop, much less that one of them had a gun. And she knew without a doubt that she'd shoot first before trying to arrest the goddamn son of a bitch.

Jaime squeezed her eyes shut as she thought of the older woman. Sandra had enough pain to last a lifetime. Why her? Sandra, who was so looking forward to the rest of her life, taken down like an animal. It made no sense. If he was after Sara, why take a shot at someone else?

But she knew the answer. It was just the thrill of it. She'd been on the force long enough to hear that answer over and over again. He was a hit man for sure but obviously not a very disciplined one. No doubt he was just a thug hired to do a job. And she should have suspected that earlier. Any professional who'd been trailing them for eight or nine days would have had plenty of opportunities to do the job and get out. Even Sara had said the same.

She moved a little farther down, stopping where a tree grew up from next to a boulder. It provided good cover and gave her a clear view of the canyon. They were totally in the shadows this time of day and while that was welcome when trying to stay out of sight, it also dropped the temperatures to a very uncomfortable level. She lay on her stomach and elbows, holding the binoculars to her chest as she scanned the area. Still no movement. She pulled the binoculars to her eyes and slowly moved them down the mountain. She nearly jumped when she saw him. He was just crossing the first stream, rifle slung on one shoulder. She held her breath as he studied the trail then walked on, following their earlier route.

Her hands had a tight grip on the binoculars as he paused at the river, looking first downstream, then up. The ravine was steep and there was no way they could have crossed over to the other side. It was straight up a sheer cliff. No. He had to choose. Upstream or down? She moved closer against the rock, fearing he could see her, but his eyes were on the river. Finally, he walked downstream, staring at the limb she had broken earlier. She nodded as he hurried, almost running along the river as it wound its way down the canyon.

But then he stopped.

What the hell?

He pulled something from his pocket, holding it at arm's length. Then his eyes lifted toward her, nodding.

"What the fuck?" She lowered her head. *Oh God no.*

She ran, ran fast, stumbling through the trees, ducking under branches. There was no time to waste. She was panting when she found them and she bent over, trying to catch her breath.

"What is it?" Sara asked urgently. "What did you find?"

Jaime looked up, locking glances with Sara. "There's a transmitter," she gasped between breaths.

"What?"

"Somebody's got a fucking transmitter," she said loudly. She looked at the group. "Drop your packs. We're bugged."

"What the hell are you talking about?"

Jaime looked at Sara. "He has a receiver of some sort. He knows we went upstream."

"Oh shit," Sara murmured.

"Search your bags. See if anything looks out of the ordinary."

"It can't be us. We bought all of this new. It was housed at the clinic." Their eyes met. "Search your stuff," Sara said quietly.

"I swear, if the bastard . . ." Jaime stared at the small thermometer attached to the top of her backpack. "Fuck," she whispered. She'd had the thermometer for years. And the tiny, circular compass at the bottom was more for looks than anything. Everyone knew that. If you were going to use a compass, you used the real thing. So where better to plant a transmitter?

"What?"

Their eyes met again. "It's me. It's goddamn me." Jaime ripped the thermometer from her pack, then felt Sara's hands close around hers.

"He doesn't know we've found it."

Jaime paused, clutching the thermometer in her fist. She nodded. "I've got an idea."

She unzipped a side pocket on her pack, pulling out a packet of waterproof matches. She dumped the matches in her pack, then slipped the thermometer inside the pouch and sealed it. She looked at Sara. "First aid kit?"

Sara dove into her pack. "What do you need?"

"Tape."

Jaime found a downed limb and broke it in half. She then took the tape from Sara, wrapping it around the limb, securing the thermometer—and the transmitter—inside the waterproof pouch.

"Now what?"

"Now we send it downstream," Jaime said. She walked to the water's edge, gently tossing the limb into the stream. They all watched as it floated downstream, away from them.

"Will it work?"

Jaime shook her head. "I don't know." She looked at them, all wet and cold, the shadows lengthening in the canyon, hinting at dusk. They didn't have much time. She looked at Sara. "You take them on ahead. Follow the stream. I'm going to go back down, see what he's doing."

"It'll be dark soon."

"Yeah. Still a couple of hours once we get out of this canyon. Go as long as you can. I'll find you."

Their eyes held. "Are you sure?"

"I'll be back before you know it. Remember, he can't track us in the dark."

Jaime left without waiting for a reply. She stumbled back down the path she'd come up, her boots slipping on rocks in her haste. She paused against a boulder, sinking low to the ground, scanning the mountainside with her binoculars. She saw him, some three hundred yards downstream. And he was walking toward her.

She shook her head. *Check your transponder.*

"Check your goddamn transponder," she murmured.

Finally he did, pulling it out of a pocket. He held it high, away from his body. Then he turned, pointing downstream.

"Oh, yeah. Downstream, you bastard," she whispered.

CHAPTER TWENTY-ONE

He turned in a circle, watching the signal bounce around the canyon.

"What the fuck?"

He looked upstream, where his gut told him they'd gone, then downstream where the signal now pointed. He shook his head. Something wasn't right.

"It's moving too fast."

It didn't matter. It would be dark soon. No sense traveling in the darkness. He would catch up to them tomorrow. And they would pay.

He let his backpack slip from his shoulders. Yeah. Tomorrow.

CHAPTER TWENTY-TWO

It would be dark in a couple of hours. All they had to do was keep moving, putting distance between them and him. He was stopping for the night. They could push on. But they were all exhausted and cold. They needed a place where they could get a fire going and warm up. But it would be hours before they could do that.

After Jaime was certain he was stopping, she scampered back up the hill, hoping to catch the others before they got too far ahead of her. She caught up with them only thirty minutes later.

"Well?" Sara asked immediately.

"You're moving too slow."

"Where is he?"

"He's stopped. He's setting up camp along the stream."

"Good. So we have time?"

"No. We've got to move." She looked at the others. "We've got to keep going. For a while, at least."

Abby stood. "Okay, Chief. Where to?"

Jaime pointed. "See the ridge?"

"Holy shit," Lou Ann murmured.

"Over the top and down the other side. Two more hours. Then we stop."

"Two?" Sara shook her head. "Jaime, we're wet, we're cold . . . we're tired. Two more hours?"

"We stop at full dark," Jaime insisted. "We can't take a chance."

Sara looked at the group of women, now short one. They were all soaking wet. "Ladies? Are we up for it?"

"Let's go," Judith said. "The farther away from him the better."

"I can make it," Beth said with a nod.

One by one, they all nodded, agreeing to the two-hour hike up the mountain.

"Okay, walk carefully. Try to disturb the rocks, the ground, as little as possible. Eventually, he's going to find our trail. We don't want to give him tracks to follow. Okay?"

They nodded again.

"And no talking. Quiet. We move up to the ridge and down the other side. Hopefully, we can find a west facing ridge where we'll be shielded and we can get a fire going."

"Fire? Oh God, that sounds good."

Jaime started out, walking lightly, stepping on rocks instead of the ground when she could. Hopefully, they would follow suit. But even as careful as they could be, twelve women hiking . . . no, eleven now . . . would leave some sort of mark. She shook her head, trying not to think of Sandra. Not now. Now she needed to focus. She had to get them out of here. Later, when things were quiet, she would allow the guilt she felt about Sandra's death to come. Later.

Twenty minutes into their hike, Jaime paused, letting everyone catch their breath. She looked up, noticing that it had suddenly gotten extremely steep. There had to be an easier route over the ridge.

"Jaime?"

Jaime turned to find Sara staring at her. "Yeah?"

"That's practically straight up."

"Yeah, I was just thinking that." The shadows were getting

longer and Jaime was afraid they would not make it over the ridge by dark. And they had to. No way they could stay on this side of the mountain, not knowing for sure where he was. They had to cross over. "You guys stay here. I'm going to hike down a little ways and see if it levels out."

"And I'll walk up. There might be some kind of trail."

Jaime hesitated. She didn't want Sara alone but—"Okay. But don't go far." She watched Sara walk off, heading in the opposite direction, then turned and walked downhill, going around the pile of boulders, looking for something, an old landslide with footholds, an animal trail, something to get them over the ridge. But she found nothing. Twenty or thirty yards past the boulder field, the mountain sloped downward. She turned around and retraced her steps.

"Anything?" Abby asked.

"No." Jaime looked past them. "Where's Sara?" In the shadows, she saw her, waving to them.

"This way," she called. "I've found a trail."

"Good. Looks like the Sarge found something," Jaime said. "Come on, ladies."

Sara met them halfway, her breathing labored from the hike. "It's a deer trail, nothing more. But I think we can make it."

"Hell, if a little deer can make it, surely we can," Abby said.

Sara and Jaime exchanged glances . . . and smiles. "Okay, Abby. Then you lead," Jaime said. "Celia? You're second."

"But—"

"No buts, no nothing. You're second." Jaime pointed at Sara. "Sarge?"

Sara nodded. "I'm third."

Jaime clapped her hands. "Let's go! Let's go! Lou Ann, move it. Ashley, Beth . . . come on, you're next. Everybody, let's go." Jaime watched as they all followed each other up the pass. It would get steep at the top . . . but they could make it. She glanced around then decided to check their back one more time. She pulled out her binoculars then looked up the trail where the women were heading. "Sara," she yelled.

Sara stopped, one hand gripping a tree branch, and turned around. She raised her eyebrows. Jaime held up her binoculars. Sara nodded. Jaime hurried off down toward the ravine and Sara watched her go with just a bit of apprehension. She looked down the deer trail that they were following, her eyes glancing off each of the women, some meeting her eyes, others not. Her professional side knew that they needed to talk about what had happened and what was still happening. Sandra was a part of them. And they needed to talk about it. But damn, there hadn't been a moment that was appropriate. Maybe tonight, once they were settled, they could talk. Perhaps revert back to the group sessions even though she'd vowed they were done with them. Regardless, they had to talk it out. It wasn't something that could be shelved until later. Sandra . . . God, Sandra was laying somewhere up on a trail they had abandoned long ago. Yes, they needed to talk about it. She turned her gaze upward, watching as Celia slowly made her way up the trail in the waning daylight.

Jaime followed the shadows, moving slowly from tree to tree, studying the riverbank, looking for signs of movement. There was none. Satisfied he had indeed stopped for the night, she retraced her steps, finding the old deer trail the others had used. She shook her head. Even in the shadows, she could follow their tracks. No doubt he'd find it easily tomorrow. But she couldn't worry about that now.

She moved quietly through the trees. When she reached the top of the trail, the others were already up on the ridge. She saw them moving among the trees and she hurried to reach them. Dusk was upon them. There was probably only another hour, if that, before full dark. And they needed to put some distance between them and the river. She pulled herself up the trail, using tree branches to steady herself where the trail was steep. She saw overturned rocks where someone had slipped and she stopped to right them.

"Jaime?"

She looked up, seeing Sara's silhouette as she leaned against a tree. "Yeah. I'm coming."

Sara moved down the trail a little ways, waiting. She wanted, needed some time alone with her. They were all running on adrenaline but eventually that would run out. They needed some reassurance and they needed it to come from Jaime.

"You okay?"

Jaime grasped the trunk of a small tree, pulling herself up. "Yeah, I'm okay. How about everyone else?"

"We need to tell them something, Jaime."

"I know." Jaime pulled herself up the last few feet, standing on a rock facing Sara. They were in the shadows but their eyes met and held. Jaime reached out, gently touching Sara's face. "How are you holding up?"

"I'm trying not to think about it."

"Yeah. Me too."

Sara saw the hint of tears in Jaime's eyes. Sandra was a client. Not a friend. But to Jaime, Sandra was a friend. Albeit, a brief friendship, but she knew that Jaime had taken Sandra under her wing. Even at the end, they had been together, talking and laughing. And that's why Sara knew Jaime was taking this harder than anyone, except maybe Celia. But Jaime was very good at hiding her feelings. She had simply taken charge and gotten them out of there. Ten nearly hysterical women and Jaime had managed to get them down the mountain and up the river without mishap. Yes, they were soaking wet and cold—but they were alive.

Sara finally held out her hand, offering it to Jaime. The fingers that closed around it were cold but Sara pulled Jaime across the rocks, never releasing her hand.

"Thanks."

Sara smiled, squeezing Jaime's hand as she walked past. "What's the plan?"

Jaime turned and shrugged her shoulders. "Are you as tired as I am?"

"Yeah."

"Then that means they're damn near exhausted."

"Most likely."

Jaime adjusted the straps on her pack. "Not even an hour before full dark. If we can get down the mountain a little ways and maybe find a sheltered ledge, we should be fine. We can get a campfire going without worrying about being seen if we can get up against the mountain."

"I think if we promise a campfire, we can get an hour's hike out of them."

Jaime nodded. "Well, let's go." She took the last few steps that brought her out on the ridge, finding everyone else sitting on rocks, resting.

"Ladies? One more hour then a campfire. Are we up to it?"

Abby stood up. "Come on, Jaime. What the hell's going on?"

"Well, we've been shot at and apparently we're being followed. I have a theory as to why, if that's what you mean."

"Sandra was shot," Abby stated quietly. "Shot and killed."

"Yes. I'm aware of that," Jaime said. "I was next to her when it happened." Jaime turned around, facing them all. "But now is not the time to discuss this. We've got to put some distance between us and him. Tonight, once we get a fire going and everyone has changed into dry clothes, we'll talk about this. Okay?"

Celia stood up and brushed at her once-styled hair, tucking it behind her ears. "Let's go. Dry clothes and a campfire sound like heaven right about now." The others followed, all standing and waiting expectantly, looking at first Sara, then Jaime.

"We go down the mountain, moving to the west. That way, we'll catch as much of the daylight that's left as we can. Hopefully, we can find a sheltered ledge or slope, something up against the mountain where we'll be shielded."

"Well, then lead the way, Chief," Celia said, pointing. "I don't want the night to catch us here."

Jaime looked briefly at Sara then started out, moving through the trees, trying to find an easy route over the ridge and down the other side. It was extremely rocky and huge boulders blocked their way. She went around and over them, sitting on her butt as she slid down the hill. The others followed suit.

CHAPTER TWENTY-THREE

"Captain Morris?"

Morris rubbed his eyes. "Yeah? What is it?"

"FBI. They want a word."

"At this hour?" He glanced at his watch. "What are you still doing here, anyway?"

Simon shrugged. "There's two of them."

Morris nodded. "Okay. Send them back."

Simon stepped aside and two suits walked in. Captain Morris stood then motioned to the visitor's chairs.

"I'm Special Agent Erickson, this is Agent Fielding."

Morris nodded, barely glancing at the badges they flashed him. "It's damn near seven o'clock. My wife's probably trying to keep dinner warm. What do you guys want now? Need to borrow another detective?"

The two agents exchanged glances.

"I don't know what you're talking about, Captain Morris."

Erickson sat down and waited until Morris did the same. "We're following a lead in an investigation. A lead that points to one of your detectives." He looked at his notes. "Jaime Hutchinson. I don't suppose she's still around?"

"You guys amaze me. Do you not communicate?"

Erickson leaned forward. "Captain Morris, what are you talking about?"

Morris leaned back, scratching his head as he stared at the two agents. "Your man Ramsey came in here the other week. Tabbed Hutchinson to help you guys watch some woman. That senator's daughter. Sara Michaels."

Erickson stood up, pacing. "Ramsey? I know of no agent named Ramsey."

"Special Agent Ramsey."

"You're saying some guy came in, claiming to be FBI and he knew about Michaels?"

"They've had death threats. And what do you mean, *claiming* to be FBI?"

"So some guy comes in here and says he's FBI and you just believe him?" Erickson asked, his voice rising.

"He flashed a badge, just like you guys did."

"And you just assumed it was legit?"

Morris smiled. "Well, I'm assuming you're legit. Your badge looked just like his." Morris's smile faded. "You want to tell me what the hell is going on?"

Erickson tilted his head. "How about you first, Captain. Your detective was identified by the owner of a sporting goods store. He said she was asking questions about Sara Michaels. We're very interested in that."

CHAPTER TWENTY-FOUR

Jaime added more wood to the fire, then stepped away, giving the others access to the warmth. They hadn't set up tents yet, they hadn't eaten. They just wanted to get warm.

"Change into dry clothes," she said. "We can lay these by the fire. Hopefully, they'll be dry enough by morning."

"What's going on? I mean, what the hell just happened to us?" Abby asked. She waved at the others. "What are we doing here?"

"After we eat, we'll talk," Jaime said. "Then we've got to discuss our plan for tomorrow. It'll be another long day."

"What about Sandra?" Celia asked quietly.

"There's a sniper," Jaime said, equally as quiet. "Now put up your tents. Change into dry clothes. After we eat, we'll talk," she said again.

"Who is he after?"

Jaime and Sara exchanged glances across the fire.

"He's . . . he's after me," Sara said quietly.

CHAPTER TWENTY-FIVE

"Simon, get in here."

"I was just heading out, Captain."

Morris motioned him in. "Just take a second." He walked back around to his desk. "This is Hutchinson's partner," he said to Erickson. "Detective Simon."

The two men shook hands, then Russ glanced nervously at Morris. "What's going on, Captain?"

"You heard from Hutchinson?"

He shook his head. "She's . . . she's on vacation. She doesn't normally call."

Morris flashed a humorless smile. "We both know she told you about this case, Simon. Cut the crap."

"Is she . . . is she in trouble?"

"We're more concerned with where she is, Detective." Erickson stood, pacing slowly across the room. "Tell us what you know."

"I don't know anything. She said the FBI pegged her to follow some senator's daughter into the mountains."

"And you've not spoken with her?"

"No. But I mean service up there is iffy at best."

"Why don't you try calling her, Russ. Make sure everything's okay," Captain Morris suggested.

"Sara Michaels's clinic wouldn't give us any information but we got a warrant. We'll head over there in the morning. We should be able to get her location."

"But you said earlier that the death threats were vague. That's what this man Ramsey said too."

"Captain, just the fact that there was an imposter in here tells us these threats are no longer vague. They also tell us that Sara Michaels is the most likely target, not the senator."

"But what purpose could he have for wanting Hutchinson out there? If they're trying to kill somebody, why put a cop on the scene?"

"Because they didn't know where Sara Michaels was going."

Morris frowned. "You're saying, they used Jaime to lead them in there?"

"It's my guess, yes." Erickson sighed. "Is she any good?"

Morris nodded. "They're in for a surprise."

CHAPTER TWENTY-SIX

"I just never made the connection. Your father is running for *president*?" Abby asked Sara.

"Afraid so."

"But I don't understand."

"Look, I'll tell you everything we know, which isn't much," Jaime said. "I'm a homicide detective in Denver. One day this FBI guy comes in and says he needs me to watch Sara here. He said there had been death threats." Jaime fixed her gaze on Sara. "So here I am, tagging along with you guys. For the last couple of days, I suspected we were being followed."

"That's why you kept sneaking off," Celia said.

"Yes. It could have just been hikers on the same trail for all I knew."

"But if he's after Sara, why would he shoot Sandra?"

Jaime shook her head. "I don't know. Sandra and I were standing next to each other. Maybe he intended the shot for me. Maybe he saw me doubling back." She shrugged. "And maybe he did it for fun," she said quietly.

"This is like a bad dream," Megan said. "I just can't believe it."

"Yes, it's a very bad dream," Sara said. "And I can't help but think that if Jaime wasn't here with us, how many more of us would he have gotten?"

"I guess it's too much to hope that somebody ignored orders and brought a cell phone with them," Abby said, looking at their group.

"I have a cell," Jaime said. "No service. And a low battery."

"Is he . . . is he like a hit man?" Megan asked. "Like in the movies?"

Jaime nodded. "Yes. He's got a high-powered rifle with a scope. I'm guessing he shot from over two hundred yards, if not more. Which gives him a big advantage. That's why we had to keep moving. And we'll have to start out in the morning as soon as there's enough light."

"I don't think I'll be able to sleep," Celia said.

"You can squeeze in with us," Abby offered.

"You'll all sleep out of sheer exhaustion. We'll be safe here tonight. There's no moon. He won't be able to travel at night. And he won't have a signal to follow this time."

"You have a plan?"

"We're off trail, so that'll slow us down, but if we can make it to St. Elmo, we might be able to find help. There are weekend homes up there, summer homes. Someone might still be there. If not, maybe we can at least find a phone." Jaime looked at Sara. "What the hell day is this, anyway?"

Sara looked at her watch. "Monday."

"Not good. It'll take us at least two days. Wednesday. Any weekenders will be gone."

"Can we even make it in two days? I mean, without being on a trail?"

"With luck. And who knows, without a signal to follow he might not even be able to track us as closely."

Sara knew Jaime was just trying to make them feel better, but the others seemed to be pacified somewhat. He was a hit man, hired to take her out. The chances that he wouldn't be able to track them were slim.

"Wash out your pots as good as you can, but conserve your water," Jaime instructed. "We're up high. We may not find water tomorrow."

"Are you sure it's safe up here?" Beth asked.

"Yeah. We're going to be fine tonight. And remember, I'm a light sleeper. Nothing's going to sneak into camp."

"I'll be glad when daylight comes. It's spooky out here without the moon."

"Do you . . . do you think Sandra will be okay?" Celia asked.

Jaime frowned. "What do you mean?"

"I mean, eventually, when we get out of here, we'll tell them where she is." Celia met Jaime's eyes. "Will she still be there?"

Jaime closed her eyes. She didn't want to think about it. She certainly didn't want to tell these women that most likely, wild animals would find Sandra before they did. So she lied. "She should be fine, Celia. It's cold at night."

CHAPTER TWENTY-SEVEN

He huddled inside his tent, his dinner long cold. The wind whistled around him, bringing cold air across the water. He again checked the receiver, and shook his head. The signal continued to move away from him at an alarming rate.

"It's in the goddamned river," he muttered. How in the hell had they found the transmitter? But it didn't matter. He could track them. They were heading upstream. He didn't think any of them were savvy enough to get them out of the mountains without a trail. Not even the cop. No, they would most likely follow the river, thinking they were safe, thinking he was following the transmitter.

"Bitches."

He didn't bother cleaning up his dinner. He crawled inside his sleeping bag, wishing he'd thought to move away from the water, where it would be warmer.

CHAPTER TWENTY-EIGHT

"I'm like Celia," Sara whispered. "I don't think I'll be able to sleep."

"You'll sleep fine." Jaime took her boots off then moved her sleeping bag to face Sara. "Come here."

Sara moved closer, her eyes shutting as Jaime's arms wrapped around her. "Why do I feel like I know you so well?" she murmured.

Jaime smiled. "Maybe because we've crammed a whole lot of togetherness into nine days."

"It's more than that. I can't quite put my finger on it."

Jaime laughed. "So you want to put your finger on it? I can help with that, you know," she teased.

Sara relaxed. "I like the way you smell."

"After what we've been through today, I'm afraid to know how I smell."

Sara smiled and turned to face Jaime. "I have a confession to make."

"Oh yeah?"

Sara cleared her throat. "This morning, when you woke up."

"Uh-huh."

"And your hand was on my breast."

Jaime stiffened. "Oh, God, Sara. I'm so sorry. You acted like you didn't know. I don't know how—"

"Shhh. Jaime, I'm the one who put it there," she whispered.

"What? But you—"

Sara took Jaime's hand. "Like this," she said, pulling Jaime's hand to her like she'd done the night before.

Jaime's hand instinctively closed over Sara's breast. "Sara?"

"I pretended not to know because I was too embarrassed," she said. "But then, when you thought you'd done it, I didn't want you to take the fall. So I pleaded ignorance."

Jaime swallowed, her hand still resting lightly on Sara's breast. She moved her hand, her fingers brushing the fabric over Sara's nipple, feeling it harden from her touch. Damn, if there wasn't a madman after them, if they didn't have nine other women within hearing distance . . . she closed her eyes, wondering what it'd be like to touch flesh.

"Maybe when this is over, we might be able to have . . . I don't know, have dinner or something. If you think—"

Sara laughed quietly. "We've got a killer after us, we're both exhausted, you're making plans to date if we get out of this alive . . . and all I can think about is making love with you," she finished in a whisper. "Right now."

Jaime's hand again covered her breast, then she pulled Sara closer. "We both know that's not possible." She brushed her lips lightly across Sara's cheek, wishing they had time.

"It's been so long since someone's made my heart pound like this," Sara admitted.

Jaime nodded, feeling the thundering heartbeat under her hand. "The feeling is mutual, sweetheart."

"Why won't you kiss me?"

Jaime smiled, finally moving her hand from Sara's breast, sliding it safely to her waist. "I'm afraid to kiss you," she admitted.

Sara sighed then finally let out a small laugh. "I've known you what? Barely more than a week? This day alone has lasted at least a week. But regardless, nine days." She rolled her head, facing Jaime. "I'm lying here in a tent with you, wanting your hands on me and I feel like I've known you for years. And yet you're practically a stranger."

"Not a stranger," Jaime whispered.

"No. I'd like to think I would not put my life in the hands of a stranger." Sara sighed and turned her head away. "And I can't believe she's dead," she whispered. "And we just left her up there."

"Sara, we had no choice," Jaime said gently. "You know that. We would have been putting all these other lives in danger if we'd tried to move her."

"I know. It's just all so horrible. Like we didn't even care about her."

"Sometimes you just do what you've got to do to survive. And we did that." Jaime shifted, pulling Sara into her arms again. "And when we get out of this, we'll give Sandra the respect she deserves."

Sara nodded, resting her face on Jaime's chest. She finally closed her eyes, letting sleep claim her as Jaime's hands moved soothingly across her back.

CHAPTER TWENTY-NINE

Sara woke first, feeling safe with Jaime's arms still around her. They were in much the same position as when they'd fallen asleep, when exhaustion finally claimed them. It was still dark out but her internal clock told her it was nearly five. She pulled her arm from under Jaime, illuminating her watch. Four fifty. They were on the west side of the mountain, so daylight would come more slowly.

"What time is it?" Jaime murmured.

"Nearly five."

"Good." Jaime kept her eyes closed, allowing herself a few more seconds of warmth, a few more seconds of contact. Then she sighed, slowly pulling her hands away from Sara. "I slept great. You?"

"Yeah. Like a rock."

"I've also got to pee."

Sara laughed. "Funny how we lose all sense of dignity up here."

"Do you think we can chance having a fire?"

"It would be nice. It must be in the thirties."

"Okay. I'll get one going if you'll wake the others."

Before long, eleven sleepy women huddled around the fire, trying to stay warm while water boiled for coffee.

"I didn't wake up once," Judith said. "I don't think I've ever been so tired."

Jaime smiled. "We'll ask you again tomorrow morning. It won't be a walk in the park today."

"Do you think he'll find us?" Lou Ann asked.

"Yes. We have to assume he's a professional."

"Will we make St. Elmo today?"

Jaime shook her head. "No."

"But maybe we'll come upon some people today," Beth said hopefully.

Jaime wanted to tell them no, they wouldn't come upon any people today, not bushwhacking across the mountains like they were. But she smiled and nodded. "Perhaps we'll get lucky."

"Water's ready," Abby announced.

Everyone spooned instant coffee into their cups, waiting somewhat impatiently as Abby dispensed the boiling water. Jaime and Sara exchanged glances then, without a word spoken, walked together.

"Is it too early to start?" Sara asked quietly.

"It should be light enough soon."

"Do you think he's already on the move?"

"No. He's down in a canyon. It'll stay dark longer down there. We should be able to get a good head start."

Sara glanced at the others, knowing most of them were listening to their conversation. She moved her hand between them, touching Jaime's arm, squeezing lightly. "I'm really glad you're here."

"Yeah? I know you're really just using me to keep you warm at night."

"Well, that too."

Jaime bent closer, her mouth at Sara's ear. "We're going to be fine, Sara. I promise I won't let anything happen to you."

Sara nodded. "I believe you."

Jaime moved away, handing her cup to Abby to fill. She blushed slightly at the grin Abby gave her.

"Despite all we've been through, it's still good to see you and the Sarge flirting."

"I wasn't flirting," Jaime insisted.

Abby bent closer. "Sandra would be happy," she whispered.

Their eyes met and Jaime nodded slightly. She sipped her coffee, glancing occasionally to the sky, trying to hurry the dawn.

By the time they broke camp and their packs were ready to go, the sky had lightened enough for them to travel. By flashlight, Jaime had shown them the route she wanted to take. They would go over the top of one peak, nearly twelve thousand feet, then hook up with a trail to Cumberland Pass. Once on the trail, they should have an easy shot to St. Elmo. The problem was getting over the peak. She had no idea how passable it was.

They walked slowly, cautiously, until full light, then Jaime picked up the pace. Once they cleared the ridge, the hike down would be easy. Then they would begin their climb.

"It's colder this morning," Lou Ann said.

"And windy," Jaime noted. "May have had a front blow in during the night."

"How far ahead of him are we?"

Jaime looked at her watch. "I'd say a good three hours. But we're also moving slower than he is. I'm hoping it takes him awhile to find our trail from last night." She ducked under the branches of a low-growing spruce then slipped on the rocks, landing on her ass. "Damn. Careful there," she called back to Lou Ann.

She found a relatively flat area and stopped, pulling out the map and compass again.

"Problem?" Sara called from around the tree.

"Just making sure we're not off course." Jaime looked up. "How's everyone doing?"

"Celia's got a slight blister. Other than that, we're keeping up."

Jaime nodded. "From the wet boots last night." She pointed up ahead. "After that ridge, we'll climb down into a small canyon.

Then we start the climb to the top." She stood, addressing them all. "This is where it gets tricky. We'll be exposed. If our guy happens to be at the top of that ridge there," she said, pointing to where they'd come. "Then we'll be in his view. If he wanted to take a shot, I'd guess it'd be over four hundred yards. A tough shot."

"Impossible shot?"

"No. Military sharpshooters can make that shot."

"Do we have a choice?"

"Not to make St. Elmo in a day, no. With luck, he won't see us. We can stick to the trees as much as possible. But like it is here, there'll be open spots."

"Let's get a move on, then," Abby said. "I, for one, don't want my ass shot at."

They made the trip down the mountain quickly, in single file, with Jaime leading the way. Conversation was nonexistent, all concentrating on the steep incline down. Celia lost her footing once but Jaime turned, catching the older woman before she tumbled down. Celia smiled her thanks.

Jaime laughed when she reached the narrow canyon bottom. "Wonderful."

"What?" Celia asked, bending over to catch her breath.

"Water," Jaime said, pointing to the small stream. "Fill your water bottles," Jaime instructed. "Don't forget to purify."

She hopped across the stream, walking upstream a few steps then dipped her nearly empty bottle into the fresh water. She looked up, watching as Sara bent down, filling her own bottle. She stared, transfixed, as Sara cupped water into her hands, then splashed her face. Across the stream, their eyes met. For just a second, Jaime forgot about their plight. She fell into the blue-green eyes, thinking she'd never seen a sexier sight than Sara Michaels splashing water on her face.

Then sounds intruded, the others jumping the small stream, gathering, waiting for instruction. Jaime stood slowly, finally sliding her eyes away from Sara, feeling nearly shaken. It was amazing how quickly she'd become attached to Sara. But as she'd told her last night, they'd crammed a whole lot of emotion into only a few days.

She took a deep breath then turned her eyes up the mountain they had to traverse if they were going to hit the old Cottonwood Pass trail that would take them to St. Elmo. It looked steeper from this angle. She tensed slightly when a warm hand wrapped around her forearm.

"Can we make it?"

Jaime stared, letting Sara's eyes capture her own. "I think so. I'm more worried about the lack of cover," she admitted. "And it'll be windy. We'll be on a north-facing side."

Sara nodded. "Single file or spread out?"

"Spread out. If we can. We might need to help each other at the really steep parts though."

Sara nodded again, realizing her hand was still resting on Jaime's arm. She squeezed lightly then let it slip away.

Jaime gave her a brief smile and headed up. "Spread out and try to use the trees and rocks for cover. About thirty yards up, we'll be visible from that mountain over there," she said, pointing to where they'd stood early that morning. "Let's go, ladies. No time to waste."

The climb was easier than Sara had thought it would be. Steep, yes, but there seemed to be enough low-growing shrubs and trees for them to use for support. She glanced occasionally both to her left and right, making sure Celia and Judith were making it okay. There was no conversation, just quiet determination as they made their way higher up the mountain. She saw where Jaime and Megan had pulled away from the others, moving some ten to twenty yards ahead of them. She paused, watching Jaime, enjoying the sight of her as she pulled herself along with the help of a spruce limb.

She was about to call to her when a rifle shot sounded. In slow motion, she turned. It seemed like many seconds passed before dirt kicked up where the bullet had hit. Before she could move, another shot sounded.

"Get down! Get down!" Jaime yelled. "Sara! Goddammit, *move!*" she screamed.

Sara dove behind a rock as another shot rang out. She covered her head with her hands, looking over as Celia hid behind two spruce trees.

"Is anybody hit?" Jaime called. Before anyone could answer, two more shots landed within feet of her. "Goddamn bastard," she said as she crouched lower. "Megan? Where are you?" she called.

"Jaime? *Jaime?* Are you okay?" Sara yelled.

"We've got to go back down," she called. "It's too windy for him to get a clean shot. We've got to take a chance and go back down."

"While he's shooting?" Abby screamed. "No fucking way!"

"We can't stay here. It's the only way," Jaime insisted.

Another shot hit the spruce where Celia hid. She cried out in fright then bolted down the mountain, screaming as she ran.

"*Celia!* Don't," Sara yelled.

Another shot landed two feet behind Celia as she stumbled down the incline. Before long, Judith followed, scrambling after her.

"Go! Everyone, run!" Jaime shouted. She rolled to her back, looking across the mountain, finding the scope's reflection two ridges over. He had a bad angle. At least four hundred yards away. She didn't think he could get a clean shot off, not with the wind blowing like it was. Only two more shots rang out as the others hurried back down the way they'd come.

"Jaime?" Sara called.

"Keep going. I'm coming." She crouched down, moving to another rock pile. "Megan? Where the fuck are you?"

"I'm . . . I think I'm shot."

Jaime crawled on her belly down the hill, sliding behind the tree where Megan lay. She saw blood on her stomach then pulled Megan's hands away.

"Lay still." Jaime lifted up her shirt, revealing the wound along her side. She felt behind her, nodding when she felt the exit wound. "Through and through," she murmured. "You got lucky.

It's just through the fleshy part." She slipped off her pack, rummaging in the side pocket, finding the Ace bandage she always packed but never used. Well, she'd used it as a decoy at the beginning of this trip. She pulled out her last clean bandana and pressed it to Megan's side. She ignored the cry of pain as Megan tried to pull away from her. "Hold still." She wrapped the bandage around her waist, holding the bandana in place. "Just to stop the bleeding," she said. She gripped Megan's hands. "I know it hurts. But we've got to get down to the ravine. We'll clean it in the water then wrap it. Sara's got some stuff. But we've got to move."

"I can't."

"Yes, you can. We can't stay here." She pointed to where she saw the reflection. "His angle is bad. The others made it down. We can too."

"I can't run. It hurts."

Jaime shook her head. "You don't have a choice." She slipped on her pack again, then peeked around the tree. There was no reflection. He was on the move. "Come on. I'll help you down."

She stood, pulling Megan to her feet. Gripping her arm, Jaime ran, struggling to keep Megan upright. She stopped behind a rock pile, letting Megan slide down beside her. "You okay?"

Megan nodded, her breath coming fast. "Too scared not to be."

"You'll be fine. It's what we call a flesh wound in the business. Our biggest worry will be infection."

"Jaime?" Sara called. "Where are you?" A pause. "*Jaime?*"

"Is everyone okay?" Jaime yelled down.

"Yes. Are you?"

"Yeah. We're coming." Jaime looked at Megan. "Ready?"

"How much farther?"

"See the dead tree? We get below that, we should be out of his line of sight. Can you do it?"

Megan nodded. "Yeah."

Jaime looked across the mountain and again there was no reflection. Apparently he knew he didn't have a good shot. She relaxed. "Let's go."

Jaime gripped Megan's arm hard, pulling her down the last

thirty yards or so, stumbling once and bringing them both to their knees.

"Sorry. You okay?"

Megan nodded and struggled to stand. Jaime pulled her up and slowed her pace. They were well out of his sight by now.

Sara ran to meet them, her eyes wide when she saw the blood on Jaime's hands. She gripped Jaime's shoulders, her eyes searching.

"You're bleeding. Where are you hit?" she asked quickly, her hands moving over Jaime's torso. Jaime stilled them.

"Not me. Megan."

Sara turned her eyes to Megan who had slid to the ground. She saw the dark stain on her shirt.

"Oh my God. How bad?"

"The bullet didn't lodge, thank God." Jaime tossed off her pack and helped Megan out of hers.

"What can we do?" Lou Ann asked.

"Anything you've got clean, soak it in the water. We've got to clean her wound then dress it," Jaime told them. She looked at Sara. "What do you have for infection?"

"Just topical. Nothing orally."

"What about for pain?"

Sara shook her head. "Ibuprofen."

"That's it?"

"I'm not a doctor. By law I can't administer prescription drugs."

"Well, we've got to do the best we can. Stop the bleeding, mainly." She turned to Megan, gently pushing her down. "You've got to lie still while we clean this."

"It hurts."

"I know. But you're going to have to deal with it. We've still got to get out of here."

Abby touched her shoulder. "Let me help. My mother was a nurse. I picked up a little."

Jaime nodded. "Good. Thanks." She stood, her hand gently squeezing Sara's arm before she walked away. "I'll try to find another way out of here."

Jaime paused to wash her hands in the stream, rubbing to get Megan's blood off of them. They were lucky. It could have been a lot worse. It was a goddamned stupid idea to try to make it over the top before he caught up with them. But it was the best route, she reminded herself. They didn't have a lot of options. And now they had one less.

She walked away from the group then turned a circle, wondering how the hell they were going to get out of here. Go downstream? It would be the easiest route but it would take them in the wrong direction. Besides, if he should see them, all he had to do was head straight down to intercept them. But upstream? God, it looked impossible. She pulled out her map, finding the tiny stream, moving her fingers over the grids as she calculated the elevation gains. If they could make it upstream and over the top, it would put them a hell of a lot closer to the trail than the original route. But could they make it? Could Megan make it?

"How's it look?"

Jaime sighed. "Rough."

Sara sat down beside her and pointed at the map. "Show me."

Jaime paused. "How's Megan?"

"I think in shock."

"The bleeding stopped?"

"Yes, for now." Their eyes met. "She needs a doctor."

"I know."

They were quiet, then Sara nudged her arm. "How far behind is he?"

"I'd say two to three hours." She glanced at her watch. "He's moving faster than we are."

"Okay. What's the plan?"

Jaime moved the map onto Sara's legs. "Here's where we are," she pointed. Her finger moved along the stream to the base of the mountains. "If we can climb up here," she said, "then over the top, we'll save about three hours from the original route. Maybe more."

Sara looked at the map then looked ahead of them toward the mountain. "Looks steep. Really steep, Jaime."

"I know."

"What about going down?"

She shook her head. "Wrong direction. Besides, we'd be heading back into his line of sight."

"What if we can't find a trail?"

"Then we'll turn into rock climbers. It's the only way, Sara."

CHAPTER THIRTY

"What do you mean it's too windy to fly?" Erickson demanded.

"Up in the mountains, they've had gusts over fifty knots. No way we can send a helicopter up there," Fielding said.

Erickson loosened his tie. "What about the team on the ground?"

"They've started out but sir, they're more than a week behind them. Chances of them catching up are slim."

"They're a week behind and if something happened and forced them off trail, then we're screwed." He slammed his fist on the desk. "We need that chopper in the air."

Captain Morris turned away then looked at Simon, motioning him into his office. "Shut the door."

"What's up?"

"They're not telling me jack, that's what's up." He looked out his window, watching the two FBI agents argue. "They left from Buena Vista but we already knew that. Simon, do you have *any* idea which route?"

"No, sir. She didn't know. She said she was going to intercept them on the trail, then follow." Russ followed the captain's gaze. "But isn't this their show now?"

"Yeah. But she's ours. They're not concerned about Hutchinson. They're only worried about Michaels. And as soon as they coordinate their team, they're out of here. Then we'll know less than we know now."

"So what do we do?"

"I'm going to call Captain Zeller. He had a detective who worked for him a while back. She was like Jaime, always up in the mountains. She retired up there, last I heard."

"Jake McCoy. She was the one shot by her lieutenant. I remember that."

"I'll see if we can get in touch with her. She knows that area. Maybe she might help us."

"You going to tell them?" he asked, motioning to the FBI.

"No fucking way."

CHAPTER THIRTY-ONE

"I don't know, Jaime."

"It's the only way."

Jaime turned to the others. "I'll go first. We'll do the buddy system. Help the one behind you and above you. It'll be steep. We'll go slow." She met Sara's eyes. "We've got maybe three hours on him. By the time he finds our route, we'll be over the top. I seriously don't think he can make it up this way alone. He'll have to take the route over the side, like we were going to do. I'm guessing by this evening, we'll be at least five hours ahead of him, if not more." She looked at Megan. "I know this is going to be hard, Megan. But it's the only way."

She nodded. "Can I go next to you?"

Jaime smiled. "Absolutely." She looked at the others. "Single file. Sara? You bring up the rear."

Sara nodded. She would rather be near Jaime—hell, they all would—but she and Jaime were the most experienced. It stood to reason they should both take an end. She glanced behind her, looking at nothing but space, wondering how close he was. They were maybe three hours in front of him, but with a rifle, he was a hell of a lot closer than three hours.

"Come on, Sarge."

Sara looked up, nodding at Lou Ann who was waiting for her. She tightened the straps on her pack one more time then started up, following the others. The climb was gradual at first, the footholds plenty. Then the placid stream turned violent as it cascaded down the mountain. She watched as Jaime and the others moved away from the stream, climbing among the boulders as they made their way higher.

"It's like a waterfall," Lou Ann said.

Sara nodded. "Sort of, yeah. It just kinda falls down the mountain, doesn't it."

"It's all so pretty up here," Lou Ann mused. "And we've all been too scared to even notice."

Sara gave a humorless laugh. "Yeah. This trip of self-confidence has been shot to hell."

Lou Ann looked down at her. "I don't know. If we make it out of here alive, it'll be the most exciting thing any of us will ever experience in our life. How can we not come out of this with more self-confidence? I mean, we just had a guy shooting at us, for Christ's sake! Did anyone get hysterical?" She laughed. "Well, other than Celia. But really, I think it's everything we learned in your lessons. We do feel confident we'll make it through this."

Sara met her eyes. "A woman died yesterday."

"No disrespect, Sara, but Sandra told me this had been the best week of her life. And she truly meant that. Did you see her in the hot springs? She was so different from the woman we first met all those weeks ago." Lou Ann paused, looking up into the sky. "We all saw what happened. Sandra never knew what hit her. She was talking to Jaime, smiling. Her last thoughts were of being happy. We should all be so lucky."

Sara nodded, wondering if perhaps Lou Ann needed to think

that, if they all *needed* to think that. But the fact remained, one of them had died.

She wiped her palms on her jeans and grabbed the tree limb that Lou Ann had just vacated, pulling herself along. She stopped, watching as Jaime reached down to help Megan. Again, how would they ever have made it if Jaime wasn't here?

"Easy," Jaime murmured, tugging Megan up beside her. "Let's rest. Let me check your wound."

Megan nodded, her eyes closed.

"How bad is the pain?" Jaime asked the younger woman.

"I don't have anything to compare it to," Megan said hoarsely. "I just want to lie down and sleep."

"I know. And I wish we had something to give you."

"Tell me again why the first-aid kit is so basic?"

Jaime laughed. "Lawsuits, my dear."

"Lawsuits. Figures. And to think I once thought about being a lawyer."

"Lay back just a little," Jaime said.

But Megan grabbed her hand before she could lift her shirt. "I'm not going to die, am I?"

Jaime turned serious. "No way. We're going to play doctor until we can find you a real one. It's just going to hurt like hell."

"It's funny. I didn't really feel anything when it happened. Just this burning."

Jaime frowned, touching lightly against the exit wound on Megan's back. It was bleeding again.

"What is it?"

"Bleeding again."

"I have this ache but it feels numb where you're touching."

"Sometimes pain is a good thing," Jaime murmured as she tightened the tape. Then she felt Megan's face, feeling the light heat on her cheeks. Could be from the exertion, but most likely, a fever was setting in. *Goddamn.*

"Everything okay?" Sara called from below.

Jaime met Megan's eyes, smiling slightly. "We're just taking a little break," she called back down. She looked up to where they had to go. The steepest part was yet to come. "We're about halfway there," she said to those below her. "Everybody ready?"

"Lead on."

"Remember, it's going to get very steep. Help the one behind you." She looked down. "Ready?" she asked quietly, squeezing lightly on Megan's arm.

"I'm game."

Jaime laughed. "That you are, my friend."

She stood, pulling herself up, and reached to help Megan stand. Through the trees, she saw blue-green eyes looking at her. Worried blue-green eyes, she noted. She offered a quick smile then turned away. She didn't have a whole lot of reassurances to give Sara. She was too worried herself.

CHAPTER THIRTY-TWO

Peter Michaels paced slowly in his study, pausing to glance at his reflection in the decorative mirror his wife had brought back from France last year. Unconsciously his hand lifted, touching the steel-gray hair on his temples. His eyes moved, meeting his own blue ones in the mirror. A slow smile formed as he studied himself. He'd been called incredibly handsome by the tabloids. He'd also been called a lady killer. He smiled broadly. He believed both of those statements wholeheartedly.

"Senator? Mr. Dodds is here."

Peter straightened his shoulders then turned away from the mirror, directing his gaze to Arthur. Arthur had been with him for years, ever since their days on the city council in Colorado Springs. However, his trust only went so far. And what he and Mr. Dodds had to discuss was not a matter for Arthur to be involved in.

"Thank you, Arthur. Escort him in, please."

"Of course. Do you also wish for Daniel to attend?"

Peter shook his head. "Actually, this is a private meeting. You can call it a night, Arthur."

"But Senator—"

"And inform Daniel that I'm expecting Mr. Ramsey as well."

Arthur finally nodded. "Very well. Good evening, Senator."

Arthur closed the door quietly and Peter returned to his desk, waiting. Mr. Dodds knocked once then opened the door. His bulky frame filled the doorway and Peter motioned him inside.

"Dodds," he greeted.

"Pete. Good to see you." He reached out, shaking Peter's hand with enthusiasm. "Ramsey should be here within the hour."

"Good." Peter sat down and motioned for Dodds to do the same. "Has it been taken care of?"

"I don't have confirmation. But that was the plan. It'll take him a number of days to return."

Peter nodded. "So we'll assume it's handled?"

"Yes. Now we just have to decide how to proceed. There has to be enough remorse over her death so that moderates are appeased. And if we're lucky, we might even draw in some liberals who are appalled that your lesbian daughter was killed."

"Of course, we don't want to piss off our base. If I show too much remorse, conservatives might get the idea that I approved of her lifestyle."

"Perhaps we can use that. You loved your daughter but God saw fit to end her life."

"As punishment," Peter said, nodding. "That could be good."

Dodds laughed. "If you use that line, there go any liberals you may have pulled on board."

"We don't need them to win. Our Christian base is sound. Moderates will join us." He grinned. "And I've always enjoyed strong female support."

"Well then, let's discuss the FBI. Eventually, your daughter's body will be found. There will be an investigation. I don't anticipate them finding anything out there. He's a professional. Besides, there's hundreds of thousands of acres for them to search. He'll be long gone."

"And the money won't be traced?"

"After confirmation of her death, the money will be transferred to an offshore account. He will already have left the country. We won't hear from him again."

A sound startled them and they both turned, finding wide eyes staring at them. Joyce Michaels stumbled into the room.

"Sara?" She brought a hand to her chest. "My God, you're talking about Sara? About killing *Sara*?"

Peter stood. "Joyce? What are you doing? How long have you been there?"

"Are you *insane*?" she said, spitting out the words. "She's our daughter!" she screamed.

"Joyce, please," Dodds said, walking to her. "Think about it. We'll never win the presidency as long as you have a lesbian daughter. It goes against everything we've preached all these years."

"I wasn't aware that *we* were running for the presidency, Mr. Dodds." She took a step back, looking at Peter. "I can't believe you're even talking about this. It's not okay to have a lesbian daughter but it is okay to condone murder?" She pointed at Dodds. "It's okay for the founder of the Family Values Association to hire someone to kill our daughter?" she yelled. "I won't let you get away with this."

"Joyce, listen to me," Peter said, walking closer. "It's the only way. We've worked too hard all these years to let it slip away just because of her."

"You can't even say her name, can you?" Joyce pulled away from his touch. "She's our daughter, for God's sake. Doesn't that mean anything to you?"

His laughter rang out, his eyes cold as he looked at her. He shook his head. "She's no daughter of mine. If she was, she would have embraced what I stand for. Instead, she's gone against me every step of the way." He walked closer, his height dwarfing that of his wife. "And we both know why, don't we Joyce?" He glanced once at Dodds, then back to his wife. "Did you think I wouldn't find out about your little affair all those years ago?"

She gasped, her eyes darting around the room as she took a step backward. She felt his desk hit the back of her thighs and stopped.

"What . . . what do you mean?"

"What I mean, my dear wife, is that I know she's not my daughter."

"But Peter, of course she is."

He walked away with only a shrug. "Spare me the lies, Joyce. Do you think a man in my position goes blindly into marriage? Do you think all these years I've let you have free rein?" He shook his head. "No. Of course not. So all those years ago, after we'd only been married a year at most, did you really think I didn't know about the man you were seeing? About the man who impregnated you?"

She shook her head, her eyes wide. "No. No, Peter. You've got it wrong."

"Do I?" His eyes narrowed. "Such a tragedy, his accident. And he was so young. Shame."

She gasped then looked down, unable to meet his eyes. But her voice was quivering when she spoke. "I beg you, Peter. You've raised her as your daughter. You can't possibly be involved in a plot to kill her."

"She's only an obstacle to me, Joyce. An obstacle. She means nothing to me."

"My God, you're such a hypocrite. You preach Christian values, yet you've both turned to murder. Murderers! *Thou shall not kill.* Since when does that not apply to you?"

Peter smiled. "It's not like I was the one who pulled the trigger, Joyce."

Her eyes widened again. "It's . . . it's already been done?" she whispered.

Dodds nodded.

She screamed, sinking down to her knees, her arms flailing wildly. "How could you? How *could* you? You won't get away with this," she screamed. "You won't get away with this!"

The outer door opened and Ramsey walked in, closing it quickly behind him. "What's going on in here?"

"Unexpected complication," Dodds said, motioning to Joyce Michaels. "Please take care of it."

"Of course."

"Who are you? Get away from me," Joyce said, trying to stand as she slapped at the hands that grabbed her. "Help! Somebody help me!"

A strong hand clamped over her mouth and the only sound was that of the electric charge as the stun gun touched her neck. Within seconds, her limp body slid to the floor. All three men stared at her.

"She could be a problem," Dodds said.

Peter shook his head. "No. Once it's all over with, she'll be fine." He shrugged. "If not, we'll just keep her drugged, won't we?"

"Perhaps the rumors of alcoholism might turn out to be helpful after all. She was so distraught by her daughter's death that she turned to drugs." He smiled. "I have a doctor at my disposal. We might even be able to get her committed this time."

Peter nodded. "Could conjure up some sympathy votes." He turned away from his wife. "Ramsey, take her to her quarters. Watch her."

"I'll call Dr. Hammond. Have him give her a sedative."

"Then we need to discuss the FBI issues. Ramsey? I assume you have updates?"

"Yes, sir. It's going as planned."

"Good." He motioned to his wife. "Let's get this handled then we'll meet."

CHAPTER THIRTY-THREE

"Can she make it to St. Elmo?"

The quiet words hung in the air and all eyes slid to Jaime. One by one, Jaime looked at them, seeing their expressions in the soft light of the campfire. Most of the gazes were the same, swimming in worry and doubt. Behind them, in the tent, Megan lay asleep, her body warm as the infection tried to take over. They had cleaned her wound again and redressed it. And the bleeding was again stopped. For now.

"The trip tomorrow will be easy. No climbing. Once we get there, if we're lucky, some of the summer residents might still be around. Or the general store might be open."

"I thought it was a ghost town."

"It is. But some of the old cabins have been restored and people live there in the summer. From what I remember, the general store rented Jeeps. But tourist season is over, so there may not be anyone around. Especially on a weekday."

"But we might find a phone?" Abby asked hopefully.

"Yes. And we might find something for Megan. Penicillin, pain pills, something."

Sara reached out to the fire, warming her hands. "If we can make it through tomorrow, make it to St. Elmo, then we should be okay."

"Well, I for one, am ready to see civilization again," Lou Ann said.

"And maybe we don't have to worry about that guy," Ashley said quietly. "I mean, maybe we lost him."

Jaime and Sara exchanged glances.

"We may have. But to be sure, I don't think we should assume that," Jaime said. "It's better to plan as if he's on our trail. That way, we'll be prepared." She looked up into the dark sky, seeing the multitude of stars sparkling overhead. No moon. At least he wasn't traveling. But she had no doubt he was still on their trail.

"So, if people live there, that means there's a road, right?"

Jaime smiled at Abby, nodding. "There are two dirt roads. One is a rough Jeep road that goes over Tin Cup Pass. The other goes down the mountain, toward Nathrop. That's the better of the two roads and obviously, Nathrop is a town with amenities, including a doctor. The problem being, it's probably twenty miles or more. So if we can't find a vehicle, we're closer to Tin Cup, over the pass, than Nathrop."

"Does Tin Cup have a doctor?"

"No. But they have year-round residents."

"Well, let's just hope we find someone in St. Elmo."

Captain Morris tapped his fingers impatiently as the phone continued to ring. He glanced up at Simon, motioning to the FBI.

"They're both on the phone."

He nodded then heard the breathless voice on the other end.

"Jake McCoy."

He cleared his throat. "Detective McCoy? This is Captain Morris, Denver PD. Homicide."

CHAPTER THIRTY-FOUR

He hovered over the fire, nearly too exhausted—and too cold—to eat. The bitches had taken a route nearly straight up the mountain, following a small chute in the wall facing. He'd tried to follow them, but soon realized he would never make it. It set him back at least a couple of hours as he backtracked to the stream and picked up their original route. It pleased him somewhat when he saw the blood. At least he'd gotten one of them. It would slow them down, if nothing else. But still, they had a good eight hours on him now. And if he couldn't find their trail tomorrow, it was as good as over.

"Goddamn bitches," he murmured as he held his hands to the fire. He looked at his useless cell phone, the battery long dead.

CHAPTER THIRTY-FIVE

Sara rolled out her sleeping bag then did the same with Jaime's. She heard the others as they all talked quietly in their own tents. Surprisingly, panic had not set in. And even more unbelievably neither had exhaustion. Oh, they were plenty tired but no doubt running on adrenaline. She only hoped the crash wasn't too severe when it finally happened.

"Hey. Ready for me?"

Sara scooted away from the door, making room for Jaime. "How is she?"

"Still sleeping. The fever doesn't seem to be getting worse. Maybe the ibuprofen has helped some. But it's swelling bad. The bullet wound is just through her fleshy part at her waist, so I doubt it nicked something inside. The swelling might just be because we can't get the bleeding stopped, not when she had to climb like we did today."

"How much longer do you think she can go without a doctor?"

"If we didn't have to travel, if we had something for the infection, maybe a couple of days. But she's strong." The small flashlight Jaime held showed their breath as it frosted around them. "It's colder than last night."

Sara pulled off her boots, left her socks on and quickly crawled into her sleeping bag. "I agree with Lou Ann. I'm ready for civilization."

"Don't mind saying, I am too," Jaime murmured as she unlaced her boots. "A hot shower. A warm, soft bed."

"Mmm." Sara closed her eyes, listening as Jaime shed her jeans and replaced them with sweats.

"Mmm?" Jaime slid into her own sleeping bag and turned to face Sara. "Want to talk about it?"

Sara's eyes opened. "Talk about what?"

"You've been very quiet today. Distant." Jaime reached over, finding Sara's hand in the darkness. "Has it finally caught up with you?" Jaime asked gently.

Sara sighed and closed her eyes again. "First Sandra—which seems like a lifetime ago, not a couple of days—and now Megan. And the rest of them, they're acting like it's nothing."

"What do you mean?"

"Lou Ann said it would be the greatest adventure any of them ever went on." Sara cleared her throat. "Providing they live, of course." Sara shifted. "I mean, she was acting like Sandra's death was acceptable. She said Sandra was happy at the end and she didn't even know what hit her. But Jaime, Sandra's *dead*," she whispered. "Do they think this is a movie or something?"

"I think they're just all trying to cope in their own way. Ashley is the most upset over Megan because they are buddies. Celia is the most upset over Sandra for the same reason. The others, well, they're probably just trying to survive, mentally and physically." She rolled onto her back, staring at the ceiling of the tent. "Think about it, Sara. They've known you for ten, eleven weeks now. Same with each other. There may be some attachments with the women they've met, but mostly, they're scared about what happened to Sandra, afraid it might happen to them. Of course they feel some sort of remorse over losing someone they knew, but it wasn't like they were lifelong friends. Right now, they're just trying to make it out of here alive. And it has to be frightening to them to put their trust in you, someone they've known a few months, and me who they've known less than two weeks."

"I guess you're right. But this whole thing is surreal. I feel like *I'm* in a movie."

"It'll be over soon. We'll make St. Elmo tomorrow. I think once we're there, we'll be safe. We'll have shelter at least. And I'm hoping we can find a phone. My cell is dead."

"Mmm," Sara murmured, then sighed. She hoped they found a phone too. She hoped they found a car. She hoped they found several cars that they could pile into and get the hell off this mountain, away from *him*.

Jaime rolled closer, pulling Sara to her. "Come on. Get some sleep."

Sara nodded. "I'm even too tired to flirt with you tonight," she whispered. But she pulled Jaime's arm tighter around her, entwining their fingers, feeling safe.

CHAPTER THIRTY-SIX

Jake McCoy sat on the porch, her long legs stretched out in front of her, the old rocking chair barely moving as she gazed out at the nighttime sky. Cheyenne sat beside her, eyes closed as Jake ran her fingers through her shaggy fur. The dog looked up occasionally, watching Jake, her intelligent eyes studying her.

"Don't act like you know what I'm thinking."

The dog yawned.

Jake rolled her shoulders then reached up, absently rubbing her neck. She hadn't told Nicole yet about the phone call. Hadn't told her she might be leaving in the next day or so. She jumped, startled when warm hands touched her shoulders.

"Sorry. I thought you heard me."

Jake shook her head. "Just thinking."

Nicole walked around the chair, squatting down beside her. Her hand went to Jake's thigh, rubbing lightly across the now-healed injury.

"Is everything okay? You've been kinda quiet this evening."

"Oh, yeah, everything's fine." Jake shrugged. "Got a phone call earlier is all."

"What is it?"

"Captain Morris, from Homicide."

Nicole stiffened. "In Denver? Is everything okay? Rick? Steven?"

Jake smiled and covered Nicole's hand with her own. "Nothing like that. He just wants me to do him a favor."

Nicole sat down on the porch and leaned against the railing, pulling her knees up nearly to her chest. "What's up?"

"He's got a detective up here, undercover. She's with a group of women. She's supposed to be watching a senator's daughter. Sara Michaels. Of Senator Peter Michaels."

Nicole nodded. "Small world. I know her."

"Oh, yeah?"

"She interviewed me several years ago when she was just starting her clinic. She's quite successful from what I hear."

"What kind of clinic?"

"The New You. It's sort of the twelve-step program to improving your life."

Jake rolled her eyes and Nicole laughed.

"Yes. I know how you feel about that, sweetheart. But I've heard good things about her clinic." Nicole reached out and touched Jake's hand, tugging lightly. "But what about your phone call?"

"There have been some death threats against the senator and his family. Which is not surprising, given his politics."

Nicole nodded. "He makes Falwell look like a liberal."

"Anyway, Detective Hutchinson was to infiltrate this group that Sara Michaels brought up here. They've not had any contact with her in ten days. The FBI is involved, which is why he couldn't go into a lot of detail."

"That's right. She takes her classes out on a backpacking trip at the end of each session. It's a confidence builder. I've read about her methods in the *Journal*."

"Well, Captain Morris is afraid—and I guess the FBI too—that they ran into trouble. It's been too windy to do flyovers, not that they could put a chopper down up here anyway. They've got a team that started out on foot from Buena Vista, but hell, they're nine days behind."

Nicole's eyes widened. "And he wants you to go out looking for them?"

Their eyes met.

"Yeah, that's what he wants. Sort of."

"What do you mean?"

"He's going to e-mail me what he's got. But they were heading up to Cottonwood Pass. If they ran into trouble, they could be anywhere, which is the problem. If it were me, I'd try to make it to the Mt. Princeton area where there's always someone about. Or to St. Elmo."

"I thought the road to St. Elmo was washed out. Besides, this late in the season, there's probably no one still there."

"The road going down to Nathrop is passable but you're right. I think the general store closes after Labor Day."

"Why don't they just call the county sheriff in Nathrop and ask him to drive up the mountain?"

"It's the FBI's gig. And it's a sensitive situation. The death threats haven't been made public. There's no way the FBI is going to involve a local sheriff in a tiny town."

Nicole unconsciously ran her fingers over Jake's thigh, tracing the scar with her fingers. "Can you make it, Jake? I mean, your leg still bothers you if you overdo it," Nicole said gently.

Jake covered Nicole's hand, squeezing it lightly. "I love you."

Nicole smiled. "But you'll be fine and I shouldn't worry?"

Jake nodded. "I'll have my cell. And I'll take Cheyenne. Depending on what he finds out tonight and in the morning, I'm thinking I'll drive to the washout above Cumberland Pass then hike in to St. Elmo. I'll start there and follow the trail down to Cottonwood Pass."

"I could get someone to cover my classes and go with you," Nicole offered.

But Jake shook her head. "No. If there's trouble, I'd rather you not be anywhere near it."

Nicole nodded and leaned forward, resting her head against Jake's leg. "I love you," she murmured, relaxing a little as Jake's fingers brushed through her hair. She would worry, yes. But she suspected Jake had something to prove by agreeing to this. That, and well, Jake just missed being a cop.

CHAPTER THIRTY-SEVEN

"Oh, my God," Abby said. "Will you look at this. Incredible."

Jaime nodded. "Pretty amazing, isn't it."

Spread out before them was the preserved town of St. Elmo, the old buildings nestled up against the mountains, the forest slowly trying to reclaim the town again.

"It could be a movie set. Look, there's a schoolhouse."

"And there's the saloon," Lou Ann said. "Man, I could use a drink about now."

They all laughed and Jaime and Sara exchanged glances. It was the first laughter they'd had in days.

"I feel like we've just gone back in time. I mean, this is like a real Old West town. Even the wooden sidewalks are still here."

Jaime ginned. "Hence the name ghost town." She pointed up ahead. "There's the general store."

Abby turned in a circle on the road. "Look, Miner's Exchange Store. Did they trade gold and stuff in there?"

"Mercantile? What's that?" Judith asked, pointing to another building.

"It was like a trading post. Like a general store back in the day," Jaime explained. She eased Megan down onto the bench in front of the general store. "You okay?" she asked quietly.

Megan nodded. "Thirsty."

"Here. Use mine," Ashley offered, holding the water bottle so Megan could drink.

Jaime stood back, sighing as she read the sign.

CLOSED FOR THE SEASON.

"Wonderful," she murmured. She took a deep breath and turned around, her eyes finding Sara. "Okay, ladies, here's the plan. Abby and Lou Ann, you stay with me. We're going to see if we can find a Jeep we can hotwire or something. Sara, you take the others. The summer cabins are down at the other end of town. There's only a handful of them, so don't be expecting a whole neighborhood or anything. The road down there leads to Nathrop. Hopefully, that's where we'll be heading soon."

"What are we looking for?"

"A phone would be nice. Or a car. Or people. But we need to see if we can find something for Megan."

"Don't you think the cabins will be locked up?" Celia asked.

"Yeah. Break in." She pointed at Ashley. "You mind staying here with Megan?"

"No, of course not." Ashley sat down beside Megan and put her arm around her as the other woman slumped against her. "We'll be fine."

After Sara and the others walked off, Jaime led Abby and Lou Ann around the general store. There, eight Jeeps were lined up, all covered with tarps. They pulled the tarp off the closest one and Jaime popped the hood.

"Well, goddamn," she murmured. "Can we not catch a break?"

"What is it?"

"No battery. Probably no fluids, either."

"What does that mean?" Lou Ann asked.

"They've been winterized." She slammed the hood down and walked to the back door of the store, peering inside through the window.

"Anything?"

"Only one way to find out," Jaime said. "Stand back."

The breaking of glass shattered the quiet of the old ghost town. Jaime looked at Abby, then Lou Ann, shrugging before sticking her arm through the broken window to unlock the door.

Abby laughed. "Breaking and entering."

Jaime smiled. "Yeah. Some cop, huh?"

"If we're lucky, maybe someone will come along and arrest us."

The general store was crammed full of anything a modern day tourist could ask for. T-shirts of varying colors fought for space on one wall, and souvenirs of every kind littered the shelves. The women walked in, the old floorboards creaking with their weight. Jaime walked behind the counter, looking for a phone. There was none.

"Probably cost a fortune to run a phone line up here." She opened up cabinets, smiling when she found a first aid kit. She ripped it open, but it contained only band aids, sterile wipes and anti-itch ointment.

"Oh my God! Look what I found," Abby said excitedly, holding up two fistfuls of chocolate bars.

"It's kinda spooky here," Judith said as she trudged quietly along with the others.

"What do you mean?"

"We've come upon a town but no one's here. Wonder if this is what it feels like to be alone in the world. Like in a movie where everyone dies but you."

"Well, partially the reason no one is here is because it's technically a ghost town. And secondly, it's after Labor Day. Most places up this high shut down then. I suppose as long as the weather stays good, a lot of these people still come up on weekends." Sara paused, her gaze lingering on what looked like a brand new cabin tucked back against the forest. "Wow. That's beautiful."

"It looks like a lodge. You think it's just a house?"

Sara shrugged then started walking down the lane. "Let's go see."

The massive cabin's porch was supported by no less than six log beams. Sara ran her hand along the smooth surface of one as she climbed the porch.

"It just seems wrong to break one of these windows," Beth said quietly.

Sara followed her gaze along the porch. The four giant plate glass windows nearly dwarfed them. "Yeah. I agree. Let's go around back. Maybe there's a small window or something."

The back of the house was nearly identical to the front, but they found a small four-paned window on the side. Sara grabbed a good-sized stick from the firewood pile to do the honors. The sound of shattering glass made them all jump back as they stared at the hole in one of the lower panes. Sara used the wood to clean the remaining glass from the pane then reached inside to flip the two locks. She grimaced as she pulled her arm back through. Blood trickled from her wrist.

"You okay?"

Sara wiped the blood on her jeans, nodding. "Okay. Just a scratch." She raised the window and looked back at the others. "Judith? You're the smallest."

"Oh, I don't know," she said, taking a step back. "I'm not good at this kind of stuff."

"Just crawl through the window then find your way to the back porch. We'll be waiting there."

"But—"

Sara smiled. "Judith, you can do this. We need you to do this. We'll boost you up."

Judith looked at them all, her hands wringing together. She finally nodded, pausing to tuck her long hair behind her ears. "Okay. Okay, I can do it."

"Good. Be careful of the glass."

They boosted Judith through the window then walked around to the back, waiting. They finally saw her walking through the house and Sara tapped on the glass impatiently.

Judith fumbled with the lock, opened the door and stepped back to let the others inside.

"It's spooky in here too," she said. "The power's off."

"I guess that's expected," Sara said. "Well, let's spread out. See if they've got any drugs stashed here. Look for a phone too," she added as they dispersed. She took a deep breath and let it out slowly. Everyone had stayed on the lower floor. She eyed the dark staircase then walked toward it. She slid her hand along the banister, a smooth rounded log, and she climbed the stairs. Sunlight poured in through the second floor windows, chasing the shadows away, and she paused, admiring the beauty of the mountains that looked nearly close enough to touch.

She finally shook herself, moving away from the view and into one of the bedrooms. It was the master suite judging by the size. She looked around the room for a phone, but there was none. She moved on into the spacious bathroom, nearly gasping as she saw her reflection in the mirror. She ran a hand through her blond hair, tucking it behind both ears. She looked nearly frightful.

"No wonder she hasn't wanted to kiss you," she murmured. *I would be scared away too.*

She looked away from the mirror, bending over to open the drawers and cabinets, feeling a bit embarrassed at snooping in a stranger's house. Her eyes widened as she pulled open another drawer. *Jackpot.*

"Hmmm, what do we have here?"

She was looking at no less than thirteen prescription bottles. She sifted through them, shaking her head. "Must be a depressing household," she murmured as she found yet another type of anti-depressant. Poor Jill, she thought, glancing at the name.

Finally she found what she was looking for—two types of pain medication, although they both contained codeine. She hoped

Megan wasn't allergic. The only antibiotics she found was a bottle of amoxicillin someone used for a toothache. She looked at the pain pills. One was for the same date.

"Thanks, Jill," she murmured after taking the three bottles and closing the drawer.

She walked back into the hallway, stopping again to admire the view. She let out a tiny sigh, wondering what it would have been like to hike into St. Elmo in the normal fashion—everyone intact—and just explore the old town as they'd planned. She smiled wistfully, wondering how many stories Jaime could come up with to entertain them. But her smile faded as the reality of their situation came back to her. One last sigh, this one harder, sharper, and she moved quickly down the stairs, hearing the others as they regrouped in the spacious—albeit dark—living room.

"Did you find anything?" Celia asked. "We found nothing stronger than wine," she said, holding up two bottles.

"Wine?"

"In the basement," Judith said. "There's practically a wine cellar down there."

Sara gave a short laugh and held up her hands. "Found some drugs."

They all came closer, inspecting her loot. Beth opened one bottle, silently counting the pills.

"Eight," she announced. Then she looked at the label. "Codeine? That's not real strong, is it?"

"It's all we've got. And we need to make sure she's not allergic. The last thing we need up here is for her to have a reaction." Sara looked past them, out the giant widows. "Has anyone seen the others?"

"I'll go find them," Judith volunteered. "I'd rather be outside, where there's sunlight."

"You didn't mind the tents and there certainly wasn't any light out there," Celia reminded her.

"That's different. Remember what I told you in our sessions? About my grandmother's house?"

"Oh, yeah. Forgot about that."

"I guess we could all go out," Sara suggested. She gave Judith a gentle smile. She'd forgotten all about her grandmother's house and how Judith had been locked in the dark attic for three days when she was a child. No wonder she'd been hesitant to be the first one to enter. "It'll be cooler outside too. Let's sit on the porch."

They had just barely settled down—Sara taking the steps and letting the others fight over the two benches—when they saw Jaime and the others walking down the road. Megan was sandwiched between Ashley and Lou Ann, leaning heavily on Ashley as she favored her left side.

Sara wasn't surprised by the relief she felt at just seeing Jaime. Before, she'd always thought of herself as a leader, as being in charge. But she realized now she wasn't a take-charge person. She was a planner. And if she had a plan to follow, she could carry it out to a T. But Jaime—Jaime was a take-charge person. Whatever the situation, Jaime had simply given them direction and they'd followed it. Without question. And that was probably the only reason they were all still alive.

But as Jaime got closer, as Sara was able to look into her eyes, she felt a different kind of relief. She thought perhaps it was a bit foolish of her to feel this way but what she saw in Jaime's eyes told her she was safe, told her Jaime wouldn't let anything happen to her. She had a nearly overwhelming urge to run to Jaime, to fling herself into Jaime's arms, but she resisted, instead answering the smile Jaime gave her with one of her own.

"Well, you all look comfortable," Jaime said as she paused at the bottom step. "Did you find the mother lode or what?"

"Sara found some pills," Celia said. "We found wine."

"Well, all right," Abby said. "Megan gets the pills, we get the wine. I like that arrangement." They eased Megan down on the top step, next to Sara.

"No Jeep?" Sara asked, reaching over to gently squeeze Megan's leg.

Jaime shook her head. "They've been stripped for winter." She walked closer. "What'd you find?"

Sara handed Jaime the prescription bottles. "Jill was well stocked with antidepressants but I found what we needed, probably not enough."

"There are other cabins. There might be something."

Sara shrugged. "If these are weekend homes, summer homes, I doubt they're going to have much. I was actually surprised to find this."

"Well, what's the house look like?"

"Oh, it's beautiful," Celia said. "Looks brand new."

"Bedrooms?"

Celia frowned. "I don't know. Why?"

"We gotta sleep somewhere tonight," Jaime said. "Or do you want to pitch your tent out here?"

Abby laughed. "Oh hell no. Not if we have a choice."

"Is it safe?" Sara asked quietly.

"Tonight, yes." She motioned with her head. "Come with me." As Jaime walked away, she tossed the pills to Ashley. "Hang on to these."

Jaime led them around the corner, Sara following closely behind. She felt the eyes of the others on them as they rounded the corner of the cabin.

"What do you have in mind?" Sara finally asked.

"Turning the power on."

"Can you do that?"

"If luck's on our side." Jaime pointed to the power box attached to the side of the cabin. "And it is. It's not locked." She shook her head. "People seldom lock their power box."

Sara watched as Jaime opened the box. The main electrical breaker to the cabin was off.

"They probably turn it off when they leave in case a storm comes up and they can't make it back here." Jaime pointed down the road. "They don't plow up here in the winter." She gripped the handle. "Okay, here goes." She paused then grinned mischievously before leaning over and kissing Sara on the mouth. "For luck."

Sara, startled, simply nodded as Jaime lifted the lever. They waited only a second, then heard an excited yell from the front.

"Hey! The porch light just came on!"

Sara raised her eyebrows teasingly at Jaime. "Must have been the kiss."

Jaime walked closer. "Must have been."

Their eyes met for a second and Jaime smiled. "Let's see if we can find the water pump. A lot of summer cabins up this high just have cisterns or holding tanks for water that they have delivered a couple of times a season." She walked around to the back of the house, Sara following. "But this house reeks of money. I'm guessing they have an actual well."

"Is that good or bad?"

"Either. They'll both have a pump. I just want to make sure they didn't turn the valve off too."

Jaime squatted down beside a faucet and turned it on. They both laughed as water poured out.

"And we have running water," Sara murmured.

"And in a short while, we'll have *hot* water. Can you imagine a clean shower with hot water?"

"The girls will love it."

"Okay, let's have a powwow with everyone." She glanced at her watch. "It's only five. A good couple of hours before dusk."

"Where do you think he is?" Sara asked quietly as they walked back to the front of the cabin.

"If he found our trail—and I've got to believe he did—then he'll be here tomorrow." She shrugged. "Early afternoon, maybe."

"If he found our trail?"

"If he's got a map, it should be obvious we're heading this way."

Their conversation came to an end when an excited Celia met them at the porch, her eyes nearly smiling.

"There's electricity! There's running water," she said with a laugh. "Never knew I'd get so excited about running water."

Sara and Jaime followed her inside. Jaime found Abby as she was snooping through the pantry in the kitchen.

"Where's Megan?"

"She's in the living room. There's a sofa in there."

"Did you give her anything?"

"No. I wanted to wait for you. I put the pills in there by her. But I did change her dressing."

"How's it look?"

Abby shook her head. "Like it hurts."

"Okay. Let me go take a look. Why don't you gather everyone in the den? It's time for a meeting." She looked behind her, finding Sara standing in the doorway. "Come on. Let's play doctor."

Megan was lying on her back, a blanket pulled up to her waist. She appeared to be asleep but when Jaime knelt down beside her, her eyes fluttered open.

"How's it hanging?" Jaime whispered.

"Hanging pretty low, doc," Megan said with a slight smile.

Jaime held up the medication. "Found some drugs."

"Good. Gimme."

"Well, if you had a toothache, we could knock it right out. Got some weak antibiotics but they're better than nothing. And some pain pills."

"Okay. Anything."

"Megan, are you allergic to anything? Penicillin?" She looked at the bottle. "This pain stuff has codeine in it. Are you allergic to that?"

"I don't think so."

"Because if you have a reaction, we're screwed," Jaime warned.

Megan shook her head. "I can't take much more, Jaime. I almost wish I'd ended up like Sandra. At least it'd be over with."

"Don't you talk like that," Jaime said, her voice hard. "Don't ever say that. You made it this far. Don't you dare give up now."

Megan rolled her head away, eyes closing. "I'm so tired."

Sara moved closer, touching Megan's shoulder. "Megan, please. I will forever be haunted by Sandra's death, feeling like I'm responsible. Please don't wish two of them on me."

Megan turned back to them, her eyes opening wearily. "Not your fault. Nobody thinks that. Just rotten luck."

Jaime squeezed her hand. "Okay, come on. Let's take some

drugs and see what happens." She looked at the bottles again. "You're supposed to eat something." She looked at Sara. "What the hell do we have?"

"We have a stove and we can boil water. I'll do a dinner real quick."

Megan shook her head. "No. I can't eat anything."

"It might make you nauseous if you don't," Sara warned.

"How about we give her a pain pill now. Then after dinner, we do the antibiotics?" Jaime looked at Sara. "She'll sleep."

Sara looked at Megan, noting the pained expression on her face. She looked back at Jaime and nodded.

"Okay. And maybe we can find something in their pantry to eat. Maybe make a decent meal." She squatted down beside Megan. "When we wake you up, you've got to eat something. Promise me you'll try."

Megan nodded. "Yes, I'll try," she said quietly.

"Good." Sara squeezed her arm, then nodded at Jaime. "I'll go see what Abby found in the pantry."

CHAPTER THIRTY-EIGHT

Jaime stood in the doorway, watching the others. They were sprawled on sofas and across chairs, all talking and smiling as if they really were on vacation. Sara moved into the room, brushing past her to stand in the middle. She turned back around and their eyes met.

"Ready?"

Jaime nodded.

Sara turned in a circle, trying to get everyone's attention.

"Ladies, time for a powwow."

"How's Megan?" Celia asked.

Jaime walked farther into the room, gently guiding Sara down onto the sofa then she turned, addressing them all.

"Megan is sleeping. I've given her a pain pill. We also have some antibiotics but I fear it's too little too late," she said. "She has a fever. And she needs a doctor."

"She's not going to die, is she?" Ashley asked, her voice quivering.

"I don't know, Ashley. Her wound is obviously infected." Jaime shrugged. "We've done as much as we can with what we've got. But that brings us to our options." She turned around, looking at them, one by one. "We can relax tonight. We can enjoy the amenities. Hot showers. A meal in the kitchen." She smiled. "And beds."

"I could go to bed right now," Lou Ann said.

"I know there's not enough for everyone, so you can choose where everyone sleeps. Draw straws or something," Jaime suggested. "But tomorrow, it's back at it. Let's don't forget the reason we're here. There's still a man out there. A man with a rifle and the intent to kill."

"You think he'll find us?"

"Yes, he will. And since we don't have a vehicle, we can't head down the mountain to Nathrop like I'd hoped. That means we hike west to Tin Cup."

"How far?"

"It's less than ten miles. But there's a road. I think you can hike it in five, six hours." She paused. "Megan is not going to be able to make it."

Ashley gasped. "We can't leave her!"

Jaime shook her head. "No, I didn't mean that. I'm going to stay with her. The rest of you will head to Tin Cup."

"No."

Jaime looked at Sara. "No? What do you mean?"

"I mean no. You're not staying behind. Either we all go or we all stay."

Jaime smiled. "Sorry, but it's not your call. Our guy has to come through St. Elmo. But he'll be looking for the whole group. He's not going to find me and Megan. And you should already be in Tin Cup by the time he gets here. You'll be safe."

"But what about you?"

"It'll be easier to hide two people, Sara."

"I don't like splitting up, Jaime. I don't like it one bit."

Jaime squatted down beside her, ignoring the others as she took

Sara's hand. "You think I like it? I'm supposed to protect you and here I am sending you out alone. But it's the only way."

"And if he finds you?"

"He's not going to find me. Besides, I do have a gun, you know." Jaime grinned. "Cop, remember?"

Sara shook her head. "I don't like it."

Jaime's smile vanished. "It's not up for discussion, Sara." She straightened up and turned to face the others. "Let's enjoy our last night up here, ladies. But go easy on the wine, Celia," she said with a laugh. "You'll need to get an early start in the morning."

"I feel kinda funny about using these people's house," Judith admitted. "I mean, if this were my house, I wouldn't want a bunch of strangers making themselves at home in it."

Jaime nodded. "I understand. And I'll make certain they're compensated for anything we use, for the broken window." She shrugged. "Same with the general store." She looked at Judith, her smile gentle. "In a life-and-death situation such as ours, we can't worry about what's right and what's wrong."

"Well if that's the case, I vote we raid the wine cellar again," Abby said with a laugh.

"Raid all you want. But remember, you've got a nice little hike in the morning. Alcohol and altitude don't mix all that well," Jaime warned.

"Party pooper," Celia teased.

Jaime laughed with the others then motioned to the door. "I'm going to go scout around a bit. Try to save me some hot water."

Sara watched her go then turned back to the group, forcing a smile onto her face. "Okay, who's up for kitchen duty?"

Abby stood. "I will. I've actually missed cooking."

"Me too," Judith chimed in.

"Yeah? Well have at it," Lou Ann said. "I'm grabbing a shower."

"Remember, easy on the hot water," Sara reminded her.

CHAPTER THIRTY-NINE

Jaime's stomach rumbled as soon as she walked in the house. A delicious aroma was coming from the kitchen and she followed the sound of laughter, finding two opened bottles of wine and three women chatting about recipes.

"Whoa, Sheriff," Lou Ann said. "I surrender." She raised both hands as giggles erupted around her.

Jaime lowered the shotgun. It was the only gun she'd managed to find as she raided a few of the older cabins, ones she suspected might be hunting cabins. She smiled broadly.

"How's the wine?"

"Best wine I have *ever* had," Celia said, raising her glass at Jaime. "Want some?"

Jaime shook her head. "Maybe later. I'm more interested in a shower right now."

Abby slid off the bar stool and clasped onto Jaime's shoulder. "Speaking of that, you're in luck, Chief. We settled on sleeping arrangements. You get the master bedroom," she said with a wink.

"Wow. How did I score that?"

Abby laughed. "You must have connections with the Sarge. Seems she won that room too."

"Well aren't I the lucky one."

Celia laughed. "You might be even luckier tonight."

Jaime felt her face blush but she laughed along with the others. Even in a crisis, Celia was still playing matchmaker.

"What's all the laughing about?"

They all turned, finding Sara watching them from the doorway.

"Just filling Jaime in on the sleeping arrangements," Abby volunteered.

They laughed again as a quick blush covered Sara's face.

"They tell me we scored the honeymoon suite," Jaime teased. "Imagine that."

"I had nothing to do with it," Sara insisted. "That one"—she pointed at Celia—"is to blame."

Jaime laughed. "Well, big-time thanks, Celia. It might be my last chance to get her alone."

"Oh, I wouldn't worry," Abby said. "I think she's hooked already."

Sara cleared her throat. "I am still here, you know. If you're going to talk about me, at least wait until I leave the room."

"You want some wine, Sara?" Celia offered. "It'll really relax you."

"And I suppose you think I need relaxing." She took the glass Celia offered her. "Actually, I came to check on dinner. It smells great."

"All done. If we can just get Annie Oakley here to shower, we can eat."

"I think she means you, Detective. I put your pack in the bedroom."

"Thanks. And I'll hurry. I'm starving." She paused at the door. "Megan?"

Sara nodded. "She had some soup earlier. I gave her the drugs. She was still out of it but the fever didn't seem quite as bad."

"Maybe just resting and not having to move around will help her."

Sara stood at the window, looking out at the night sky. The stars were brilliant, twinkling by the millions, sharpened without the light of the moon. It would rise later, after midnight, and hopefully she would be in the middle of a peaceful sleep. Then she smiled. Or not.

She glanced nervously at the bed, wondering how far she and Jaime would take things tonight. Was it appropriate in their situation to while away a few hours by having sex? Was it presumptuous to even think Jaime wanted that?

No. Not presumptuous. During dinner, the teasing had been merciless. Even Judith had chimed in. And Jaime had taken it all in stride, time and again Jaime's eyes catching hers. But the looks they shared weren't always teasing. In fact, by the time everyone started retiring for bed, their glances grew smoldering, promising.

She turned as the door opened, her hand letting the drapes fall back into place. Jaime paused at the door, watching. Sara felt her heart pounding just a little too fast as Jaime walked into the room.

Jaime stared, the shadows making it hard to see Sara's face, hard to make out her expression. She glanced quickly at the bed, then back at Sara. She closed her eyes briefly, taking a deep breath. She was tired. Mentally exhausted. Hell, physically exhausted. And she just wanted—*needed*—a release.

So she closed the door, kicking it shut with her foot. She walked into the middle of the room, then hesitated.

"I really hope you . . . you want what I want tonight."

Sara walked closer, stopping mere feet in front of Jaime. She tried to catch her eyes but the shadows hid them.

"I want to make love, Jaime. I want you to take me away from all this, if only for a few hours."

Jaime nodded, a brief smile touching her face. "Good."

Sara took a step closer. "Good?"

Jaime took her hand and twisted it behind her back as she pulled Sara flush against her. "Good, because I didn't want to waste time with small talk," she murmured as her lips finally covered Sara's.

With her free hand, Sara pulled Jaime closer, her mouth opening, her eyes closing, pushing the nightmare away as she lost herself in Jaime's kiss.

"Oh, yeah," Jaime whispered as she pulled away. "I knew it would feel this way."

Sara opened her eyes again, her heart beating wildly. "This way how?"

"Heart pounding, butterflies inside." She slid her hand higher, cupping Sara's breast. "You were such a tease in the hot springs. I can't wait to get you naked."

Sara laughed quietly. "*I* was a tease? Good Lord, Jaime, you even had all the straight women fawning over you. I certainly didn't stand a chance."

In one motion, Jaime pulled Sara's shirt over her head, leaving her naked from the waist up. Her hands immediately found Sara's breasts, covering them both as her thumbs rubbed lightly across her nipples.

Sara tilted her head back, eyes closed. She moaned softly when Jaime's mouth moved across her throat, pausing to nibble against the pulse that pounded there.

"I'm going to make love to you, Sara," Jaime murmured against her skin. "I'm going to be inside you. I can't *wait* to be inside you." She moved her mouth to Sara's ear, her tongue snaking inside. "And I'm going to have my mouth on you. I'm going to make you come, Sara."

Sara's knees literally buckled at Jaime's words but Jaime was there, holding her tight. Then Jaime's hands slipped inside her sweat pants, easily pushing them down past her thighs. Sara's hands finally moved, tugging at Jaime's shirt, pulling it from her jeans.

"Hurry," she whispered as her hands lowered Jaime's zipper.

Blindly, Jaime pulled the comforter away, leaving cool, clean sheets. She pulled Sara down beside her, impatiently kicking the jeans off her legs before straddling Sara's thighs. Her mouth lowered, capturing Sara's breast. The nipple was hard against her tongue and she closed over it, sucking it into her mouth, feeling Sara's hips rise to meet her own.

"God, take these off," Sara murmured, anxiously pushing the black cotton underwear off Jaime's hips. Naked, finally, she cupped Jaime's hips, drawing her closer, opening her legs to make room for her. "Yes, yes, yes," she whispered.

Jaime's hips molded themselves to Sara and she left her breast, her mouth finding Sara's again. Her tongue was captured and drawn into Sara's mouth and she moaned, her tongue battling Sara's for control. Then she gasped as Sara's hand moved between them, cupping her intimately, Sara's fingers slid into her wetness, finding her swollen clit. Jaime's hips bucked, moving against Sara's hand, her thighs opening wider.

"You're so wet," Sara murmured.

"Please go inside me," Jaime whispered. Her hips rose again, then lowered, impaling herself on Sara's fingers.

Sara tried to push against Jaime but Jaime's force was too much. She held her tightly, her hand nearly swallowed by Jaime's thrusts. She felt her tremors, felt Jaime tightening against her fingers. She drew Jaime's mouth to her own, holding on as Jaime pounded against her. Jaime's orgasm rocked them both, her hips rising, pulling Sara's hand with her, before crashing back down onto the bed. She swallowed Jaime's scream, gathering her close as her tremors subsided.

"So wonderful. Oh, so wonderful, Jaime," she whispered against her mouth. Jaime's skin was damp and she lightly brushed her fingers across her face.

"That didn't go as planned," Jaime murmured.

Sara smiled. "It went according to my plan."

Jaime rolled to her back, pulling Sara with her. "I thought I was the seducer here."

"Whatever gave you that idea?"

Jaime opened her thighs, pulling Sara against her. "That feels good."

Sara's hips moved, rolling gently against Jaime's. "Oh, yeah." She closed her eyes. "In case you didn't know, I'm about to explode here."

Jaime pulled Sara's mouth to her own, their kisses gentle now, not hurried. "I want you to explode. I want you to explode against my mouth."

Without protest, Sara let Jaime roll her over, pushing her against the bed. Her thighs parted, her breathing ragged as she felt Jaime move down her body.

"I swear, I've dreamed of this since I laid eyes on you," Jaime whispered, her mouth pausing briefly at Sara's breast before moving lower.

"Would you believe me if I said I had too?" Sara whispered back.

Jaime's mouth moved across her stomach to the curve of her hips, her tongue wetting a path, pausing to taste the soft skin in its wake.

Sara's eyes slammed shut as she felt Jaime cup her hips, felt Jaime pull her closer, felt Jaime's mouth as it moved down to her thigh, teasing her before finally—with hands spreading her legs apart—finding its target. Sara's breath left her when Jaime's hot mouth closed over her, gently sucking her clit, then teasing with her tongue. With one hand gripping the sheets, the other moved to Jaime's head, holding her tight, silently begging for more.

Jaime obliged, gripping Sara's hips and lifting her higher, then fastening her mouth on Sara's clit, sucking her hard, feeling Sara's hips smashing against her face. Sara arched again, then stilled, her breath hissing in and out before exploding in a scream she tried to stifle against the pillow. Jaime didn't relinquish her hold, her mouth taking all Sara had to give, finally slowing as Sara collapsed against the bed.

"God, Jaime . . . that was . . . incredible," she whispered, her eyes still closed, her fingers still tangled in Jaime's hair.

"Incredible, huh?"

Sara grinned. "If my brain was working properly, I'm sure I could come up with a better adjective."

"I like incredible."

Jaime pushed herself up and crawled beside Sara, wrapping an arm around her waist as she buried her face in the pillow Sara used.

Sara took Jaime's hand, sliding it to her breast, holding it there. She closed her eyes and sighed, feeling happy for the first time in what felt like months, years. She wondered, if they hadn't had a murderous madman on their heels, if she and Jaime would feel the same urgency they felt tonight. But did it matter? They *did* have a murderous madman after them.

"I feel safe with you, Jaime," she said quietly. She squeezed Jaime's hand, tightening it around her breast.

"I'm not going to let anything happen to you. I promise."

Sara leaned closer, brushing her lips across Jaime's forehead, feeling Jaime's hand tighten on her breast. She sighed again, the sound turning into a moan when Jaime rolled to her back, pulling Sara with her. She leaned on her elbows, her body slipping between Jaime's legs again.

CHAPTER FORTY

Sara opened her eyes slowly then closed them again. Her internal clock told her it was nearly dawn, time to start their day but she simply wanted to snuggle deeper against the warm body that held her.

And she did just that, slipping her hand between them, caressing Jaime's breast that lay exposed. It was amazing, really, for two people who didn't know each other all that well to be able to touch as if they'd been together a lifetime. But last night, their touches—their kisses—had been as free and natural as if they'd done it hundreds of times before.

She opened her eyes again but the darkness prevented her from seeing Jaime's face. She smiled anyway, imagining the splatter of freckles that dotted her tanned cheeks. Without thought, her hand slipped lower, moving across smooth skin, following the curves of Jaime's hips. Jaime's flesh was soft to her touch—soft and warm—and her eyes slid closed as her hand moved across the firmness of her buttocks. She moaned quietly as her hand squeezed, pulling Jaime flush against her. As her heart raced, she dipped her head, her mouth finding Jaime's nipple, closing over it, sucking it inside.

"Mmmm."

Sara smiled at the sleepy voice, enjoying the feel of Jaime's nipple as it swelled inside her mouth. Jaime rolled slightly, giving Sara more room, and with her free hand, she moved between their bodies, finding the moisture between Jaime's thighs.

"Yes," Jaime whispered, her legs parting.

Sara used her knee to spread Jaime's thighs, her fingers blindly moving into her wetness. Her mouth had not left Jaime's breast. But as soon as she touched her, she wanted more. Her breathing was ragged as her mouth kissed its way down Jaime's body, not pausing anywhere long enough to matter, simply moving along the curves until she felt hot wetness against her face. She groaned once, then cupped Jaime's hips, bringing her closer to her mouth.

"God, *yes*," Jaime whispered, her eyes slamming closed as Sara's mouth covered her. Her hips jerked, meeting Sara, her head falling back as Sara's lips closed over her aching clit. She covered her face with a pillow, unable to stop the sounds of pleasure as Sara's mouth . . . her tongue moved over her.

As Jaime's hips moved with Sara, Sara's own hips dug into the bed, wanting—needing—release.

"Come up here. Turn around," Jaime gasped. "Straddle me."

Blindly, Sara moved, turning on the bed, her hips straddling Jaime's face, letting herself be guided down as Jaime's hands cupped her hips. She groaned loudly when Jaime's mouth found her. Then she leaned down, her mouth again fastening on Jaime's clit. Together, their mouths worked, devouring each other until, hips moving against mouths, they couldn't stop the waves of orgasm. Sara came first, her hips pressing hard against Jaime's face. Her scream caused her to nearly bite down on Jaime and Jaime's own hips arched as she exploded into Sara's mouth.

They both lay still, trying to catch their breath. Then Jaime stirred, her hands sliding over Sara's hips, turning her around again, guiding her back up to the pillows.

Sara buried her face against Jaime, her eyes closed, her hands pulling at Jaime. She struggled to get close enough then finally felt Jaime's arms close around her.

"You probably won't believe me," she murmured, her mouth moving against Jaime's skin. "But I've never in my life done that." Then she laughed quietly. "Or maybe you can believe it."

Jaime smiled, then pulled Sara tighter against her, letting her eyes slip closed again.

They were quiet as they all crowded around the island in the kitchen, sharing a quick, thrown-together breakfast. Jaime had already told them they needed to be on the trail within the hour. And she, like the rest, knew it was cold outside. Probably the coldest morning yet.

"How long do you think it'll take us to hike to Tin Cup?"

Jaime shrugged. "Five hours, give or take."

"And then when we call the local sheriff, how long before someone gets back here to you and Megan?"

"Abby, quit worrying. We'll be fine. I've got a hiding place for Megan. Our guy's not going to find her."

"What about you?"

Jaime stared, watching as everyone stilled, their eyes moving between her and Sara. It was a conversation—an argument—that she and Sara had started earlier that morning and never finished. And she didn't want to finish it now in front of everyone.

"I'll be fine, Sara," she said, echoing the words she'd whispered to Sara while they were still in bed together, still holding each other, still touching.

Sara turned away, walking purposefully into the den where Megan still lay. The others watched her leave, then collectively turned their attention to Jaime. She sighed, her shoulders sagging as she silently shook her head.

"She just cares about you," Celia said quietly. "Can't help that."

Jaime let a quick smile cross her face, then sobered, her eyes moving among them.

"I know. But this is it, ladies. We made it this far. And in about five hours, you'll be completely safe. And that's all you have to worry about, getting the hell out of here. Let me worry about Megan."

"Well, we've been through a lot in the last week. Can't blame us for being concerned about you," Abby said.

"And Megan," Ashley added.

"And I appreciate that. But your being worried is not going to change anything." She glanced once into the room where Sara stood watching a sleeping Megan, then looked quickly back at the others. "Finish up. It's time."

Jaime turned, standing at the door, watching Sara. They'd made love with such abandon last night—and this morning—that she had a hard time separating herself from what she was feeling . . . and what she knew to be best. A part of her wanted to lock Sara away with Megan, gambling she'd be safe. But heading farther away toward Tin Cup was the safer of the two options. And she doubted the others would make it without Sara. They were troupers but still novices when it came to the mountains. No, Sara needed to lead them out of here.

"I know what you're thinking," Sara said quietly, still facing Megan, her hands still shoved in the pockets of her jeans.

Jaime walked closer, her voice low. "Is that right?"

Sara turned and met Jaime's eyes head on, her own softening as images of their lovemaking flashed through her mind. Her hand trembled slightly when she reached out, placing it firmly on Jaime's stomach, then inching it higher, resting just below Jaime's breasts.

"I'm scared, Jaime," she whispered. "I want . . . I want to stay with you."

Jaime shook her head. "We talked about it, Sara. You'll be safer with the others. Don't forget, it's *you* he's after."

"I think at this point, he's after all of us." She let her hand slip away as she turned back to Megan. "I'm afraid if I leave, I won't ever see you again. I have a really bad feeling about you staying here."

Jaime walked closer, standing directly behind Sara. Her hands drew Sara back against her and she closed her eyes at the contact.

Sara too let her eyes slip closed. She took Jaime's hand, pulling it tighter against her, feeling safe.

"Please let me stay with you."

"Absolutely not," she whispered into Sara's ear. "But I'll let you make me dinner next Saturday night."

Sara smiled, feeling somewhat comforted by Jaime's obviously blatant attempt to reassure her everything would be fine by next week. So instead of arguing the point, she nodded.

"It's a date."

"Great." Jaime pulled away but not before squeezing tightly on Sara's hand. "Then let's get you out of here."

CHAPTER FORTY-ONE

Jake took the corner too fast, nearly skidding as she rounded the curve above Mirror Lake.

"Damn, you'd think it was your first assignment," she murmured, glancing quickly into the rearview mirror to watch as Cheyenne hung her head out the opened back window.

She purposefully slowed, telling herself it would do no good to race up Cumberland Pass. She had spent a restless night. Hell, she'd spent a restless day and a half prior to that. After Captain Morris's initial call, she'd wanted to rush out into the mountains, despite his suggestion she wait until the FBI ground unit checked in. It'd been well over a year since she'd left Denver, since she'd been on the force, but her gut told her not to wait. But as Nicole said, it'd be like looking for a needle in a haystack if she just took off across the mountains, hoping to simply walk upon them.

When Captain Morris called again last night, saying they had found their trail and it appeared they took the high route to

Cottonwood Pass, she'd studied the map endlessly, trying to put herself in their position. And her only conclusion was St. Elmo.

And if she was wrong, then yeah, a needle in a haystack.

But she tried to relax, telling herself not to rush up the pass. She'd drive as far as she could, until she came to the washout in the road, then hike in the rest of the way. It would be an easy hike. So despite the cooler temperatures this morning, she opened her window and hung her arm outside, enjoying the brisk breeze as the pine-scented air rushed past her face. She acknowledged the surge of adrenaline for what it was. After all, it was approaching nearly two years since she'd done anything even remotely resembling police work. Her hand unconsciously rubbed her thigh, the scar tissue of the long-healed injury a constant reminder of her former life.

She pulled her hand away as she shook her head. It didn't matter. She wouldn't give up the life she and Nicole had made up here for anything. So she would do Captain Morris a favor, she would help find his detective, then she would retreat once again to the small cabin they called home. A cabin she'd been painstakingly remodeling and adding on to for the last year.

"It feels kinda strange to be hiking without Jaime."

Sara nodded and glanced back over her shoulder at the quickly fading sight of St. Elmo.

"You think they'll be okay?"

Sara looked at Celia and gave a reassuring smile.

"They'll be fine."

"Come on, Megan."

"I can't."

"Yes, you can. You have to."

They were still a good fifty yards from the old abandoned cabin Jaime had chosen as their hiding place. Weeds grew around it, obscuring any long-ago footpaths, and a Douglas fir had taken hold, growing practically at the cabin's front door. All four windows were boarded up, and through the overgrown weeds and small saplings, she'd found the back door. It was hanging loosely by rusted hinges and she broke through the old lock easily. Far from the comforts of the house they'd slept in last night, nonetheless, this old cabin would be a much safer hiding place.

If only Megan could make it.

"Just a little farther."

"Leave me, Jaime. Just leave me," Megan groaned as her legs gave way.

"Like hell." She pulled Megan up again, holding her around her shoulders. "I know it hurts. I know you're exhausted. But it's almost over, Megan. Once the others get to Tin Cup, they'll send help. Before dark, we'll be out of here. I promise. Now you gotta stay with me."

Megan closed her eyes, but nodded weakly. "Okay. Okay, Jaime. I'll try."

"Good. That's my girl."

Megan tried to smile. "I heard after last night, Sara was your girl."

Jaime's face turned scarlet but she didn't hold back her laugh. "That's what you heard, huh? Well, if you weren't in such a delicate condition, I might tell you about it."

Megan managed a small laugh. "That's okay. I think Abby did a good enough job already with the details."

They stopped to rest and Jaime pointed at the old cabin. "We just have to get to there."

"You're putting me in *there*?"

"Got a cot set up already."

"I'm thinking spiders and rats and stuff."

"No way. I chased them all out this morning. There's a couple of chipmunks that have taken up residence, though. I let them stay."

"I'm not crazy about spiders, Jaime."

"Well, I'll get you a stick and you can whack at them if they get too close. Now come on, let's get you tucked away."

Through the brush they made their way to the back of the cabin. Megan leaned against the side as Jaime pulled the back door open, the rusty hinges squeaking loudly, protesting after so many years of neglect.

"Come on."

She helped Megan inside, using her small flashlight to guide them. Once inside, she turned the light off, and they both watched as the sunlight sneaked through the cracks in the walls and ceiling, dancing across the room. It was eerie.

"It's beautiful," Jaime whispered.

"It's filthy."

Jaime turned the light on again, flashing it around the room, exposing the spider webs that decorated the furniture and fixtures. Then she shined it against the wall, illuminating the cot she'd brought over early that morning. She stole the sheets from the house they'd stayed in last night. At least they were clean. Leaning against the cot was the shotgun she'd found last night.

"Lie down here."

She eased Megan down, then helped her swing her legs up. "Comfortable?"

"It'll do."

Jaime squatted down beside her and took her hand. "I've moved the dresser against the front door so that's barricaded. The only way in is the back door." She handed Megan the small flashlight. "Keep this. And I put a couple of water bottles down here beside you," she said, holding one up to show her. Then she picked up the shotgun and laid it beside her. "Keep this too."

Megan shook her head.

"Yes. Just in case, Megan."

"I can't."

Jaime patted her hand. "Just in case."

She stood but Megan grabbed her hand when she moved to walk away.

"You're going after him? But you promised Sara you wouldn't."

"I'm going to the edge of town, the way we came in. And if I see him, then yeah, I'm going after the bastard."

Megan let her hand fall away, nodding. "Okay. I'm too tired to argue."

"It's going to be fine, Megan. Try not to worry. By this evening, you'll be in a hospital room."

"Now there's something to look forward to," she said dryly.

"Okay, hold up," Sara said, turning to face the others, her eyes looking past them to the trail they'd just come down. Yes, she'd promised Jaime. Yes, leaving was probably the most sensible thing to do. But it just didn't feel right. The farther she got from St. Elmo, the worse she felt. The nagging, itching feeling she'd tried to shake just wouldn't go away no matter how often she told herself she was doing the right thing.

"What's wrong?"

Sara shook her head. "Something."

"What?"

She took a deep breath then pointed ahead of them. "You stay on this road until you come to the Cumberland Pass cutoff. Then you take the road to the right. It's a straight downhill shot into Tin Cup. You can't miss it."

Abby stepped forward, her hands spread. "Sara? What are you doing?"

"I'm going back."

"No way. Jaime said we were not to turn back no matter what. Jaime said we weren't to stop until we reached Tin Cup."

"Well I don't give a shit what Jaime said," Sara said loudly. "I've got a bad feeling, okay? And I don't think she and Megan should be there alone."

"We're safer away from there, Sara. You know that," Celia reasoned.

"Yeah. *We're* safer. What about them?" she asked, pointing back the way they'd come. "What about *them*?"

"What can you do?" Lou Ann asked. "Jaime's the cop. She knows best, Sara."

Sara turned away, her eyes looking skyward. Yes, Jaime knew best. She sent her away to be safe without regard to her own safety. She told herself it had nothing to do with the fact that they'd been intimate. That didn't matter in the least. It was Megan she was concerned about. Not Jaime. Jaime could take care of herself.

Her shoulders sagged. Who the hell was she kidding? Of course it was Jaime she was worried about. And the fact that they'd become lovers made it all the more difficult to separate.

"I'm going back." She pointed down the road. "And you are all going that way. To Tin Cup." When Abby opened her mouth to speak, Sara held up her hand. "Don't argue with me, Abby."

CHAPTER FORTY-TWO

He had long ago stopped cursing himself. It was doing no good. But he had their trail. Did the bitches really think they could hide from him in St. Elmo? No, he'd get them all. And he'd start with the cop and end it with the bitch Michaels.

Damn. He'd told Ramsey not to get the cops involved. He'd told Ramsey he could track them on his own. He didn't need a goddamned tracking device to follow them. But no, Ramsey didn't want to take a chance. A female cop wasn't going to be a problem, he said.

"Stupid bastard," he mumbled as he pulled the collar of his light jacket up higher around his ears, trying to ward off the cold wind that had hit that morning. "Stupid bastard," he said again.

CHAPTER FORTY-THREE

As Jake climbed higher up Cumberland Pass, the cold wind turned bitter and she called Cheyenne in, raising the window to keep out the cold. Cheyenne's sharp bark brought her attention back to the road and she slammed on her brakes, barely avoiding the group of women who scrambled to the side and out of her way.

"Jesus Christ!"

She skidded to a halt, her eyes as wide as those that stared back at her. She opened her door and got out, wanting to make sure no one was hurt. The women all started talking at once, some pointing behind them, others pointing up ahead.

Jake held up both hands, trying to silence them.

"Whoa there, ladies. Calm down. Is anyone hurt?"

Again, everyone started talking at once and Jake shook her head, again holding up both hands.

"Come on now. Give me a break here." She pointed at one of them. "You. Talk."

Abby stepped forward, her head cocked. "You damn near ran us down. Who the hell are you?"

Jake raised an eyebrow. "Jake McCoy. Who the hell are you?"

"You got a phone?"

"You got a name?"

Abby shifted nervously, looking away from Jake's intense stare, then glancing at the others. "I'm Abby."

Jake nodded then looked over the group. "Sara Michaels?"

Abby's eyes widened. "How do you know Sara?"

Jake shrugged. "I'm a . . . I'm a cop," she said, surprised at how easily the words flowed. "I understand somebody might be after her."

Abby put her hands on her hips. "Well that's a bit of an under-statement."

CHAPTER FORTY-FOUR

Jaime moved along the edge of town, keeping to the trees as she made her way to the general store. She'd gone back to the house they'd stayed at last night, trying to make it obvious that they'd been there. Been there and were now gone. She purposefully left the kitchen a mess, hoping he'd see they'd eaten and taken off. What she wanted to avoid was him doing a cabin-by-cabin search. If he slipped past her—or got past her—she didn't want him finding Megan. Shotgun or not, she doubted Megan would be able to shoot.

But she wasn't planning on letting him slip past her.

She paused under the thick boughs of a low-growing spruce tree, scanning the outskirts of the old town with her binoculars, looking for movement. Of course if he was smart, he'd be behind the trees, looking for movement in town. She had to remind herself he had a rifle. A rifle with a scope. She had to stay behind cover.

When she saw nothing out of the ordinary, she moved again, keeping to the shadows. She looked back over her shoulder the way she'd come, expecting to see the old dirt road empty. But the flash of red startled her. She snatched up her binoculars, staring.

"Goddammit!" She lowered her binoculars. *I'll kill her.*

She jumped up, running. She ran into the trees, sprinting back the way she'd come. She stumbled once, nearly falling, but caught herself. She stopped, trying to catch her breath, trying to judge where she was. Through the forest, she made out their cabin from last night. She took a deep breath, then ran, assuming Sara would go there first. The tree cover gave way to the small clearing beside the house. She raced to the house, diving behind the back, away from the road. She saw her just as she rounded the corner.

"Sara!" she hissed as loud as she dared.

Sara stopped, her eyes widening when she saw Jaime. She ran toward her, her smile fading at the angry glint in Jaime's eyes.

"What the *fuck* do you think you're doing?" Jaime demanded.

"I . . . I was afraid to leave you behind."

Jaime grabbed her, pulling her onto the back deck and through the door they'd broken into yesterday. Once inside, she held Sara against the wall, her hands tight on her shoulders.

"Sara, goddammit, you've got to think. You're running around with a bull's-eye on your back."

Sara glanced at the bright red New You sweatshirt she'd worn that morning. It was the warmest thing she'd packed. She closed her eyes, nodding.

"I guess you're mad," she stated quietly.

"I'm beyond mad." Jaime released her grip on Sara's shoulders then pulled her into a quick, awkward embrace.

"I had a bad feeling, Jaime. That's all."

"Yeah? Well what kind of a bad feeling do you think I'd have had if he'd seen you just now and gotten a shot off?"

"Look, I told you last night and I told you again this morning, I didn't like the idea of us splitting up."

"Sara, the whole point of this is for you to be safe. You're not now."

"The whole point is not just for me to be safe. I don't outrank anyone else in this group. I don't deserve more consideration. He's not just after me anymore. He's after all of us. You included."

Jaime's eyes flashed. "*I* need you to be safe. And you were safe when you walked out of here with the others."

"*You* need me to be safe? Will it be a black mark on your record if something happens to me? Is it going to set your career back?"

Jaime was startled by the anger in Sara's voice. Her eyes softened immediately.

"Sara, I don't give a damn about my career. I need you to be safe for *me*, not my job. It's totally selfish, trust me."

"Then why can't I be selfish too?"

Jaime closed her eyes, her heavy sigh quite audible in the empty house. Well, it was too late now. She couldn't very well send Sara out of here again. It was too late for that. She opened her eyes again.

"Okay. The first thing we've got to do is get you out of this red Santa suit."

"I'm sorry, Jaime. I just—"

"No. It's okay. To be quite honest, I was worried as hell as soon as you left my sight."

Sara nodded. "Megan?"

Jaime smiled. "How do you feel about spiders and stuff?"

CHAPTER FORTY-FIVE

He climbed higher, pausing to catch his breath as he peered through the trees, just barely able to make out the buildings of the old ghost town. Earlier, when he first reached St. Elmo, he moved off the trail and into the woods. He had visions of the bitches hiding, waiting for him, all armed with sticks and stones, ready to attack. Well, he wasn't stupid. He would hike along the ridge above town then come in from the back side.

And then he would decide. If some of the summer residents were still about, if tourists were out and about, he'd have to abort the mission. He wasn't going to take a chance at getting caught. No, he'd just disappear, leave the country. They'd paid him half up front. And after all he'd been through for the last week and a half, he felt he was due that, even if he didn't get his target.

But he'd done his research. He knew all about St. Elmo. All along it was going to be his destination after the kill, his means of escaping out of these mountains. He knew the general store closed after Labor Day. He knew most of the summer residents left then too. And he knew the town would be mostly deserted until the snows came and brought skiers with it. No, he felt confident that there would be no one about during the middle of the week, especially on such a cold, windy day like today. He'd still get his target.

And then some.

So he pushed on, making a trail where there was none as he made his way above St. Elmo.

CHAPTER FORTY-SIX

Jake walked as fast as she dared, pleased that her leg was not protesting the pace. The short hikes she and Nicole took around the cabin were leisurely at best. Even on the occasions they hiked to the hot springs, they didn't push. But now, she pushed, letting Cheyenne run in front of her.

After getting the story from the women—a story she tried to decipher as all eight insisted on talking at once—she made a quick call to Captain Morris, letting him know she'd found their party, albeit short his detective and the Michaels woman. Then she packed all eight of the women into her Land Cruiser and sent them down the pass to Tin Cup. And despite Morris's plea to keep this quiet, that the FBI didn't even know she was on the scene, she'd also placed a call to the sheriff in Nathrop as well as to Chad Beckett in Gunnison. Both were en route.

And she would beat both of them to St. Elmo.

But from what she'd gathered from their story, this Jaime

Hutchinson seemed capable enough. She'd gotten the group this far with only two casualties, one of whom needed medical attention. As she walked, she studied the treetops, judging the wind speed. She shook her head. The swirling wind was too gusty to chance a helicopter.

They were on their own.

"I can't believe you came back. What were you thinking?"

Sara took a sip of water, then handed Megan the bottle. Yes, what was she thinking? She closed her eyes for a second, again remembering Jaime's touch, her kisses. Yes, that was what she'd been thinking.

"I was worried about you. Both of you. And as I suspected, Jaime stashed you somewhere with plans to play cowboy with this guy."

"Yeah. And left me with a shotgun." She touched Sara's arm. "Do you know how to use one of these?"

Sara shrugged. "I've been skeet shooting before. Whether I could point it at a person and pull the trigger is another matter." As Megan's eyes widened, Sara smiled and gently squeezed her hand. "But don't worry. We're not going to need it. Jaime won't let him get to us." Then she touched Megan's forehead. "You don't feel quite as warm. Maybe those antibiotics have helped some."

"I don't know. To be honest with you, I'm so numb I'm not sure how I feel."

Sara nodded. She didn't know what to say so she remained quiet. Megan had already heard all of their consoling words. What she needed was a doctor. So she turned out the small flashlight Jaime had left with them and leaned back against the wall next to Megan.

And waited.

CHAPTER FORTY-SEVEN

Jaime was hiding in the forest, out of sight of the main trail but after an hour without movement or sound, she grew anxious and very worried. She scanned once more with her binoculars and again saw nothing out of the ordinary. In fact, it was too quiet. But she could attribute a lot of that to the gusty winds that had been blowing all morning. Even the normal chatter of the birds was missing.

She shook her head. Something wasn't right. She could feel it in her gut. She frowned, looking down the trail then back toward town. The street was still deserted. Then she looked farther, past the street, her eyes following the old road out of town, the road the girls had taken that morning. Her eyes widened.

"Son of a bitch," she muttered.

He's coming in from the back side.

Jake came to a sudden stop when she saw movement through the trees. She touched Cheyenne's head, silently telling the dog to keep quiet. She waited then saw him. A tall man carrying a burgundy backpack—he looked like an ordinary hiker. So she stood still, watching as he lowered the binoculars he'd been looking through. He turned suddenly, as if sensing her presence.

"Well, hey there," he called. "You startled me. Haven't seen any other hikers in days." He motioned with his binoculars. "Thought I saw a bear."

Jake nodded, her body still tense, wary.

"You alone?" Jake asked.

"Yeah. You?"

Jake nodded. "Just a day hike." She released her hand, allowing Cheyenne to move away. The low growl in the dog's throat told Jake everything she needed to know.

The man moved again, taking a step closer, their eyes fixed on each other.

"You been to St. Elmo before?" he asked.

Jake nodded. "Many times."

"Many people out and about this time of year?"

Jake shook her head. "No, not really."

She felt a chill as a smile slowly formed on his face and his eyes turned cold.

"That's what I was hoping."

She felt her adrenaline surge when he pulled a rifle out from behind his back. Without thinking, she dove headfirst to the side of the trail, sliding down quickly behind the fallen boulders. She ducked her head as the first shot rang out.

"*Cheyenne!*"

She saw only a flash as Cheyenne ran behind her. "Good girl," she murmured. She pulled the dog closer against the rocks. "Now stay put." She ducked her head again when a second shot was fired.

"Come on out now, little girl. Got no place to run to."

With her weapon drawn, she scooted down lower, trying to get an angle on him. He was walking closer. She didn't have a good shot but she wanted him aware that she had a gun. Between the limbs of the spruce tree she fired, her shot landing near enough to his feet to kick up rocks. It was his turn to take cover and she fired once more as he took refuge behind his own rock pile. They were maybe fifty feet apart. Too close for comfort but far enough away for Jake to feel somewhat safe. She tucked her head against her chest as the dirt kicked up behind her from another round.

Safe? Who was she kidding?

Jaime stopped dead in her tracks as the unmistakable sound of a rifle shot rang through the forest.

Sara.

She ran back into town, still trying to keep to the trees when a second round was heard, instinct making her duck her head. She stumbled, nearly falling, then righted herself. But she stopped again when more shots were heard.

"What the *fuck*?"

Not a rifle, but a handgun this time. A big one. She ran on, finally reaching the back side of the large cabin they'd stayed in. She leaned against the side, gasping to catch her breath. But her head jerked up when another rifle shot was heard, followed by two large caliber rounds from a handgun. She shoved off the wall, moving more slowly now as Sara and Megan's cabin came into view. It looked undisturbed.

But she had no time to savor the relief she felt. Gunfire erupted again.

"Sara, no! You can't go out there."

Sara paced, waving the shotgun wildly as more gunfire was heard.

"She's going to need help."

"Not from you. You don't even know how to use that thing."

"He's got her cornered somewhere, I just know it."

"Sara, please. You can't leave me here."

Sara closed her eyes, nodding. "I know, Megan. I'm just so scared." She jumped as another shot rang out. "I'm scared for Jaime and I'm scared for us."

She moved back to the cot, the shotgun clutched tightly in her hand, wondering if she could possibly use it if it came down to that. Then she remembered Sandra.

Yeah. I could pull the trigger.

"Put the gun down, you bastard," Jake yelled. She heard him laugh and she did the same. "Yeah, right. Maybe he'll surrender," she whispered out loud. His answer was another shot fired into the tree above her. She closed her eyes, telling herself she needed to be careful. Nicole would kill her.

"How long we going to do this, lady? I've got a whole box of shells here."

And she believed him. Unfortunately, she only had one extra clip for her own weapon. But she wouldn't have to hold him off forever. If this Detective Hutchinson didn't come, then she had no doubt the sheriff from Nathrop would be here soon. She glanced at her watch. Over an hour since she'd called him. He had been out near Buena Vista, but still, he should be here any minute. No, she didn't have to hold him off long. So she peeked around the tree again, firing blindly to where he was hiding.

Jaime was near the edge of town now and she kept hidden. The shots were close, but the sound was distorted by the mountains. She wasn't sure where they were coming from. Then the handgun sounded again and she thought she made out muted voices.

With her weapon drawn, she crouched low, nearly slithering among the trees, trying to stay in the shadows. She fell once, her boots slipping on the rocks, and she landed hard on her knees. She caught herself with her hands and her gun went flying.

"You're going to shoot yourself if you're not careful," she murmured as she scrambled after her gun. Once on her feet, she ducked low as the shooting started again.

As she moved parallel to the road, but still in the trees, she spotted the burgundy backpack. She pressed herself against a tree, her eyes widening. She'd recognize the burgundy backpack anywhere. Goddamn bastard. And who the hell was he shooting at?

And who was shooting at him?

She took a deep breath, waiting as another round of shots were exchanged. Then she stepped from behind the tree, her weapon pointed at him.

"Hey, you," she yelled. He turned quickly, surprise showing on his face as their eyes fixed on each other. "Yeah, you." She walked closer. "Drop your goddamn rifle."

His smile was cocky. So was his laugh.

"Now why in the world would I do that?"

"Because I'm assuming you don't want me to shoot your sorry ass."

"You must be the police detective who was so kind to carry my tracking device." He shrugged. "I don't believe you're allowed to shoot your suspects."

"Drop your goddamn rifle," she said again, her weapon pointed directly at his chest.

He smiled again. "I'm a firm believer that police work is for men, not women."

She cocked her head. "Oh, yeah?" She fired quickly, her shot landing mere inches from his boot. He jumped back, his eyes wide as he looked at her. "I said drop your goddamn rifle."

Jake heard voices, then a shot. A handgun. Large caliber. She nodded. The detective, most likely. She moved farther down the mountain, sliding on her belly, wincing as rocks dug into her thigh, reminding her of why she wasn't on the force any longer. She shifted, her hand going to her thigh and rubbing lightly across the scar. She waited a few seconds for the pain to subside enough for her to go on. She looked back at Cheyenne and held her hand up.

"Stay." The dog whimpered once and she shook her head, meeting the intelligent eyes of her furry friend. "I mean it."

❧

Jaime walked closer as he slowly lowered his rifle to the ground. She nodded, then motioned with her head.

"Move away."

"Sure. Sure. Just be careful with that thing."

She smiled. "Yeah, you know women and guns. You better hope I'm not PMSing." When he stepped away from the rifle, she relaxed. "Now, who the hell was shooting at you?"

"Don't have a clue. Some woman."

"A woman? Hell, man, it's just not your day, is it?" Jaime laughed as she bent to retrieve the rifle.

He laughed too, then quickly reached behind his back and pulled out a handgun. Jaime dove to her right as she fired twice, rolling down the mountain away from him. One of her shots got him in the shoulder and he went to his knees. He fired quickly in her direction but she ducked low, both shots going over her head.

"Stupid ass," she murmured. What did she think? That she could simply arrest him without a fight? She rolled again, then sat up, firing as he tried to run. He went down then turned, pointing his gun at her. She pulled the trigger without thinking, all three rounds hitting him squarely in the chest. Her heart was pounding so loudly she had to stop, taking deep breaths to try to calm herself. Then out of the corner of her eye, she saw movement. She whipped around, training her weapon on the woman who emerged from the trees.

"Drop your goddamn gun!" Jaime yelled.

The woman shook her head, her own gun pointed at Jaime. "No. I don't think so. You first."

Jaime's eyes widened as she took a step forward. "I said drop your goddamn gun," she repeated, her voice low and threatening.

Jake held up one hand. "Whoa now, calm down. I'm assuming you're Detective Hutchinson. Denver PD. Homicide?"

Jaime arched an eyebrow but did not lower her weapon.

Jake finally relaxed, lowering her own gun. "I'm Jake McCoy." At Jaime's blank stare, she added, "Special Victims. Retired."

Jaime's stare was intense, questioning. Then she let out her breath, finally lowering her weapon.

"Your Captain Morris called me a couple of days ago." Jake smiled. "I guess he was worried about you."

"Well goddamn. Jake McCoy. Yeah. I remember. Sure, Special Victims. Your lieutenant shot—"

"That's me," Jake said quickly. "Retired now." She pointed at their guy who lay sprawled on the bloody rocks. "Who's this?"

"Hell if I know."

They both turned at the sound of someone running toward them. Simultaneously, they raised their weapons as Sara burst from the trees.

Jaime lowered her gun, then lightly touched Jake's arm. "She's with me."

Sara stopped, her eyes wide as two guns lowered. She was winded from running but as soon as she met Jaime's eyes, she lunged forward, flinging herself at Jaime.

"It's okay," Jaime murmured as she barely caught herself before Sara could take them both to the ground. Then two frantic hands moved across her torso, then her arms. Jaime grasped Sara's wrist, stilling her hands. "I'm okay."

"Are you sure? There was so much shooting. I was afraid—"

"But I'm fine, Sara. I'm fine. Now you need to go back and get Megan. We're getting out of here."

Sara nodded, finally acknowledging the other person there. She stuck out her hand. "I'm sorry. I'm Sara Michaels. Are you okay?"

Jake smiled then shook her hand. "Jake McCoy. Yeah. I'm fine. Just happened to be in the area."

Sara nodded again. She looked past them to the man laying on the rocks. She gasped, then turned to Jaime, eyebrows raised.

"Yeah. It's him. We're safe now."

"Who is he?"

"Don't know yet."

Sara closed her eyes, then walked slowly into Jaime's arms, burying her face against her.

"It's over," she whispered. "It's really over."

"Yes, it's all over, sweetheart." Jaime pulled back slightly. "Now go get Megan. She's probably worried."

Sara squeezed Jaime's hand then turned away.

When she left, Jaime gave an embarrassed laugh. "Kinda crossed that line there between professional and personal," she admitted.

Jake laughed. "Been there, done that." She turned, gave a whistle and waited as Cheyenne bounded up to her, allowing the dog to sniff her, letting her know she was okay. "This is Cheyenne."

Jaime reached down to pet the dog's head, then motioned to their dead guy. "You got a phone on you? I need to call my captain and let him know where we are."

"Already did that. I ran into your girls on the road. Gave them my truck and sent them on to Tin Cup. I called the sheriff in both Nathrop and Gunnison. And your captain was going to notify the FBI team that was working on the case. I think everybody is en route." She looked up. "Although it's too windy to get a helicopter up here. I'm guessing the winds are fifty knots or more."

"En route? Well, great. Because I can't wait to get my hands on Special Agent Ramsey."

Jake flipped open her phone and walked into a clearing. "Let's let Morris know you're okay," she said as she punched in the number.

Jaime nodded. "I'll see if this guy's got any ID on him."

Jake watched as she dug into the man's pockets, then turned when her call was answered. "Captain Morris? I found your detective." She nodded. "She's fine. Found the assassin, too." She frowned, glancing at Jaime. "The FBI is going to want to talk to him, huh?" She and Jaime exchanged a smile. "Well, I think they're going to need some sort of an interpreter." She shook her head. "No, I don't know if he's a foreigner or not. But I do know he's very dead."

CHAPTER FORTY-EIGHT

"Senator?"

Peter glanced up, then motioned Arthur into the room. "What is it?"

"The FBI is on the phone. They want to speak with you."

He took a deep breath and let it out slowly. "Fine. Please let Mr. Dodds and Mr. Ramsey know I'd like to see them. They're both down in the bunker."

"Of course, sir." He turned to leave, then stopped. "Your wife . . . I heard she wasn't well. Is there anything I can do?"

"When did you hear that?"

"This morning. One of the maids said that Dr. Patterson was summoned last night."

Peter smiled reassuringly. "She's fine. She had a little . . . little spell again last night is all."

"Very well." He pointed at the phone. "The FBI is on line two."

"Thank you, Arthur."

His smile vanished as soon as Arthur closed the door. This was most likely the call they'd been waiting on for days. The call to let them know that they'd found Sara. And that Sara was dead. As he picked up the phone, he reminded himself to show the proper amount of grief at the news.

"Senator Michaels here. What can I do for you?"

CHAPTER FORTY-NINE

Eleven women crowded into the hospital room as soon as the doctor allowed. Megan, dressed in her hospital gown, gave them all a smile as she squeezed Jaime's hand.

"He said you all did a remarkable job of keeping the wound clean. And the stolen antibiotics did help."

"Wonderful. But what did they do to you? You've been in there two hours."

"They flushed the wound—which let me tell you was not pleasant—and then I've got this drain tube thing. I've had more shots than I can remember and he tells me I'll sleep until morning."

Jaime squeezed her shoulder then bent low. "I'm really glad you're okay, Megan. I was worried as hell there, you know."

"You saved my life, Jaime. I won't ever forget you."

Jaime cleared her throat. "Oh, hell, it wasn't just me." She stood up, motioning to the others. "Everybody had a part in this." She looked at Sara, silently asking for help.

Sara smiled at the misting of tears in Jaime's eyes, then moved forward, thinking this was as good a time as any to address them all.

"Ladies, we had a hell of a trip. And"—she paused—"we lost Sandra along the way." She swallowed down the lump in her throat as she met their eyes, lingering on Celia as the older woman wiped tears from her eyes. "I won't even bother reciting the original purpose of this trip. If you didn't learn perseverance and self-confidence from our little trek through the mountains, then you won't learn it anywhere."

"Yeah, we learned it all right. I'm just not sure any of us ever want to do it again," Abby said, and the others chimed in with laughs.

"Well, I hope this isn't the last communication I have from you all. I know we exchanged addresses and phone numbers and e-mail addresses but once you leave here and get back into the real world, we may all fade from your memory," Sara said, glancing quickly at Jaime before continuing. "I've made arrangements to get you back to Denver. And the clinic has rooms for you at a hotel just down the street from the airport. I want your last night to at least be comfortable. You all know my secretary, Tracy. She's going to make all of your flight arrangements so she'll be in touch with you in the morning." She laughed. "All but you, Megan. You're staying here overnight."

"Can I stay with her?"

"Ashley? Are you sure?"

"Yeah. She might need a friendly face around." She shrugged. "Besides, I don't have anything to rush home to."

"Thanks. That'd be great, Ash," Megan said.

"Okay then. Let's say our good-byes to Megan and hit the road."

One by one, they went to Megan, wishing her well. Then each of them stopped in front of Jaime and Sara, giving tight hugs to both women.

"You saved all our lives, Jaime. Not just Megan's. I won't ever forget you either," Lou Ann said.

Jaime didn't know what to say, so she just nodded. Then Abby squeezed her hard and patted her cheek. "Thanks for the skinny dipping lessons, Chief. It ranks right up there on the fun scale."

"Glad we could all get naked together," Jaime said, drawing laughs from the others.

Celia was the last to leave the room. She took Jaime's hand, shoving a camera into it. "It was Sandra's. There's a bunch of the two of you on it. I thought maybe you'd like it." She shrugged. "I don't know of any family she has. I think she'd rather you have it anyway."

"Oh, man," Jaime murmured. She squeezed the camera, then pulled Celia into a tight hug. "Thanks. She was a special lady."

"She thought you were too."

CHAPTER FIFTY

As soon as the van pulled away, Special Agent Erickson and Agent Fielding were waiting.

"We'll take the chopper to Colorado Springs, Ms. Michaels. Your father is expecting you. Then we'll transport Detective Hutchinson back to Denver for debriefing."

"The woman I was telling you about. Sandra Kellum. Have they found her yet?"

"They're on the trail but they've not come upon her yet. They'll let me know as soon as they do."

Sara glanced at Jaime. "You gave them the coordinates?"

"They'll find her, Sara. Come on. Let's get you out of here."

As they walked toward the helicopter, Sara moved closer to Jaime. "I'm not crazy about flying and I've certainly never been on one of these before," she yelled as the sound of the rotors nearly drowned her out.

"We'll be fine," Jaime said loudly into her ear. "I'll be right beside you."

Jaime climbed in first, then helped Sara on board. The two agents followed. After Jaime got them buckled in, she took the headset Agent Fielding handed her, slipping it over her ears. She motioned at Sara but Erickson shook his head.

Sara looked at the three of them, wondering if she should feel slighted, but as soon as the helicopter lifted off, she gripped the seat hard, watching as the ground disappeared at an alarming rate.

"So Hutchinson, this McCoy person—a former Denver police detective—she just happened to be in the area?"

Jaime met his steady gaze then shrugged. "That's what she said."

He smiled but it never came close to reaching his eyes. "Quite the coincidence."

Jaime grinned. "Yeah. We were damn lucky she was out hiking today."

"This guy, any idea who he is?"

Jaime shook her head. "I thought that was your specialty."

"We'll find out soon enough. The county coroner has released him to us."

Jaime nodded, glancing at Sara. She was white as a sheet. Jaime reached over and squeezed her arm. Sara met her eyes and offered a weak smile. Jaime leaned closer, covering the mouthpiece on her headset. "You okay?" she yelled.

Sara nodded, then gasped as the helicopter lurched to the side. She clutched Jaime's hand, squeezing hard.

"Got some turbulence," the pilot said. "Going to drop her down a little. Hold on."

Sara leaned back, watching as the trees got closer again. She saw a river and noted they seemed to be following its path.

Jaime nodded, following her gaze. "Arkansas River," she yelled. "We'll be in Colorado Springs in no time."

CHAPTER FIFTY-ONE

He paced quickly in his office, his feet moving back and forth across the carpet. It was the worst possible outcome. Not only was Sara still alive but the FBI had the body of their hired killer.

"It's not that bad, Senator," Dodds said again. "He's dead. He can't tell them anything."

Peter Michaels turned, glaring at Dodds. "Not that bad? We've paid him half a million dollars. Don't you think they'll trace that?"

Dodds shook his head. "It's been transferred so many times through bogus accounts, there's no way it'll come back to us." He moved closer. "We can still do this. The FBI is dropping her in our lap. We'll say thanks and a job well done, then send them on their way."

Michaels shook his head. "I had no problem with your plan, Dodds. In fact, it was genius. But if you think we're going to bring her here and then carry out our plan *here*, you are sadly mistaken. It's too risky."

"I doubt we'll have another chance. Ramsey can handle it."

"No. We can't take a chance."

Dodds smiled. "Peter, it's not really your decision to make. We have millions and millions of dollars invested in you. If you don't win the presidency, it's all for nothing. All these years will have been wasted. Do you understand what I'm saying?"

Peter squared his shoulders. "Do you understand what *I'm* saying? It's too risky. We had our opportunity and we missed." He straightened, standing to his full height, dwarfing Dodds. "I'm still in charge here."

Dodds laughed then turned away. "No, Peter, you're not in charge. You've never been in charge." He opened his cell phone and pushed a number, waiting only seconds. "Ramsey? Come up here, please." Dodds turned back around. "No, Peter, you are not in charge." He smiled again. "We own you, Peter. We own every single bit of you." He walked to the window and pulled the drapes aside. "We'll still take her out. We have to take her out now. Once the press gets wind of this, everyone in the nation will know you have a lesbian daughter." He turned, looking pointedly at Michaels. "And it will be such a shame that she survived an assassin's bullet but couldn't survive a car accident." His smile vanished. "We took care of your wife's affair all those years ago, Peter. It's only fitting his daughter should die the same way."

CHAPTER FIFTY-TWO

Sara's relief as Colorado Springs came into view was short-lived as the helicopter passed over the city and headed to the east. Years ago, her father's estate had been miles out of town, sprawled out on the plains, far from neighbors. Now, the city crept closer and closer, inching mere blocks from the guarded estate.

As they approached the helicopter pad, Sara involuntarily reached over and clutched Jaime's hand. She had a bad feeling, a feeling she couldn't put into words. She didn't want to see her father. She didn't want to be interrogated by him. And she didn't want to be left here alone. She hadn't been to the complex in years and she hadn't had a face-to-face meeting with her father in more than five years. The last one had been so disastrous, she was thankful her mother had not pushed for them to work out their differences yet again, something they'd been trying to do ever since he found out she was gay.

"We'll drop Ms. Michaels off here, Detective. We've got a car waiting. You'll go back to Denver with us," Erickson said, his voice filling the headset. "We'll need a complete debriefing, start to finish."

"Sure. Whatever," Jaime said. She held Sara's hand tightly as the helicopter touched down, jolting them only slightly as it came to rest on the pad. The constant hum of the overhead rotor blades eased somewhat as the engine idled. Their door was opened from the outside and when Sara fumbled with her strap, Jaime reached over and unbuckled her.

"Thanks," Sara said nervously.

Jaime only nodded and followed Sara from the chopper, both ducking their heads as they were led away. They stopped beside a shiny black Lincoln with darkened windows. Agent Fielding opened the back door and held it, nodding at Jaime.

"Can you give us a second?" she asked.

"Sure. But just a second. Special Agent Erickson will escort Ms. Michaels to the senator. He's waiting."

When they were alone, Jaime shyly took Sara's hand. She smiled gently, knowing Sara was still spooked by the whole ordeal.

"Are you trying to hide the fact that we're holding hands?" Sara asked with a wink.

Jaime blushed. "I didn't want everybody talking about you. I mean, your father's out there."

Sara walked closer. "He knows I'm gay, Jaime. And I couldn't care less what any of these other people think."

Jaime nodded. "Will you be okay?"

"I don't really want to be here," Sara admitted. "I certainly don't want to be left here. I have this terrible feeling they're going to lock me away for security reasons and I'll never see the light of day again."

Jaime squeezed her hand. "They're not going to do that. They just want to make sure you're safe, that's all. And they want to find out who this guy was and who hired him."

Sara nodded. "I know. But this isn't my life. I never wanted any part of it and it pisses me off now that I'm affected by it."

Jaime raised her eyebrows teasingly. "You got to meet me."

Their eyes held.

"Yeah, I did, didn't I?" Sara cleared her throat. "Have I thanked you properly for saving my life?"

"You don't have to thank me."

"Of course I do."

Sara moved closer, her hand sliding up Jaime's chest to curl around her neck. She closed her eyes as she pulled Jaime to her, their mouths meeting slowly, gently. She still wasn't used to the way her body reacted from Jaime's kisses. She opened her eyes and took a deep breath, trying to slow her racing heart.

"Wow," Jaime whispered.

Sara nodded. "Will I ever see you again?"

"I thought we had a dinner date? You were going to cook for me, remember?"

Sara laughed. "Oh yeah. It's still a date then?"

"Absolutely."

They pulled apart at the subtle clearing of the throat behind them. Agent Fielding stood waiting.

"Ready?"

Sara nodded. "If I must." She glanced once more at Jaime, their eyes meeting for a brief intense second, then she pulled them away.

Agent Fielding pointed. "If you'll go with Special Agent Erickson, ma'am."

"Thank you, Agent."

As she walked away, she glanced to the west, seeing the hulking shape of Pikes Peak as it hovered over the city, much like a sentinel standing guard. As a child, she used to love looking at the giant mountain. She always felt protected by it. She hoped it still held that same magic for her.

"Wow."

Jaime glanced at Fielding. "What?"

"That was some thank-you kiss. I've never gotten one like that."

Jaime slapped his shoulder with a laugh. "Then you're not doing something right, man."

As she followed Fielding into the back seat of the car, she watched Sara being greeted by three men. She assumed one to be her father but she did recognize the other agent, Special Agent Ramsey. *Bastard. Going to take all the glory, no doubt.* She shook her head and closed the door behind her.

Sara managed not to flinch from the angry glare of her father. She met his gaze head-on.

"Well, Sara, I see you still know how to cause a scene."

Sara laughed. "Was that a scene?" She shrugged. "I thought it was pretty mild."

He clenched his jaw. "You call kissing another woman in my presence mild? Don't you have even one ounce of respect in you?"

"Respect? You expect me to show you respect?"

"No, Sara. I expect no such thing." He turned to Special Agent Erickson. "Thank you for bringing her here safely. You'll keep me informed of course?"

"Yes, sir. As soon as we know something, I'll be in touch."

"Then have a safe trip back to Denver," he said dismissively. He gripped Sara's elbow hard. "I'm sure you want to see your mother."

CHAPTER FIFTY-THREE

"So, what kind of investigation will you do?" Jaime asked as they maneuvered back to the interstate.

"With what, Detective?"

"With what? With our dead guy, of course. He was obviously a hire. Surely you have some idea as to who's been calling the shots."

Erickson looked over his shoulder from the front seat. "That's nothing you need to concern yourself with, Detective. It's an FBI matter."

Jaime laughed. "Oh, I see. But it wasn't an FBI matter a couple of weeks ago, I guess?"

"What are you talking about?"

"I'm talking about the fact that you solicited a lowly Denver detective's help, that's what."

"Oh, yes. I forgot about the alleged agent who needed your help. I suppose we should be thankful you and your captain fell for it."

Jaime leaned forward. "What the hell are you talking about?"

"Your captain said some guy claiming to be an agent coerced you into finding Michaels' party on the trail."

"What? What do you mean, claiming to be an agent?"

Erickson shrugged. "They used you to lead them to Michaels."

"They? You mean Ramsey? Ramsey's not FBI?"

He shook his head. "Don't have an Agent Ramsey on this case. Don't even know a Ramsey," Erickson said. "Told your captain as much."

Jaime gripped the back of the front seat hard. "Turn the god-damn car around!"

CHAPTER FIFTY-FOUR

"You remember Mr. Dodds, of course," Peter said. "This is Ramsey."

Sara nodded as she followed the three men toward the mansion. "Where's my mother?"

"She's resting in her quarters."

Sara's eyes lifted to the second floor balcony which was her mother's suite. It appeared to be closed up.

"Her room down in the bunker, Sara. Not up there."

Sara frowned. "The bunker? Why?"

"Your mother has not been herself lately," Mr. Dodds said.

"She's under a doctor's care," Peter added.

"What's wrong? Why wasn't I told?"

"You haven't exactly been accessible, Sara. But not to worry. She's being taken care of."

Sara paused beside the door as Ramsey held it open for them. She frowned. *Ramsey?* Something was nagging at her, something just below the surface but she couldn't quite grasp it. She paused at the door, her head tilted sideways, brows drawn together.

"Sara?"

She shook her head, then turned toward the sound of her father's voice.

"I'll have Arthur take you to your mother. I'll be along shortly."

Sara nodded, feeling a genuine smile form as Arthur approached. Arthur had barely been out of college when he'd joined her father's very first campaign, that for city council many, many years ago. She'd always gotten along well with Arthur, finding him to be a buffer between herself and her father during her awkward teenage years, years when she was noticing girls instead of boys.

"Well Miss Sara, how are you?"

"Hello, Arthur. Good to see you again."

"Your mother has been asking for you." He grasped her hand and linked it in the crook of his elbow. "I'll take you to see her."

Sara nodded, her smile fading when she glanced at her father. His eyes were always so angry when he looked at her. Even as a child, he'd always looked at her with contempt, like he was mad at her for something she had yet to do. She certainly didn't understand it then. And even now as an adult, she couldn't believe that all of this anger was over her sexual orientation. But no. They'd always clashed, well before she was coming of age. When she was younger, she used to think his anger toward her was because she was a girl and not the son he must have wanted. It was easier to think that rather than believing your own father simply despised you for no reason at all.

Arthur flipped on lights as they descended into the bunker. She shook her head, wondering at the paranoia her father suffered through, even now. *Really. A bunker?* Who had a bunker? As a kid, she was always embarrassed by it, refusing to let any of her friends know it even existed. She was embarrassed by it, yes. But she had also been afraid of it. It was dark. It was hollow. Many a night she'd woken up with nightmares, imagining her father locking her away under the earth, refusing to let her come to the surface. She felt a chill and she tried to shake it off. How easy would it be for her father to imprison her here?

"She's down here," Arthur said, motioning down a long hallway.

"Why is she down in the bunker, Arthur? Why not her suite?"

Arthur shook his head. "I'm not sure, Miss Sara. Her doctor, Dr. Patterson, came the other night. But before that, Mr. Dodds brought in his own doctor. I think his name was Hammonds. Real young guy."

"Is she okay? I mean, is it serious?"

"Like I said, your father hasn't told me anything." Arthur looked over his shoulder, then lowered his voice. "The staff tells me she's being kept sedated."

Sara stopped. "What do you mean?"

"She's not been very coherent on the occasions I've been allowed to visit with her."

Sara shook her head. "She was fine the last time I talked with her. What could possibly have happened?"

Arthur tapped lightly on the door then opened it. Sara was not only surprised to find someone else in the room, but she was surprised to find her mother in bed, sheet pulled nearly to her neck.

"Mrs. Reynolds. How is she?"

"Still sleeping."

He nodded. "Why don't you take a break?"

"The senator instructed me not to leave." She glanced at her watch. "She's due her next dose in an hour."

Arthur smiled. "This is Sara. Her daughter. Let's give them a moment, please. The senator is aware she's here."

"Of course." She got up. "Nice to meet you, Sara. I've heard a lot about you. I'll just be in the hallway."

Sara nodded as the older woman left the room. She looked at Arthur as she moved to her mother's bedside. "Who is she?"

"She's been on staff for the last three years. She oversees the housekeeping crew."

Sara pulled the sheet off her mother, her eyes wide as she stared at her. Yes, she appeared to be asleep. She gently shook her shoulder.

"Mother? Wake up. It's me, Sara." There was no response. "Mother?"

Sara felt her skin. It was cool to the touch. Cool and clammy. She lightly patted her mother's face, then with more force when there was still no response.

"Arthur? What the hell? It's like she's unconscious." Sara lifted up one of her mother's arms and released it, watching as it fell lifelessly to the bed. "What has he done to her?" she asked quietly.

"I'm afraid I don't know anything. For the last several months, your father has been keeping counsel solely with Mr. Dodds. I've been reduced to little more than a messenger, I'm afraid."

"Arthur? You were always his right-hand man for as long as I can remember. What happened?"

"The run for the presidency, I suppose. Dodds has brought in this Ramsey guy. It's all very secretive." He shrugged. "I appear to be the odd man out."

Ramsey? She drew her brows together, finally remembering Jaime's words that night by the river. *"Ramsey. Squirrelly white dude."* Was it a coincidence? She frowned, trying to remember the conversation. Jaime said the FBI guy that approached her, Ramsey, said he'd spoken directly to Sara. But Sara had only talked with Erickson and Fielding. Never a Ramsey.

Muted voices in the hallway brought Sara back to the present. She glanced at Arthur then moved her eyes to the doorway as her father filled the space.

Sara pointed at her mother. "What have you done to her?"

He smiled. "She hasn't been herself lately, Sara. She's been distraught over these death threats. Her doctor recommended that she be sedated."

"Sedated? She's practically catatonic. What doctor would do this? Do this and leave her here without being monitored? I can't believe Dr. Patterson authorized this?"

"It's not really your concern, is it Sara? I have everything under control."

"What are you talking about?"

"I said turn this fucking car around," Jaime yelled. "Ramsey. He was there."

"I'm telling you, there is no Ramsey," Erickson said again.

"And I'm telling you, the guy who called himself Ramsey, the guy who flashed an FBI badge, was there with the senator."

Erickson and Fielding exchanged glances.

"Are you certain?"

"I am positive," she said.

"Because if you're not certain, we can't just go barging into the senator's home. He's got his own security, for one thing. Not to mention the Secret Service agents assigned to him during the campaign."

"It was him. I never forget an asshole. There were two men with the senator when you brought Sara to them. One was Ramsey."

Erickson nodded. "Okay. We'll go back. But if you're wrong, you're taking the fall, not me."

"Yeah. Whatever. Sue me," she muttered, holding on as the driver made a sharp turn on I-25, then bounced them through the median and onto the southbound lane.

Sara caught her breath as Dodds and Ramsey followed her father into the room. She'd known Dodds most of her life and was used to the looks of disgust he normally gave her. Ramsey, however, she was not used to. His eyes were cold, empty. A predatory smile appeared as he watched her.

She swallowed the lump of fear in her throat, then addressed her father. "I believe she needs to be in a hospital. She looks comatose to me."

"No, Sara. She's fine. She's just heavily sedated. And if she's not . . ." he said with a shrug. "Doesn't really matter, does it?"

Sara's eyes widened. "What are you talking about?"

"I'm talking about her, I'm talking about you. I'm talking about this so-called marriage." He turned to Arthur. "You may go, Arthur. I no longer require your services today."

"Yes, sir. But I tend to agree with Miss Sara. Your wife does not look well, sir. Perhaps I should call Dr. Patterson."

"Yes, you always did tend to agree with Sara, didn't you? Well, as I said, you are dismissed, Arthur. There is nothing here that concerns you."

"Very well." He bowed slightly in Sara's direction then excused himself.

As soon as Arthur was gone, Sara realized how completely alone she was. Alone and at the mercy of her father. She squared her shoulders, determined not to show the fear that was threatening to strangle her breath.

"We have a slight predicament, Sara," her father stated. He motioned to Ramsey who walked fully into the room, standing between Sara and her mother. "You see, your mother overheard something she shouldn't have. Therefore, we've had to keep her sedated. She's what you might call under house arrest," he said with a laugh.

"House arrest? Surely you're not serious."

"He's very serious," Dodds said. "And enough of this small talk, Peter. Let's get this over with."

"What are you talking about?" Sara demanded. She jerked away when Ramsey moved to take her arm. "Get away from me."

"I don't know how you did it but you foiled our plan, Sara. But all good plans have a backup."

She stared at Dodds, shocked by his tone. The soft-spoken man she remembered had a dangerous gleam in his eyes, a gleam that was mirrored by both her father and Ramsey.

"What are you talking about?"

"He's talking about the man who was hired to kill you, Sara."

242

Sara's breath caught at her father's words. "You? You did that?" she asked, her voice now shaking with fear. "You would consent to having your own daughter killed?"

He laughed. "That's the funny part about it all. You see, you're not really my daughter." He pointed at the bed. "She had an affair. She thought I wouldn't find out."

"Oh my God," Sara whispered. She glanced at her mother who lay still, unconscious and oblivious to them and their conversation.

"Yes. And even if I had not known of the affair, I still would have figured it out, Sara. No child of mine could possibly turn out like you. You've made a mockery of me and my life. You go against everything I stand for." He walked closer. "And you stand between me and the presidency."

"You are insane. I think you've really lost your mind." She moved away from him but her mother's bed prevented any further escape. "Did you actually think you could get away with it?"

"Yes, Sara, we did. And we will. Do you think this is our first time?" Dodds said with a laugh.

"What do you mean?"

"Your biological father, of course." He snapped his fingers. "Ramsey, take her to the holding cell."

"Holding cell?" Sara again jerked her arm away from Ramsey but he grabbed her. "I said, let go of me!" she yelled. Without thinking, she slammed the back of her fist against his face, stunning him. A sidekick to his hips knocked him down. Before she could go after Dodds, Ramsey reached out an arm and took her legs out from under her. She landed hard on the floor then felt the cold barrel of a gun pressed against her forehead.

"Not real smart, Sara," Dodds said as he squatted down beside her. "Careful. Ramsey's got an itchy finger." He laughed quietly. "Now get up."

Sara got to her feet, her eyes filled with fear as she met the cold, indifferent eyes of her father.

"Take her."

CHAPTER FIFTY-FIVE

Jaime tapped the seat impatiently as they carefully maneuvered through traffic. As the driver came to a stop at a yellow light, she threw her hands up.

"Jesus Christ! It's a wonder you didn't get rear-ended," she said loudly. "Nobody stops at yellow lights!"

"Will you calm down, Detective."

"No, I will not calm down! I thought we were in a hurry. Whatever happened to weaving in and out of traffic, running lights and blaring the horn at anyone who got in the way? That's what they do on TV."

"We're not in a police cruiser, Detective. And technically, we're not in crisis mode," Erickson said.

Without thinking, Jaime pulled out her weapon, pointing it directly at the driver. "I say we're in fucking crisis mode! Now run this goddamn red light!" she yelled.

"Put the gun down, Detective. This is not helping," Erickson said reasonably."Run the goddamn light!" she screamed.

They all pitched backward as the driver floored it, shooting them through the intersection as cars skidded to a halt around them, all blowing horns at them.

"Okay, that's more like it," she said, lowering her weapon. "We don't have time to piss around here, Erickson."

Erickson turned around in the seat, pointing his finger at her. "Don't think you won't be cited for that, Detective."

"Well thankfully, I don't work for you."

"And you never will. Discipline is apparently not your strong suit."

Jaime laughed. "Sticks and stones, Agent."

"I'm serious. Your captain will hear of this. You *do not* pull a weapon in the goddamn car."

"Whatever," she murmured. She clapped the driver on the shoulder, nearly smiling at the wide eyes that looked back at her in the rearview mirror. "Just get us there."

Sara only thought she'd known fear. But with hands tied behind her and the unmistakable feel of a gun pressed against her back, the fear they'd lived with in the mountains—with an assassin on their trail—was nothing compared to the hopelessness she now felt. There was no Jaime to come to the rescue, there was no ghost town to hide her and no retired police detective to mysteriously show up and lend help.

And the person she'd known as her father had turned into a madman. Her mind was reeling with questions as she preceded Ramsey down the long, dark hallway, her boots clicking loudly in the deserted bunker. Had her mother really had an affair? And had her biological father really been murdered by these people? No wonder a murder-for-hire to get rid of the lesbian daughter was so easy for them. They'd done it before. Perhaps many times. Apparently, the nightmare of the last two weeks was quickly coming to an end. Her mother was sedated to the point of unconsciousness and her lone ally in the entire estate was Arthur, but he'd been dismissed for the evening. She realized how totally alone she was.

Alone and on her own.

"Where are you taking me?"

"Shut up. That doesn't concern you."

"I beg to differ. I'm the one with a gun pressed to my back." When he didn't respond, she tried another approach. "You're Ramsey, the guy who pitched the death threats to the police. To Detective Hutchinson." Again he said nothing. "Would have been funny if the real FBI contacted them too. I guess your plan would have backfired."

"The FBI was too busy chasing down bogus leads we'd planted. They weren't concerned with you until we put a bug in their ear."

"A bug so they could find my body," she stated. "Sorry that didn't work out for you. But you know, you probably should have used a different name. I mean Ramsey? Not very common. When Hutchinson mentions you to the FBI, don't you think they'll come looking for you?"

"Keep quiet. Like I said, it doesn't concern you. After tomorrow, nothing will concern you," he added with a laugh.

"Now keep your mouth shut when we get there," Erickson said as they approached the locked and guarded gate to the senator's estate. "We don't have a warrant, so we're at their mercy as to whether they let us in or not."

"A warrant? We don't need a warrant, for God's sake."

"He has security or have you forgotten that, Detective? They'll have to notify the senator when we get there. There's nothing to say he's got to see us."

"Well, the way you get around a warrant, Special Agent, is to say we need to visit some more with the senator's daughter. And yes, we'll be happy to wait inside while you call him," Jaime said. "All we need is to get inside the front door. See, no warrant because we were escorted in."

"We're not the local police, Detective. Anything we do will be scrutinized. And any hope of prosecution is hampered by not following protocol."

"Fuck protocol. And why the hell are we worrying about prosecution at this point? We need to be worrying about saving her life."

"I realize that, Detective. But we have rules."

"And fuck your goddamn rules. We just need to get inside the house."

"That's all well and good but we probably need more than just getting inside. Rumor has it the senator's got a fully functional bunker below ground."

"A bunker? What the hell?"

"He's paranoid, from what we hear," Fielding explained. "The bunker is supposedly safe from nuclear attack as well as chemical warfare."

"It's fully stocked with supplies to last a full year," Erickson added. "Along with a functional communication system."

"A bunker? Who in the hell has a bunker?"

"Rich, powerful, paranoid men."

"Or someone who's got something to hide," she said. "Well, I guess we know where they've taken her."

"Yeah, we just got some more information as we were heading back to Denver," Erickson said as they stood next to the car on the massive circular driveway. "We thought we might as well get with her now instead of hauling her ass up to Denver tomorrow."

The man smoothed his trim beard, nodding. "I'm sure she'll appreciate that. Let me find out where they are."

Jaime was about to suggest they wait inside when the front door opened. One of the men who was with the senator earlier came out.

"What is it, O'Riley?"

"FBI came back," he said. "They have some more questions for Ms. Michaels."

The man paused only a moment as he stared at them, then nodded. "Of course. Why don't you come inside? I'll give the senator a call."

Jaime let out a relieved sigh as they followed him into the mansion. She barely took the time to look around, her eyes glued to this man.

"I'm Arthur, Senator Michaels' aide. They are actually in the bunker with Miss Sara." He looked quickly over his shoulder, making sure they were alone before continuing. "I'm actually relieved you're here," he said, his voice low. "I was contemplating calling the local police."

"What is it?" Erickson asked.

"The senator and Mr. Dodds have been acting very strange for the last several weeks or so. Along with this Ramsey that Dodds has brought in. And what they've done to Mrs. Michaels should be a crime." He cleared his throat. "I most likely will lose my position with the senator if he learns what I've told you but I'm extremely concerned for Miss Sara."

"Arthur, we're concerned for Sara as well. What exactly is going on here?"

"Look," Jaime said impatiently. "Can't we walk and talk at the same time? Where's the bunker?"

"Yes, that's where they have her. That's where they've been holding Mrs. Michaels as well."

"Holding her how?"

"She's heavily sedated. She's only been allowed to regain semi-consciousness once in the last several days." He turned, motioning for them to follow. "My loyalties to the senator go only so far. When I fear their lives are in danger—Sara's and Mrs. Michaels'—then it's time for me to act. To think I was willing to call the local police after the way he spoke to Sara when he dismissed me—" He stopped, pulling out a key card which he swiped. The walls opened up, revealing a dimly lit staircase going down into the bunker.

"What do you mean?" Jaime asked.

"Something's just not right. Miss Sara had a look of pure terror on her face when I left her with them. Perhaps she was afraid she'd end up like her mother. Perhaps it was something else."

He started to precede them down the stairs, but Jaime stopped him with a hand on his arm. She pulled her weapon, Erickson and Fielding doing the same.

"Stay behind us."

"Hutchinson, don't go cowboy on us," Erickson warned.

"At the bottom of stairs is a hallway. The living quarters are to the left. The main complex, along with the offices, is to the right," Arthur explained.

"Where were they when you left?"

"They were still in Mrs. Michaels' suite," he said quietly as they crept down the stairs. "There's been a staff member staying with her. Mrs. Reynolds. She's been administering the medication. She may be in the room or he may have dismissed her as well."

"Do you have any influence over her?" Erickson asked.

"No. She was hired by the senator. She reports directly to him."

Jaime leaned against the wall when Erickson touched her arm, silently telling her they would go first. She drew her brows together. She *hated* being outranked. When they passed her, she motioned for Arthur to follow then she took up the rear, watching their back.

"The next door down," Arthur whispered loudly. "It's closed now. I would assume they've left."

Erickson and Fielding each flanked the door. Jaime tugged on Arthur's arm, moving him behind her and up against the wall. She took her position in front of the door, weapon pointed. Erickson held up two fingers then silently counted before turning the knob. It was locked.

Before Fielding could lift his leg to break it, Arthur stepped forward and grabbed his arm.

"I have a key."

"Well, that'd just be too simple," Jaime murmured, watching Erickson snatch the key from Arthur's hand.

The room was empty but the bed was not. Jaime assumed it was Mrs. Michaels who lay there. The woman's skin was pale, ghostly. Arthur went to her immediately, touching her cheek, then bending low, listening.

"Very shallow breathing," he said. He reached over, fingering the IV drip, then pulled it out of her hand. Blood pooled where the needle had been and he covered her hand with the sheet.

"Should you do that?" Jaime asked.

"That's how they've been keeping her sedated. Through the IV," he explained.

"Why in the world would they do this?" Fielding asked. "She's like a prisoner in her own home."

"She saw or heard something she shouldn't have," Jaime guessed. "Why else?"

"I agree," Erickson said. "Fielding, call it in. Let the local police know the situation. And get an ambulance out here," he added. He then turned to Arthur. "Tell us about this bunker. Where could they have taken Sara Michaels?"

CHAPTER FIFTY-SIX

Peter paced in his office as Dodds and Ramsey discussed—argued—the situation. He wanted Ramsey to take Sara away and he didn't want to know what happened. Just like Dodds had done all those years ago with Joyce's affair. He handled it and Peter didn't know the details. A car accident was a car accident.

But no, Dodds didn't want that. He wanted to keep Sara hostage awhile, a day or two, just in case something went wrong. Peter took a deep breath. As if their hired assassin getting killed wasn't cause enough for alarm.

And Ramsey, Ramsey wanted to kill her right here in the bunker and dispose of her body tonight. His plan was to drive her out to Dodds' ranch in the plains and burn her. Peter shuddered at the thought.

"I'm telling you, a murder is too risky. It's got to be an accident," Dodds insisted.

"Then we do them both at the same time," Ramsey said.

Peter stopped pacing. "Both?"

"Peter, we can't take a chance with Joyce. You know that." Dodds smiled. "Besides, having both your wife and only child killed will generate more sympathy from voters than we could ever imagine."

"Talk about risky, Dodds. I think that's going too far."

"As I said earlier Peter, it's no longer your call."

"How do you propose to stage an accident for both of them?"

"A car accident appears to be the easiest," he said. "Of course we'll need a driver. Which of your men are you willing to sacrifice, Peter? I think this would be a good opportunity to get rid of Arthur."

Peter's eyes narrowed. "What are you saying?"

"We can't very well have Sara drive, now can we? And it'll be days before Joyce is coherent enough to get behind the wheel. We rig the brakes, just like before. Have Arthur drive them to your cabin in Woodland Park for a short vacation after Sara's ordeal. Halfway up the pass, the brakes will fail while taking one of the sharp curves, sending them into the ravine. Unfortunately, a faulty gas tank that's been leaking will cause an awful explosion." He turned to Ramsey. "You can make that work, can't you?"

"Of course."

Peter stood in disbelief as they planned the murder of his wife and Sara. And Arthur. He wasn't concerned with Sara. He had no feelings there. And Arthur, well, he'd served his purpose. But Joyce—despite her affair in the early years of their marriage—he still had great feelings of affection for her. The blinding love he'd felt at the beginning had been doused by her affair but he'd gotten past it. Their marriage was not perfect but they worked well together. And of course, the media loved Joyce. The fact that he'd managed to keep his own affairs secret over the years was simply an added bonus. He was roused from his musings by the ringing of his cell.

"What is it, O'Riley?" His brows drew together as he listened. "They what?" He flicked his gaze to Dodds. "Very well. I'm sure they're down here now. Thank you, O'Riley."

"What is it?"

"The FBI came back. Arthur let them inside. They wanted to see Sara again."

Dodds whipped around, his eyes going to the door. Then he glanced at Ramsey.

"Get her. *Now*."

"This place is like a maze," Arthur said as he led them down yet another hallway. He pointed to a set of double doors to their right. "Control room."

"Control room? What is this, a spaceship or something?" Jaime asked.

"Well, you almost have to be a rocket scientist to understand all the controls in there. For the power source, air quality, vent lockdown in case of a breach. Things like that."

"Crazy," she muttered.

He stopped when they reached another set of doors. "The offices are in this wing," he said. "I'm sure this is where they are."

"Do you think they're armed?" Erickson asked.

Arthur shook his head. "Not the senator, no. And I wouldn't think Mr. Dodds would have a gun." He shrugged. "But Ramsey, I never did trust him. If anyone's got a gun, it's him."

"Okay, Arthur. I want you to go back and check on Mrs. Michaels, then wait for the police. And make sure no one comes down here."

"Are you sure? I mean, I know my way around down here."

"You did a good job, Arthur," Jaime said. "But we don't want to take a chance on something happening to you. Besides, don't want you losing your job, man."

He nodded. "Okay. Okay sure. I'll go sit with Mrs. Michaels then."

As soon as Arthur was out of earshot, Fielding laughed. "He looked like he was about to piss his pants."

"Can you blame him? He probably feels like he's in a Hitchcock movie."

Before they went inside, Erickson stopped them. "Remember, this is our show, Hutchinson. You're just along for the ride. Don't do anything stupid."

"You guys want to take the senator down, go ahead. I'm just here to get Sara."

Once inside the hallway, Jaime felt a chill. She wasn't sure if it was the air temperature, which felt to be in the fifties, or simply the shroud of dread that settled over her. The only sound was the air that hummed through the vents overhead. She realized how unnaturally quiet it was.

Then suddenly, down the hall in another area, they heard the clicking of a door as it was unlocked. They all looked at each other then increased their steps as they quietly moved down the hallway.

Jaime heard muffled voices and tilted her head. *Sara.* She tensed, ready to run but Erickson held up his hand.

"Listen," he whispered.

"Let go of me, you bastard!"

"Shut the fuck up. Now come on."

Jaime moved forward, ignoring Erickson. "Sara!" she screamed. *"Sara!"*

"Jaime? Oh my God! Jaime! I'm here!"

"Shut the fuck up!"

The sound of a fist hitting a face brought them all running down the hall. They skidded around the corner blindly, in time to see another door close in their faces.

"Goddamn," Jaime murmured. She reached for the door knob, but it was locked. "Fuck!"

"Stand back," Erickson instructed. "We'll shoot it opened."

"Have you lost your mind?" Jaime said. "We don't know what's on the other side of this door. You could shoot Sara. Hell, you could shoot the senator."

"You got a better idea?"

"As a matter of fact, yes." From one of her back pockets she produced a key card. She held it up and grinned. "Swiped it from Arthur."

He nodded. "Okay. On three."

He held up his fingers, silently counting. On three, Jaime inserted the key card. As soon as they heard the distinctive click, Erickson threw the door open.

Sara screamed then was silenced by a hand over her mouth and a gun pressed to her head. Ramsey held her tight as he moved closer to the other two men. The senator's eyes were wide. The other man—Dodds—moved away from Ramsey, distancing himself. All three held their weapons on Ramsey, the only one with a gun.

"Drop the gun, Ramsey," Erickson instructed calmly. "No one needs to get hurt here."

"Shut up," he snapped.

He looked at Dodds, as if for help, but Dodds moved away, clutching the senator's arm.

"We're so thankful you're here. He's been like a madman," Dodds said.

Jaime frowned. *What the hell?* Then she looked at Sara, met her frantic eyes. Sara glanced at her father and Dodds, fear showing in her eyes. Jaime took a deep breath then stepped forward, pointing her gun at Ramsey's head.

"Let her go."

"Get back, Detective. I swear to God I'll shoot her."

"You're not going to shoot her," Jaime said. "For one thing, you'll be dead half a second later." She chanced a glance at the senator. "And secondly, if you shoot her, you'll be doing them a great favor."

Ramsey's eyes widened, doubt showing for the first time.

"Their original plan to kill Sara would be accomplished," she said reasonably. "Then we shoot you." She shrugged. "You take the fall. These guys get charged with nothing. Hell, he might even be elected president."

"What are you talking about?" Dodds demanded. "That's just crazy. We've done nothing. He burst in here with Sara—"

"Shut up!" Ramsey screamed, his gun moving from Sara to

Dodds. "I'm not taking the fall. This was all your idea. I had nothing to do with it," he yelled.

"Somebody do something! He's holding my daughter!" the senator said loudly, speaking for the first time.

Sara closed her eyes, then opened them, finding Jaime. She shook her head, telling Jaime all she needed to know.

"Come on, Senator. You don't expect us to believe that Ramsey here thought all this up on his own, do you? I mean, hell, he showed up with an FBI badge, instructing me to follow Sara here. For protection," she added sarcastically. "He had some lovely pictures of Sara and your wife. Even of you. They looked like family photos, actually. Like maybe you supplied them to him when he was putting together the little file he had about these alleged death threats."

"I don't know who the hell you are but you don't speak to me that way." He turned to Erickson. "You. You're FBI. Arrest this man," he demanded.

"Kinda hard to do, seeing as how he's got a gun pointed at you, Senator."

Ramsey finally moved his hand, freeing Sara's mouth. His gun alternated between Dodds and the senator.

"Tell them," he said. "Tell them what's going on."

Before Sara could speak, Dodds stepped forward. "Stop this nonsense, Ramsey. Put the gun down. Let's end this."

"You're not getting away with this, Dodds," Sara said. "They did it. They tried to have me killed. Their plan, their idea. Ramsey is just hired help."

"Sara, think about what you're saying," the senator said, his hands outstretched. "I'm your father. I would never try to kill you."

"You bastard," Sara whispered. "You're not talking your way out of this one, Senator."

"Put the gun down, Mr. Ramsey," Erickson said. "We'll work this out. No bloodshed."

"I'm not taking the fall," he said again. "I was just following orders."

256

"I understand. Now let her go. Everything's going to be fine."

Ramsey shook his head. "No. No. He's got a gun."

"He who?"

Jaime's eyes widened as Dodds reached inside his suit coat. "Gun!" she yelled. As soon as Dodds pulled the trigger, all three fired, knocking him back against the desk and over it. Ramsey and Sara were in a heap on the floor. Jaime ran to them, her heart stopping when she saw blood on Sara's shirt.

"Oh, God. Don't move," she said quietly. "Don't move, sweetheart."

Sara's eyes fluttered open. "I don't feel anything," she whispered.

"I know. That happens. Help is on the way." Jaime gripped Sara's hand hard. "It's going to be okay."

"Jaime, I mean I don't feel anything," she said again as she tried to sit up. "I don't think it's my blood."

"Oh Jesus. Are you sure?" Jaime gently lifted her shirt, revealing smooth, unblemished skin. Jaime closed her eyes. "Thank God."

"Are you okay?"

"Yeah. Come here. Let's see about Ramsey."

Sara moved, looking down at the man who had most likely saved her life. His shirt was covered with blood and his hand was pressed to his upper chest.

"It was all their plan," he whispered hoarsely.

Sara nodded. "I know." She tilted her head. "But you had the gun."

"Dodds?"

"He's dead, man," Jaime said. "How bad are you?"

"He got me up high. Been hit worse."

"He was aiming at me," Sara stated.

"Yeah. Kill you, then it's their word against poor Ramsey here." Jaime took a pocketknife out and cut part of Ramsey's coat. "Here, hold this on the wound. It'll help with the bleeding."

Sara watched them then moved her eyes to her father. No, the *senator*, she corrected. He was sitting dazed in one of the oversized visitor's chairs beside his desk. His eyes wide, he simply stared at Dodds' body which lay in an unnatural heap behind his desk. Erickson and Fielding were both on their phones, talking frantically.

Trying to find out how to spin all this, no doubt. Well, no amount of spin and damage control could possibly get the senator out of this mess. She'd see to it. Not after what he'd done to her mother. She turned.

"Jaime? My mother?"

"Arthur's with her. Ambulance should be here by now."

Sara walked over, squeezing Jaime's arm. "Thank you. Again. For saving my life."

Jaime smiled. "It's my job, ma'am," she said quietly.

"And you do it very well." Sara let her hand drift to Jaime's stomach, rubbing lightly, intimately. "I want to go be with my mother. Is that okay?"

"Sure. Go on. It's going to be awhile before we wrap it up here, anyway."

Sara glanced one last time at the senator, wondering what in the world he'd been thinking when he concocted this plot. But he never looked at her. His eyes were still fixed on Dodds'.

CHAPTER FIFTY-SEVEN

Sara knocked lightly on the hospital door, then pushed it open. Bright sunshine streamed in through the window, landing softly on her mother. She turned when Sara entered, a smile transforming her face.

"Sara. Come in, darling."

Sara moved to the bed, taking one of her mother's hands, feeling warmth that hadn't been there for the last two days. Her eyes looked clear, alert.

"You're looking better," Sara replied before bending to kiss her cheek.

"Still a little groggy but the brain seems to be working again." She motioned to the chair beside the bed. "Sit. We should talk."

Sara nodded. "Do you feel up to it?"

"Doesn't matter. I've put it off long enough." She sighed. "I watched the local news this morning. They even had him in handcuffs. I can't imagine his embarrassment. I suppose he wishes he had been killed along with Dodds."

"I'm just thankful he didn't weasel his way out of it," Sara said sharply. Then she squeezed her mother's hand. "I'm sorry. He's your husband."

"He ceased being a husband a long time ago, Sara. Our marriage was simply amicable and convenient. We didn't argue or fight. I smiled when the cameras were on and said all the right things. But when the doors were closed and the cameras were off, we went our separate ways."

"Was there someone else for you? For him?"

"Oh, he's had women all along. I'm sure he thinks I didn't know." She shook her head. "Not for me. There was just the one time." She met Sara's eyes. "And I should have told you years ago. There just didn't seem to be a purpose. He was already dead."

"Tell me about him," Sara said quietly. "When did you meet?"

Her mother's eyes turned dreamy and she closed them for a moment. Sara waited while her mother remembered.

"It was our first or second year of marriage, I guess. Your father had—I'm sorry, *Peter* had just joined the law firm and was working seventy, eighty hours a week. We seldom saw each other." She smiled at Sara. "I told you once I was a professional student. Well, I was taking grad classes. He was a young professor. I think it was love at first sight. I was completely enamored by him. He was all the things your father wasn't." She closed her eyes. "I'm sorry . . . *Peter* wasn't."

"It's okay. I've spent thirty years thinking of him as my father."

"But I should have had the courage to tell you the truth."

"You're telling me the truth now. Finish your story. He was all the things . . . *your husband* wasn't," Sara stated quietly.

"Peter was always handsome but he had that aristocratic air about him. He was always so controlled, so *refined*. Bryan—his name was Bryan—was charming and mischievous, and he made me laugh. It just felt good to be around him, you know. One of those kinds of people. You just want to embrace them."

Sara nodded. "Yes, I know."

"But of course I was married and Bryan knew it. So we flirted harmlessly. Or what we thought was harmless. We were actually falling in love." She shook her head. "But I couldn't. Peter had such huge aspirations for his life, our life. Even then, he was planning his political future. He was a brilliant trial lawyer and he was quickly making a name for himself. And he was worming his way into the inner circle of the very rich and powerful of this state. And I knew my place. So an affair with Bryan was out of the question."

"Divorce?"

"A divorce would be seen as a failure and Peter could not afford any failures in his life. No, I knew he would never allow it."

"But you obviously *did* have an affair with Bryan."

She nodded, her eyes softening. "We were out on a picnic after class one day. A thunderstorm caught us. We were soaking wet by the time we made it back." She laughed. "I knew right then it would happen. He lived in this small cottage right by campus." She took Sara's hand, squeezing tightly. "Oh, Sara, it was the most beautiful thing. We spent hours together. And afterward, when I knew I had to leave, he told me he loved me." She shook her head. "But I couldn't tell him. I had no right to tell him. I was married to another man."

"But you did love him."

"Oh, yes. He owned my heart. But Peter owned my life," she said sadly.

"So that's when you got pregnant?"

She nodded. "Yes. It never occurred to me to use protection and I wasn't on any birth control. Peter wanted us to have two children. I mean, what politician doesn't have kids? But I never got pregnant. I assumed it was me, not Peter. So I was quite surprised when I missed my first period." She met Sara's eyes. "Shocked. Scared. In my heart, I knew it was Bryan's. But I broke the news to Peter one night over a bottle of champagne. He was very excited, I remember."

"When did you tell Bryan?"

"I waited until the semester was over. He asked if he was the father. I told him no." She looked away. "I think I broke his heart that day."

"So you didn't see him after that?"

"I saw him occasionally around campus. He always told me how beautiful I looked pregnant," she said softly. "It was on those occasions that he broke my heart."

Sara stood and walked to the window, looking out into the sunshine. She wasn't sure what she was feeling. Her heart ached for a man she didn't even know existed until a few days ago. She turned back to her mother.

"You should have told him."

"I know, Sara. But I couldn't. And as it turns out, I didn't have to. I think he knew all along. A few months after you were born, he came to see me. He took one look at you and burst into tears," she whispered. "There was no doubt you were his child." She cleared her throat. "Everyone always commented that you got Peter's blue eyes." She slowly shook her head. "Bryan's eyes used to turn the color of the ocean sometimes. Blue, with a hint of green. Just like yours."

Sara closed her eyes, nearly embarrassed by the tears she was shedding for a man she never met. A man who, as it turned out, was her father.

"I'm sorry, Sara. I'm sorry I wasn't strong enough. Bryan would have made a wonderful husband . . . and a terrific father. But I wasn't strong enough to make a change."

Sara nodded. "How did he die?"

"It was a car accident. It happened . . . it happened on your first birthday. When I heard the news, I thought how terribly ironic it was."

"But it was no accident," Sara stated.

"Apparently not. It never occurred to me that Peter knew. All these years, it never once occurred to me. And even then that he would go so far as to have him killed. I just can't believe it."

Sara gave a humorless laugh. "Well, believe it. Because the man chasing us in the mountains was very real." Sara walked to the window again and stared out. "One of our group was shot down right in front of us. Sandra." A sad smile crossed her face. "One minute talking and laughing, the next, laying there dead within the blink of an eye." Sara turned back around. "That's how I was supposed to die." She cleared her throat. "I'm almost sorry he didn't end up like Dodds."

Her mother shook her head. "Believe me, this humiliation he's suffering is far worse than death. Everything he's worked his whole life for, all the plans he made, all of it gone. He always wanted to be the headline story on CNN. Now he is."

Sara moved back to the bed and sat down again. She leaned forward, resting her elbows on her thighs, her hands clasped lightly together.

"What will you do now, Mother? Will you stay at the complex?"

"No. I doubt I'll even go back there to pack." She smiled. "I need someplace new, someplace where he's never been. Perhaps Arthur might choose to accompany me. I haven't been on my own in so many years, I don't even know how to run a household."

"I think Arthur will agree to go with you. He was very concerned about you. If not for him, the FBI probably wouldn't have gotten down to the bunker."

"Yes, Arthur and I do share a fondness. But what about you, darling? What will you do? Go back to your clinic and pretend none of this happened? Do you think your clientele will abandon you?"

"I don't know. If it were any other women, I wouldn't be surprised to have lawsuits pop up. But those ladies were tough as nails. We bonded as one. It was us against him. Of course the publicity will probably curb our enrollment awhile. Two shot, one killed. Can't be good for business."

"It wasn't your fault. And it had nothing to do with your business. I doubt your clinic will suffer. But what about you? I wish you had someone, Sara. You've always been so picky about your dates."

Sara laughed. "Picky?"

"I really liked that attorney you were seeing a couple of years ago. She was very attractive."

Sara nodded. "Yes, she was. And we had absolutely nothing in common. Besides, she had political aspirations and I wanted no part of that." Sara glanced at her mother quickly, then away. "But I . . . well, I have met someone."

"You have? Why haven't you told me?"

Sara stood and again walked to the window. "I just met her recently." She turned around and shoved her hands into her pockets as she watched her mother. "She's a detective. She pretended to be an injured hiker and she was sort of absorbed into our group."

"What do you mean pretended?"

"It's a complicated story. She thought the FBI had assigned her to watch me, when in fact it was just a ploy to get her to lead the sniper to me."

"Oh my."

"We became lovers."

"Oh my."

Sara smiled slightly. "I'm a little frightened by what I feel. I mean, there was an attraction between us long before the sniper showed himself. But I don't know if what transpired after that was a result of the circumstances we were in or if it's true, you know?"

"Oh, I see. You were in extreme danger and you reached out for her, is that it? You needed an emotional attachment of some sort and she was available?"

"I don't know if that's the case or not." She walked back to the bed, meeting her mother's eyes. "Is it possible to fall in love with someone so quickly?"

He mother smiled gently and reached to take her hand. "You think you might be in love with her?"

"She makes me laugh." Sara smiled. "And she's a storyteller. And she got my group of conservative women to strip naked—twice—and jump in hot springs." Sara blushed. "And I took one look at her and nearly melted on the spot."

"What about her, Sara? Have you talked about it?"

"No, we haven't talked about it. We're having dinner Saturday night. At my place," she added.

"Then don't try to analyze it, Sara. Just see where it goes. If it was just the circumstances, you'll know soon enough."

Sara nodded, remembering the way her body reacted when Jaime kissed her. No, she didn't want it to be just the circumstances. But how were they to get to know each other? After the close quarters they'd shared, after all they'd been through, she thought they were past the dating stage. And dinner? She didn't want to have dinner. She wanted to get Jaime naked and make love with her. She blushed slightly, then turned away, but not before hearing the quiet laugh of her mother.

"Sara?"

"Hmm?"

"What's her name?"

Sara smiled as she met her mother's eyes. "Jaime."

CHAPTER FIFTY-EIGHT

Jaime couldn't believe her nervousness as she stood by her car. Sara's home was quite impressive, the quiet neighborhood landscaped with spruce trees and boulders, a view of the western mountains not marred by the cityscape at all. It was nice. And Jaime was still nervous.

She rubbed her damp palms together then stepped on the sidewalk, walking slowly to the front door. She didn't know what to expect from Sara, maybe that's why she was anxious. They'd talked on the phone nearly every day, but still, they'd not talked about *them*.

"Are you stalling?"

Jaime jumped, startled, as Sara stood at the door, holding it open. "Jesus, you about gave me a heart attack." Jaime held her hand to her chest dramatically. "I hope you know CPR."

Sara smiled. "I know mouth-to-mouth exceptionally well."

Jaime's heart literally skipped a beat as their eyes met. She didn't know which frightened her more. The uncertainty of their relationship or the look in Sara's eyes.

"Need me to show you?" Sara teased.

"Yes, please."

Sara's smile faded as she drew Jaime to her, their mouths meeting slowly, tenderly, reacquainting themselves after a week's absence. Sara's body did what it always did when Jaime kissed her. It melted.

Jaime pulled away while she still could, before her hands finished their journey to Sara's breasts. Her heart pounded in her ears and she tried to catch her breath.

"I love the way you kiss me," Sara whispered.

Jaime met her eyes. "I missed you."

Sara nodded. "I missed you too."

"I was a little afraid," Jaime admitted.

Sara nodded again. "Me too."

Jaime smiled. "Good. Glad we got that out of the way."

Sara laughed. "Come inside. I don't need to give the neighbors anything more to talk about."

"Why? Do you often kiss strange women on your doorstep?" Jaime asked as she followed Sara.

"Are you strange, sweetheart?"

Jaime stumbled, the endearment causing her heart to miss a beat. "Sara?"

Sara stopped and turned, her own heart jumping wildly in her chest as she met the intense stare from Jaime.

"Hmm?"

Jaime swallowed nervously. "Would it be terribly forward of me to . . . well to suggest that we delay . . . delay dinner?"

Sara felt her heart race, pounding in her chest, nearly choking the breath from her. She walked closer to Jaime, her hand sliding up Jaime's stomach, resting between her breasts.

"You want to make love?" she whispered.

"Yes, please," Jaime breathed.

Sara closed her eyes for a second, then moved her hand a few inches to cup Jaime's breast.

"Me too."

Jaime moaned as Sara's hand squeezed her breast then she bent her head, capturing Sara's mouth. Their kisses were no longer gentle. Tongues battled frantically as hands touched flesh. Jaime was pleasantly surprised to find no bra in her way.

"Do you have any idea what you do to me?" Sara murmured against Jaime's mouth. "I swear, I lose all control when you touch me."

Sara moved away and stripped off her shirt, exposing her breasts to Jaime's greedy eyes. Without a word, she took Jaime's hand and led her up the five steps to the split-level and into her bedroom. She didn't bother with the covers. She drew Jaime to the bed, her hands shoving between her legs, cupping her through her jeans. She wanted her. She couldn't control this wild hunger she had. She had ached with it all week. She wanted her now and her fingers were frantic as they shoved inside her jeans. Her tongue pushed against Jaime's and she moaned when she felt her flesh, hot and wet to her touch.

Jaime lay back, sensing Sara's need for her. She unbuttoned her jeans, giving Sara room. Her legs parted, ready for her.

Sara plunged inside of her, deep and hard, and Jaime surged up to meet her, her hips undulating against Sara's fingers. Sara pulled out, sliding through her wetness, moving over her like silk and she stroked her faster and faster until she felt Jaime arch hard against her fingers. She captured Jaime's mouth, catching the scream as Jaime climaxed.

Perspiration dampened her brow and she closed her eyes, shocked by her need, shocked by her aggressiveness. She let her head rest on Jaime's chest, smiling as she realized they were both still mostly clothed.

"I wanted you," she murmured. "I swear, I have ached for you."

Jaime rolled them over, pinning Sara beneath her. Her knees spread Sara's thighs, their jeans rubbing together as they strained to get close.

"You have no idea what ache is," Jaime whispered.

Jaime knelt between Sara's legs, her fingers quickly working to unbutton Sara's jeans. She pulled them down, then struggled to kick her own off as Sara worked the buttons on Jaime's shirt. They were a tangled mess and Sara laughed in frustration.

"Christ, can you get naked already?"

"I'm trying. God, I'm trying," Jaime said, finally freeing her buttons and tossing the shirt on the floor. She paused, her eyes finding Sara's. Soft, gentle smiles formed, then Sara slowly reached out, her fingers brushing Jaime's nipple.

"So beautiful," she whispered.

Jaime took Sara's hand, bringing the fingers to her mouth. She kissed them softly, her tongue wetting them. She felt Sara tremble.

"Let me love you."

Sara nodded numbly, lying back and pulling Jaime to her. She spread her legs, then moaned quietly as Jaime settled between them. Her eyes drifted closed as Jaime's soft mouth moved across her throat, finally finding her lips. As always, Jaime's kisses simply rendered her powerless. Their mouths moved together, tongues slowly, lightly caressing. Sara nearly whimpered when Jaime pulled away, her mouth going again to her throat, gently nibbling at the pulse that pounded there. Sara held her close and brushed her fingers through Jaime's hair, guiding Jaime to her breast.

Jaime's mouth covered her, her tongue raking lightly across the swollen nipple. Sara moaned and Jaime bit down gently.

"God, Jaime," she breathed, arching her hips against Jaime's thigh.

Jaime released her nipple and found her mouth again. Kisses no longer gentle, their mouths fought for control. Jaime moved her hand between them, sliding down Sara's body, seeking and finding the wetness she knew would greet her. Her knee forced Sara's thighs apart and she entered her, watching Sara's face as it transformed in pleasure, her own eyes finally sliding shut as Sara enveloped her.

"Jaime . . . please," Sara whispered, her hips moving, meeting each thrust of Jaime's hand. "Please . . . your mouth. I want your mouth to take me." She was so near orgasm but she simply *craved* the feel of Jaime's mouth—and tongue—upon her. Her hips slowed and she urged Jaime downward.

Jaime let her fingers slip from Sara. Their eyes met and Jaime watched Sara's turn from blue to green, watched as she still struggled to catch her breath.

"Please," Sara whispered again.

As their eyes held, Jaime felt a connection with Sara that she'd never experienced with another person before. A connection so strong and pure, it nearly stopped her heart. She nodded weakly, her hands already pushing Sara's legs apart. She was trembling as she gathered Sara to her, her hands cupping Sara's hips, bringing her to her mouth. She groaned when she tasted her and her mouth opened, moving over Sara's hard clit, sucking it into her mouth. Her tongue swirled over it, back and forth, trying to hold on as Sara's hips bucked against her face.

Sara foolishly thought she was in control, thought she could set the pace but she lost all power over her body. She knew she was nearly delirious, knew her mouth was opened as she struggled to draw breath, knew her hips were moving wildly against Jaime's hot mouth but surrender was all she could do. With her head flung back and her fists grasping the comforter, she held on while Jaime nearly devoured her like a starving woman. Jaime's shoulders pushed against her, driving her legs apart, moving her farther up the bed with the force of her desire.

Sara could take no more. She felt as if she were drowning, sinking into blackness, her orgasm building like a tidal wave. A kaleidoscope of colors nearly blinded her as she came, but still, Jaime's mouth held her, continuing her assault on her as wave after wave rammed into Sara, causing her to call out Jaime's name again and again.

Sara's body finally gave way and she lay limply on the bed. Only then did Jaime's mouth leave her.

"I thought my body was going to explode," Sara murmured. "Actually explode." She rolled her head to the side as Jaime moved up beside her. "That's never happened to me before."

Jaime's hand was trembling as she reached over to touch Sara's face, her fingers moving lightly against her skin.

"What's wrong?" Sara asked. "You're shaking."

"I don't know," Jaime said quietly. "I feel kind of strange," she admitted.

Sara sat up, watching Jaime. "Strange?" She took Jaime's hand and kissed it, then brought it to her breast, smiling as Jaime's fingers surrounded it. "No, not strange. I would just say nice."

Jaime cocked her head. "Nice?"

Sara nodded. "Yeah. Falling in love feels nice. Doesn't it?"

Their eyes held and Jaime forgot to breathe. Then she smiled, her eyes never leaving Sara's.

"Falling in love . . . yeah, it feels really, really nice."

END OF WATCH by Clare Baxter. 256 pp. LAPD Lieutenant L.A Franco Frank follows the lone clue down the unlit steps of memory to a final, unthinkable resolution.
1-59493-064-4 $13.95

BEHIND THE PINE CURTAIN by Gerri Hill. 280 pp. Jacqueline returns home after her father's death and comes face-to-face with her first crush.   1-59493-057-0 $13.95

PIPELINE by Brenda Adcock. 240pp. Joanna faces a lost love returning and pulling her into a seamy underground corporation that kills for money.   1-59493-062-7 $13.95

18TH & CASTRO by Karin Kallmaker. 200 pp. First-time couplings and couples who know how to mix lust and love make 18th & Castro the hottest address in the city by the bay.
1-59493-066-X $13.95

JUST THIS ONCE by KG MacGregor. 200 pp. Mindful of the obligations back home that she must honor, Wynne Connelly struggles to resist the fascination and allure that a particular woman she meets on her business trip represents.   1-59493-087-2 $13.95

ANTICIPATION by Terri Breneman. 240 pp. Two women struggle to remain professional as they work together to find a serial killer.   1-59493-055-4 $13.95

OBSESSION by Jackie Calhoun. 240 pp. Lindsey's life is turned upside down when Sarah comes into the family nursery in search of perennials.   1-59493-058-9 $13.95

BENEATH THE WILLOW by Kenna White. 240 pp. A torch that still burns brightly even after twenty-five years threatens to consume two childhood friends.
1-59493-053-8 $13.95

SISTER LOST, SISTER FOUND by Jeanne G'fellers. 224 pp. The highly anticipated sequel to No Sister of Mine.   1-59493-056-2 $13.95

THE WEEKEND VISITOR by Jessica Thomas. 240 pp. In this latest Alex Peres mystery, Alex is asked to investigate an assault on a local woman but finds that her client may have more secrets than she lets on.   1-59493-054-6 $13.95

THE KILLING ROOM by Gerri Hill. 392 pp. How can two women forget and go their separate ways?   1-59493-050-3 $12.95

PASSIONATE KISSES by Megan Carter. 240 pp. Will two old friends run from love?
1-59493-051-1 $12.95

ALWAYS AND FOREVER by Lyn Denison. 224 pp. The girl next door turns Shannon's world upside down.   1-59493-049-X $12.95

BACK TALK by Saxon Bennett. 200 pp. Can a talk show host find love after heartbreak?
1-59493-028-7 $12.95

THE PERFECT VALENTINE: EROTIC LESBIAN VALENTINE STORIES edited by Barbara Johnson and Therese Szymanski—from Bella After Dark. 328 pp. Stories from the hottest writers around.   1-59493-061-9 $14.95

MURDER AT RANDOM by Claire McNab. 200 pp. The Sixth Denise Cleever Thriller. Denise realizes the fate of thousands is in her hands.   1-59493-047-3 $12.95

THE TIDES OF PASSION by Diana Tremain Braund. 240 pp. Will Susan be able to hold it all together and find the one woman who touches her soul?   1-59493-048-1 $12.95

JUST LIKE THAT by Karin Kallmaker. 240 pp. Disliking each other—and everything they stand for—even before they meet, Toni and Syrah find feelings can change, just like that.
1-59493-025-2 $12.95

WHEN FIRST WE PRACTICE by Therese Szymanski. 200 pp. Brett and Allie are once again caught in the middle of murder and intrigue. 1-59493-045-7 $12.95

REUNION by Jane Frances. 240 pp. Cathy Braithwaite seems to have it all: good looks, money and a thriving accounting practice . . . 1-59493-046-5 $12.95

BELL, BOOK & DYKE: NEW EXPLOITS OF MAGICAL LESBIANS by Kallmaker, Watts, Johnson and Szymanski. 360 pp. Reluctant witches, tempting spells and skyclad beauties—delve into the mysteries of love, lust and power in this quartet of novellas. 1-59493-023-6 $14.95

ARTIST'S DREAM by Gerri Hill. 320 pp. When Cassie meets Luke Winston, she can no longer deny her attraction to women . . . 1-59493-042-2 $12.95

NO EVIDENCE by Nancy Sanra. 240 pp. Private Investigator Tally McGinnis once again returns to the horror-filled world of a serial killer. 1-59493-043-04 $12.95

WHEN LOVE FINDS A HOME by Megan Carter. 280 pp. What will it take for Anna and Rona to find their way back to each other again? 1-59493-041-4 $12.95

MEMORIES TO DIE FOR by Adrian Gold. 240 pp. Rachel attempts to avoid her attraction to the charms of Anna Sigurdson . . . 1-59493-038-4 $12.95

SILENT HEART by Claire McNab. 280 pp. Exotic lesbian romance.

1-59493-044-9 $12.95

MIDNIGHT RAIN by Peggy J. Herring. 240 pp. Bridget McBee is determined to find the woman who saved her life. 1-59493-021-X $12.95

THE MISSING PAGE A Brenda Strange Mystery by Patty G. Henderson. 240 pp. Brenda investigates her client's murder . . . 1-59493-004-X $12.95

WHISPERS ON THE WIND by Frankie J. Jones. 240 pp. Dixon thinks she and her best friend, Elizabeth Colter, would make the perfect couple . . . 1-59493-037-6 $12.95

CALL OF THE DARK: EROTIC LESBIAN TALES OF THE SUPERNATURAL edited by Therese Szymanski—from Bella After Dark. 320 pp. 1-59493-040-6 $14.95

A TIME TO CAST AWAY A Helen Black Mystery by Pat Welch. 240 pp. Helen stops by Alice's apartment—only to find the woman dead . . . 1-59493-036-8 $12.95

DESERT OF THE HEART by Jane Rule. 224 pp. The book that launched the most popular lesbian movie of all time is back. 1-1-59493-035-X $12.95

THE NEXT WORLD by Ursula Steck. 240 pp. Anna's friend Mido is threatened and eventually disappears . . . 1-59493-024-4 $12.95

CALL SHOTGUN by Jaime Clevenger. 240 pp. Kelly gets pulled back into the world of private investigation . . . 1-59493-016-3 $12.95

52 PICKUP by Bonnie J. Morris and E.B. Casey. 240 pp. 52 hot, romantic tales—one for every Saturday night of the year. 1-59493-026-0 $12.95

GOLD FEVER by Lyn Denison. 240 pp. Kate's first love, Ashley, returns to their home town, where Kate now lives . . . 1-1-59493-039-2 $12.95

RISKY INVESTMENT by Beth Moore. 240 pp. Lynn's best friend and roommate needs her to pretend Chris is his fiancé. But nothing is ever easy. 1-59493-019-8 $12.95

HUNTER'S WAY by Gerri Hill. 240 pp. Homicide detective Tori Hunter is forced to team up with the hot-tempered Samantha Kennedy. 1-59493-018-X $12.95